THE
DRAGONFLY

Published in the UK by Aurora Metro Books, 2017

67 Grove Avenue, Twickenham TW1 4HX

www.aurorametro.com   info@aurorametro.com

Cover design © copyright 2017 Greg Jorss
    http://www.upsidecreative.com.au/

Editor: Cheryl Robson

Production: Simon Smith

Aurora Metro Books would like to thank Matthew Rhys Daniel and
Ivett Saliba.

Printed by CPI Group (UK) Ltd, Croydon, CR0 4YY.

ISBNs:
978-1-911501-03-9 (print)
978-1-911501-04-6 (ebook)

THE
DRAGONFLY

KATE DUNN

AURORA METRO BOOKS

ACKNOWLEDGEMENTS

My thanks to Cheryl Robson, Andrew Walby, Ellen Cheshire and Simon Smith at Aurora Metro for their dedication to publishing emerging women writers – I'm lucky to be a beneficiary of their commitment; to my agent Laura Longrigg for her indefatigable faith in me and to my husband Steve and my mum Prue for holding me close while I was writing.

Zita Adamson, Carole Pugh and my uncle Simon Williams have all been readers of early drafts of *The Dragonfly* and have given me constructive criticism and encouragement at every turn, which made all the difference in the world.

Any nautical mistakes in the book are entirely my own, and my husband and I have committed a good many others while racketing around the European waterways. I'm more grateful than I can say to Phil and Maja Rollings for sharing so many of the adventures with us, and to Prue; Hilary and Lily; Tom, Stella, Gabriel and Louis; Judith and Steve; Jed – and Jack, my boy, for holding the ropes in the locks, getting the croissants in the morning, being good humoured in a crisis and sharing a medicinal glass of wine on deck when the day is done.

For Steve,

My north, south, east and best.

CHAPTER ONE

Along the cobbled quay the Paris sunshine lay as lightly as a leaf. Colin stood on the wooden pontoon, listening to the gossipy sound of the boats as they fretted and strained against their moorings. He checked the *Dragonfly's* ropes one last time, tightening and tying off the forward line. It was more of a fidget than a proper check, something to do to make him feel that he could, after all, be master of the situation. He set the line on the *Dragonfly's* bow, wishing with all his might that he could tighten and tie off the terrible thread of events that had brought him here to the Arsenal marina in Paris; tighten and tie it off, then cut the cord.

He stood up, holding his fist against his mouth. The faint smell of the canal was on his skin: the vegetable / mineral smell of last year's leaves and car tyres and diesel oil. The lapping of water against the hull failed to console him and he couldn't stop himself from going over and over the crisis that had brought him here so urgently.

For a moment he was back at home in Bath that May morning, the first decent day of summer, wondering about the paint-drying potential that this whisper of warm weather might present. He had felt the stirrings of restlessness; he rattled the change in his pocket and thought about making another cup of tea.

He had learned down the years that the only remedy for this… sensation, was to do something practical like, for example, building a boat at the bottom of the garden. After Sally left him he went to the library and borrowed a book, then he extended the garage to make a workshop which covered the whole of the patio and half of the veg patch as well. There was no one to stop him anymore. That's where he built the *Dragonfly*, diagram by diagram, plank by plank, a fourteen foot day boat for fishing. The resinous smell of a sheet of marine ply was still a tonic and the thought of it decided him. He'd pop down and do a little bit of sanding on the hull, prior to touching up her paint work. The new season had started already. No time like the present.

He had felt better in his workshop: surveying the sleek lines of the *Dragonfly* in the soft burlap light restored him to himself. He ran his hand along the flank of the boat as though it were a living creature. He liked to have the radio on in the farthest corner of the workbench because it gave him the illusion that someone else might be listening in another room. He'd wired up an extension from the house so that he could hear the doorbell because he often had to take deliveries. He'd ordered an impeller rebuild kit and it was due any day. He was sanding away, getting a rhythm going until the air was filled with particles of paint of a lustrous duck egg blue. If he wasn't careful, he'd sand her right back to the wood and then he'd really have a job on his hands. Sure enough, at nine-thirty the doorbell rang. That would be the postman with his parcel. He made his way up the garden, dusting his hands off on his trousers, and opened the front door.

The postman handed him a package. "Everything alright? Nice spot of weather. These are for you as well," and with that he was gone, back up the path.

Colin stood in the doorway riffling through a sheaf of pizza deals, estate agent flyers, an advert for a tree surgeon. Tucked in the back was an airmail letter. He peered at the postmark. After a moment or two he allowed himself to look at the handwriting. At the sight of Michael's spiky lettering, he was conscious of an accelerating rush of blood to his heart. He held the envelope to his mouth, thinking. The travelled scent of the paper stalled him for a second. He inhaled with care then put the letter on the telephone table. He'd open it later. Not now. He sat down abruptly at the bottom of the stairs.

A letter from his boy. After all these years.

He leaned forward, picked up the flimsy envelope, tore it open and unfolded the single sheet of paper it contained. "Colin," it began. Not "Dear Colin," or "Dad," or even, "Dear Dad." He digested the hurt.

"This is to inform you that Charlotte has died, very suddenly. It was an accident. She fell down the stairs at home. Delphine is coping as well as possible, although both of us are very sad. I thought that you would want to know.

Michael."

The letter was word perfect and he guessed that it had been copied out. He wondered how many drafts it had taken to reduce the news to its bare essentials. Charlotte, dead. A sound escaped from him and he swallowed. He would write straight back, offer to come to Paris – this was his moment, his chance to help. He'd write straight away. He read the message from his son again, faltering over the last line, alert to its layers of meaning. Not Dear Dad, just Colin. He held the impeller rebuild kit tightly to his chest.

More than a fortnight passed. He was in the kitchen cooking supper, humming along to the radio, when the doorbell rang. Standing on the doorstep were two police officers, a woman and a young constable with razor rash on his neck and large hands that he didn't seem to have quite grown into.

"Are you Colin Aylesford?"

He was holding a dish cloth. He'd been chopping vegetables for a stew. "Yes?" He was conscious that he'd left the frying pan on the gas.

"Is Michael Aylesford your son?"

Colin stiffened. The young copper's Adam's apple rose and fell in his throat as he spoke. "May we come in for a moment?"

"Yes, of course. Come in–" he said, without moving.

"Just for a moment. Won't keep you long."

He remembered the whiteness of the policeman's neck, the razor rash, the slow motion swallow, the words rising.

"We have some bad news, I'm afraid."

With an independent and unauthorised action, Colin's knees gave way and he slumped on the wooden chair in the hall, where he used to keep his briefcase before he took early retirement.

The policeman closed the front door and removed his hat.

"We've been contacted by the French police. Your son has been arrested in connection with the death of his partner Charlotte Duvoisin."

He felt as if he was falling from a great height, as though the ground, or something far, far worse, was rushing up to meet him.

"Arrested?" he said, comprehension, in that instant, beyond him. "But… it was an accident, she fell down the stairs, his letter said."

"The autopsy report indicates that Madame Duvoisin was pushed. That considerable force was used."

"Force?" he said. "There must be some mistake." He was getting the measure of it. There had been a terrible misunderstanding. "She fell. His letter said." He had it in mind to find Michael's letter and show it to them, to clear the matter up once and for all. He half rose to his feet. "It was an accident."

The policeman pinched his upper lip between finger and thumb, pulling at it, taking his time. "The thing is," he began, "according to the coroner's report it certainly wasn't an accident, and anyway," he appeared to be searching for ways not to say what he had come to say, "your son has made a full confession to the French police."

~~~

Colin hitched the trailer on to the back of his car figuring that he'd need a base in Paris that didn't cost much if he was going to stay for any length of time. He drove to Portsmouth to catch the first available ferry.

He hadn't seen his boy for nearly ten years, and now this.

Shaking his head, he groped in his pocket for the street map. He needed to orientate himself. He would fight for Michael's freedom, no matter what it took.

CHAPTER TWO

Michael could see the corner of the prison hospital wing from his window. If he leaned at an angle he could see an overflow pipe with a green algae stain spreading down the wall. His deceptively spacious, six square metre accommodation contained a bed for himself and a bed for his cellmate – he gave an involuntary shiver – two chairs, a table, two cupboards. It was... sufficient. He even had a number. He was a number. VN1692F was code for who he was, for who he had become.

He sat heavily on his bed. He had no idea there were so many minutes in the day. He'd just got back from recreation – he walked round three sides of the yard rather than go straight across the middle in order not to make himself too visible. The kangas checked him regularly and he wondered if they considered him a suicide risk; they had taken his shoelaces and belt as a matter of course, although it crossed his mind that they might be checking to see if Laroche had eaten him alive.

He wouldn't though – kill himself – even if he could, because of his daughter, Delphine. If he sat very still and closed his eyes and listened out he could almost catch a glimpse of her. It was never so much as seeing her in motion; it was more like a collage of all the photographs he'd ever taken of her. The spritz of her unbrushed hair. Her sturdy little body. Her telegraphic smile. The grubby tide line round her neck – more than that, the particular, unmistakable texture of her skin. His arms felt empty of her. The one measly phone call they were allowed each week was nowhere near enough. Yesterday morning, he couldn't recall the sound of her laugh and that made him sad for the rest of the day. On the whole, trying to picture her feature by feature (and failing sometimes) was easier than trying to picture how she would be managing at her grandmother's, without him. It was also much, much easier than thinking about Charlotte. He drew a shaky breath. There was altogether too much time to think.

The door flung open and Laroche loped in. There was an etiquette, Michael was learning, which meant that you didn't speak until the door had been closed and the key turned and withdrawn.

They waited.

"Woss up?" Laroche slung himself on his bed. His head was shaved so that you could see the scars on his scalp, even the stitch marks. He had red-rimmed eyes and pale lashes. "Wotch you looking at, you Rosbif ponce?"

Michael tried to overcome his automatic recoil. "Nothing, I wasn't–" He had been staring at Laroche's arm. "–looking." His cellmate was skinny and his arms were thin, with corded, brutal muscle. Amongst the badly done tattoos and the faded striae of teenage cutting, he was trying to discern if there were needle marks. It was a way of rationalising his own absolute terror: working out just how scared he needed to be. "How was your meeting?" he asked, because sometimes – now – conversation felt safer than silence. "With your lawyer?"

Laroche hawked, then rolled the phlegm around his mouth, giving his jaw a workout. "S'alright." He afforded him an idle, appraising glance, and swallowed. "You interested are you, then?"

Michael had an interest, for research purposes, for reconnaissance. Know thine enemy...

"Armed robbery, second offence, not looking good. Thass what he said. If you want to know." He let his head fall to one side, the better to study Michael. "Not in your league, though. Not a wife killer, like you."

~~~

He felt more secure in the cell, with only one of the lags to keep his eye on. On the way to the canteen Laroche remarked, as if resuming an earlier conversation, "– though you don't look as though you could hurt even a tiny little fly. Wanna know something?"

Michael couldn't get used to the white ceramic brightness of the hallways: floor to ceiling tiles that could be easily hosed of thrown food, or vomit, or blood. He couldn't get used to the netting strung between the walkways to catch the jumpers, or the pushed, although he thought that Delphine might quite like a jump in them and tried to imagine her bounding and rebounding, joyously, to take his mind off – all of it.

"Chapot has opened a book on you. You didn't know that, did you?"

"Chapot?" said Michael, looking behind him.

"Fifty euros says Joubert will get medieval with you by the end of the month. You didn't know that, did you? Did you? Well, you know now."

"Which one's Chapot?"

Laroche shook his head. "You gotta man up, dude, that's what you gotta do. Joubert fucking hates wife killers. Which is strange, when you think about it, because he's in here on suspicion of killing his own."

Michael hesitated. "What is… 'get medieval' – exactly?"

"Shit man, you don't stand a chance."

~~~

"Your father has been in touch. He wanted to be sure you had everything you needed," said his lawyer.

Michael couldn't help noticing that the view from meeting room three didn't involve any part of the hospital wing. He let his eyes rest on the distant dome of the Paris Observatory. He'd wondered if the letter to his father had been a mistake as soon as he had written it. He felt some primal need to tell one of his own people, a kind of filial reflex – *Dad! Dad!* – that he regretted almost immediately.

"Monsieur Aylesford asked if it would be possible to see the statement you made to the police. I said I needed authorisation from you before I could release a copy. Michael–?"

"Sorry? I'm sorry. I was…" He glanced round as though he had only just realized his avocat was in the room with him. "Sorry?"

"Your statement. Your father was wondering if he could–" The avocat had a provincial look to her: beige mac folded over the back of her chair, tailored skirt, pastel, floral blouse. She was doing her job. She was trying to help him. She bit her lip. "OK," she said, changing tack. He wondered if she found him difficult. He didn't mean to be. "We need to talk about your plea. As your representative, I urge you strongly to reconsider. A guilty plea is not the solution here. We can make a case. If nothing else, you need to think about your little daughter."

"OK, OK–" he interrupted. "My father can see my statement. That's OK. But I won't change my plea. End of."

"You'll get less than twenty years, but not much less. That's what you're looking at. You need to think about it very carefully."

"I have thought about it…"

"It's your decision. I can only advise you."

Michael's gaze was drawn back to the horizon. The woman began closing her laptop; he heard the slow electric sigh of it shutting down.

"Your father also asked if he might see Delphine – would you have any objections?"

"Objections?" The note of incredulity in his own voice silenced him.

When Charlotte had gone into labour, his father had turned up at the hospital.

"It's a *girl*," he breathed, "A baby girl."

"That's wonderful…"

"She weighs three point two kilograms and she's got brown hair, a little quiff of it, and she's doing fine…"

"How is Charlotte?"

Michael hesitated. He wiped his forehead with his sleeve. "She's had a rough time of it."

"I've bought her these. It's all I could find. I didn't want to come empty-handed. I'll get her something proper tomorrow–"

Michael regarded the tired yellow carnations. He bowed his head. There was no way round it. "She doesn't want to see you, Dad."

"Oh." His dad's hand, holding the flowers, dropped to his side. "Well, of course, if she's not up to it, I'll pop back – tomorrow. I could come in the morning. I'll pop back then…"

"She won't see you. She doesn't want to."

For several seconds Colin stared at the floor, at the fake grain of the linoleum. "Right," he said in the end.

"I could bring Delphine out to see you…"

"Delphine?"

"We're calling her Delphine." He hesitated. "If you like I could…"

His father stood there in the corridor, the rusting smell of staunched blood overlaid with disinfectant. He seemed heavy with questions he hardly knew how to frame. "Look," he held out his hand to articulate what he was trying to say; the gesture seemed wretched.

Michael took a step back, glancing over his shoulder at the entrance to the ward.

"Can't we–?"Colin broke off. He shoved the flowers at his son. "Actually, I wouldn't want to disturb her – them, I mean. Give these to her for me, will you? Tell her I–"

Michael could feel the scarlet stain of hurt and disappointment burn his face.

"Better this way. You know. For the time being…"

The time being lasted nine long years, years in which neither of them could quite get over themselves. Colin had never met his granddaughter. Delphine had never seen her grandpa. Looking back was like staring down the wrong end of a telescope at two tiny figures moving awkwardly through their own, small tragedy, reduced in size to almost nothing now, to almost nothing.

"Well?" the lawyer repeated.

"No," he said, finally "I don't have any objections, if her grandmother agrees."

The avocat rose to her feet and as she turned to put her coat on, she let slip her supplementary question. "Your father has asked if he may visit you. I need to know. He will have to be put on an approved list."

Michael flinched. "I can't. I'm sorry. I'm just not up to it," he said.

The woman shrugged and rapped on the door for the warder. He waited until she had gone and the door had been closed behind her, until the key had been turned and withdrawn.

Then he buried his face in his hands.

CHAPTER THREE

The apartment block in the north east of the city was faced in cream coloured render which absorbed the light, reflecting nothing back, so that the building had a sort of density, heavy with the lives of people living there. Next to the entrance was a brass panel with a buzzer and a nameplate for every flat. *Duvoisin.* Colin found hers very quickly. He rang the bell.

"Allo?" The speakerphone whistled and hissed, as if the cables had been routed under the Atlantic.

"Madame Duvoisin? It's Colin Aylesford–"

The frayed static of the intercom continued, uninterrupted. He half-expected her to hang up on him. "Madame Duvoisin?" he said more urgently "It's–"

She buzzed him in.

Once inside, he didn't wait for the lift, he took the stairs two at a time. She lived on the seventh floor. He leaned against the wall outside her flat, his lungs thick with air, wondering what on earth he was going to say to her.

Madame Duvoisin opened the door a slit's width.

"I'm–" he began. "I'm terribly sorry about Charlotte." At the mention of her daughter's name the woman rested her head against the edge of the frame, so that the angle of the wood cut a groove into her brow. He could see the fine frost

21

of her hair scored across her scalp; he was so close he could see particles of powder clouding her cheek, the weary folds of her skin.

"What is it you want from me? Why have you come?"

"Well…" This was not going to be easy. "In our different ways…we've both lost–" he broke off. He thought she might close the door in his face. "I'm sorry, I'm sorry, it's not the same for me, I know…"

"You don't know."

"Although my son's on remand–"

"There is nothing you can say to me."

They stood staring at each other, taut with the hunger of their separate losses. "Come in," she sighed. She made a small, stealing gesture, as if she were drawing a cardigan around her shoulders.

Colin followed her into the flat. She stood at the entrance to the sitting-room with her back to the light, so thin she was nearly transparent; he could make out her collarbone, the ridges of her shoulder and the blue veins knotting her wrists.

"The thing is, I just don't understand how it happened…" he said. He couldn't stop himself.

"Ask–" when it came to it, she couldn't say his name, "– your son."

"I've…" he hung his head. "He won't…"

She merely contemplated him, allowing the sense of his humiliation to accrue until it filled the hall.

"I spoke to his solicitor. He refuses to see me," he swallowed. "I'm just trying to understand – what happened?"

"Read his statement." She riffled through a pile of papers and handed him a copy of the document. "It's all there, down in black and white."

Colin scanned the pages ravenously. Michael had testified to the police that he and Charlotte were at home together with their daughter. They were standing on the landing at the top of the stairs. Charlotte had her coat on and was carrying her suitcase. She was in the act of leaving. In the act of leaving Michael.

The moment when she had turned to go elided with the one in which Michael had raised his hand to stop her and the blow sent her flying.

She fell all the way to the bottom of the stairs, followed by her suitcase. The child had come running from her bedroom, but Charlotte died before either of them could reach her.

He rubbed the heels of his palms into his eyes.

"He was a good boy. He wouldn't hurt – anyone. He just wouldn't."

How would you know, her bitter gaze demanded. "I think it is a long time since you have seen him, non?"

"He always tried to do right by her," he said obstinately. "He would never have hurt her."

Madame Duvoisin pressed the tips of her fingers to her mouth. She let them rest there. "If you are suggesting," when she took her hands away, she studied them as if she thought they might be flecked with blood, "If you are trying to suggest that Charlotte was, in any way, responsible–"

"No. No, I'm not saying that–" he blurted out.

"If you are suggesting that my daughter is to blame–"

"No, I'm not saying that. I'm not saying that." Colin didn't want to think it.

"I cannot help you." She drooped a little; she looked exhausted. "You have to try and help yourself."

"I had thought that we could help each other..." he said sadly.

A sound escaped from her, jagged and mirthless. "Do you want to help me?

"Of course, if there's something I can do... anything..."

"Alright," she answered, putting him to the test. "Alright. If you want to help me..." She took a moment to consider her words. "Take Delphine."

"*What?*"

"She's your granddaughter too. Take her. Take her for the summer. I'm too old; it's too much for me... There are six weeks of holidays now, and the trial is coming and I cannot–"

"But I'm living on a little *boat*–"

"She's with a friend this afternoon, but tomorrow you can take her. If you want to help. Maybe it is your turn now..."

"But I don't – she doesn't – we don't know each other. And besides–" he was trying not to panic, "I don't speak French. How would we...?"

"Delphine goes to the International School. Her English is... adequate."

"But what would Michael say?" he went on wildly, "He might not want..."

She stopped him in his tracks. "I think in the circumstances he will not refuse me." There was a scrape of anguish in her voice. She leaned close so that he would fully comprehend what she was saying. "Every time I look into her face, I see your son."

~~~

Colin shaded his eyes. At the far end of the marina, he could see the traffic glimmering in the Place de la Bastille. He took in the elegant apartments, the office blocks, the charcoal scratchings of trees. The street above was thronged with workers on their lunch break. He noticed the bicycles for hire, the road sweeper, two stout old men resting on a bench, smoking not talking. A police car came skidding into view and his gaze swept over the old lady with the little girl at one end of the footbridge, leaning against the railings, watching the boats.

The child was sitting on a huge bag, the sort you can buy in a pound shop, made from shiny woven checked material that leaches colour when it's wet. He could see that she had on a little denim skirt, some kind of bobbly tank top over a stripy T-shirt and slouched over one eye, a man's hat of lavender grey tweed, halfway between a beret and a peaked cap. He wondered if the hat was Michael's.

He bit his lip. To tell the truth, he didn't know what to say to her, or how to be. Should he kiss her on the cheek? Both cheeks? Should he ruffle her hair, or shake her hand? Madame Duvoisin glanced at her watch; she fingered a button on her blouse, staring along the line of boats towards the river. Spotting Colin at a distance, she half raised her hand, so that he had no option but to wave back and hurry towards them.

"This is Delphine," Madame Duvoisin said with a tight inclination of her head.

"Hello," he answered.

The old lady prompted the child to greet him, "Bonjour Grand-père."

"In English," Madame Duvoisin said, in an admonishing tone.

"Hello *Grandpa*," Delphine shot her grandmother a needling glance.

"I have told Delphine you will be going on a little trip. She is very excited."

He could see the child's flip-flop moving, sketching arcs on the tarmac. She was still sitting on her bag, her head hanging so that the hat obscured her face.

"Because it is the holiday she may stay up until eight-thirty, but it is essential that she is in bed after that, she is not sleeping very well since…" Madame Duvoisin tailed off. She blinked a couple of times and then, as though she was speaking from a script which had been difficult to learn, she ploughed on, "I've given her some pocket money and I've told her to telephone me once a week." She turned to the little girl, "It will be a big adventure for you, non? To stay on a boat with your grandfather? To make a *grand voyage*?" The child was signalling with wide, alarmed eyes. The old lady hesitated, "She wanted me to be sure to tell you that she doesn't like betterave – I think that you say beetroot – or butter that is without salt."

"That's a relief, I don't like beetroot either. Or hard-boiled eggs. When I was at school, about your age, they used to make us eat egg and beetroot salad. Nightmare." As an opening gambit, it had limited success. The child looked away.

Madame Duvoisin gripped the face of her watch, peering at it in order to make out the time, "It is not a good idea to drag this out, I think…" she observed in an undertone. She cleared her throat. "Which boat is yours?"

"It's on the end, along there…" Colin gestured at the quay far beneath them.

"Very nice," she answered stiffly, staring at the large gin palace which obscured the *Dragonfly*.

"My one's behind that, actually…"

Nobody said anything.

Feeling protective, Colin went on, "Perhaps you'd like to have a look at her, so you can see…"

Madame Duvoisin managed a smile, her lips a closed line. "I'm sure everything will be fine…" Her eyes were screwed up against the brightness of the afternoon.

On the harbour wall he noticed a scrawny pigeon butting at a discarded carton of frites. There were one or two cemented to the bottom and the bird was trying to climb inside the greasy cardboard, turning its head one way and then the other, beaking after the chips.

"So, you have everything you need, Delphine?" asked her grandmother, glancing along the passarelle towards the metro station.

The child nodded. She stood up from the bag and with formal solemnity they kissed each other three times on the cheek and said their goodbyes. Not wishing to intrude, Colin watched the pigeon finish off the frites then fly away. For a moment he found himself wishing that he could do the same.

~~~

The child was smaller than he had pictured: smaller, fiercer and bafflingly *French*. In her own way she looked extremely stylish. He could see her, a few years down the line, riding pillion on a motor scooter with a Gitane hanging from her lower lip. He swallowed.

"I like your hat," he ventured, and then hesitated. "Shall I take this?" He reached for her luggage.

"Non." She grabbed the handles of the bag and started to drag it towards the top of the steps.

"Why don't I…?" He broke off. She tugged the bag off the first step, then the second, until it began to gather its own momentum, bumping down behind her, threatening to flatten her. "Careful–!" he shouted, dashing down after her.

KATE DUNN

"Je peux me debrouiller," she snapped, as if he were responsible for all of it, the whole damn mess. She was about to drag her belongings off down the quay, but he touched her arm, just for a second, before she went steaming ahead.

"If you speak French," he said, as gently as he could, "I won't be able to understand you. I don't speak French, you see."

The child turned round. She had the good manners not to roll her eyes to the heavens, but her wish to do so was implicit in the look she gave him.

"Except bonjour," he ventured. "I can say that. *Bonjour*. And I can also say '*Tell me the way to the cathedral.*' Ou est le–?"

"I can manage." She spelt the words out then started to walk away from him, more slowly than before. A faint tide line of rubbish – twigs, sweet wrappers, cigarette butts – gathered round the bag as she dragged it along.

"I rather hoped that you might teach me," he fell into step beside her.

"Where is your boat?"

"On the end. Look, why don't you let me…" he eyed her bag, then her, and didn't bother to finish his sentence.

He was keen to show her the *Dragonfly*. It was the only thing in this sticky, complicated situation that he was looking forward to. "Here we are," he said with a small flourish as they walked past the prow of the gin palace and his valiant, lovely little boat came into view.

He couldn't be certain, but he thought that the word *merde* slipped from her in a whisper.

"I built her. From scratch. Never built anything in my life before, but I built the *Dragonfly*. I borrowed a book about how to do it from the library. Built her in my back garden. She's fourteen foot long – a day boat, for fishing."

THE DRAGONFLY

The child was looking at him, her face uncomprehending, "Do you like fishing?" he asked, to fill the gathering silence.

The child shook her head.

"Come aboard, why don't you?" He leapt down onto the deck then held out his hand, expectantly.

She looked at her bag, then at the boat. She folded her arms.

He tried to picture what it would be like to see the *Dragonfly* for the first time, but he could only view her through the lens of his own pride and delight: the flowing line of her, so close to the water; her beautiful duck egg blue paint and the compact precision of the cabin with its three tiny portholes on either side.

He made beckoning motions with his arm. "Come on," he said encouragingly.

The child had anticipated the problem before him. "I cannot install myself…" she said, her mouth all bunched to one side. "It is not possible."

Once again he gestured her down, "Oh, you'll get used to it in a jiffy."

"If I am staying on the boat," she hopped off the pontoon and onto the deck, "Then there's no room for my sac. If my sac is staying on the boat," she clambered back onto the pontoon and to demonstrate heaved her luggage over the edge so that it filled the deck entirely, causing the *Dragonfly* to sit ominously low in the water, "Then I must stay on the ground."

"Ahh. Yes. I see. I do see what you mean." Colin scratched his head. "Well, obviously, it's you that we want on the boat," he reached towards her bag, as if to move it back on to dry land.

"I cannot make boating without my sac. It is not possible," the child cried, her voice so hot and conflagrationary that he glanced around to see if anyone had heard.

"OK, OK–"

29

"It is everything I have. I need it. I cannot make boating without it."

Rattled by the way in which things seemed to be disintegrating at a *nought to sixty in under a minute* speed, Colin spoke cautiously, "Right…"

She hesitated a moment and then, putting down a marker for future arguments, she pointed out crossly, "I am here for my grand-mère only, because she is asking…"

"And I'm here for your dad…"

"Then we have a problem, non–?"

"…and for you, of course." He stared at the bag. "What exactly have you got in there?"

Before he could unzip the zip, the child had jumped back on board almost capsizing the *Dragonfly* and flattened herself onto the bag. "My affairs," she snapped.

At least they were both on the boat, with the wretched bag. The two of them stared at one another.

"Look," Colin began. "Why don't you unpack your stuff, then we can work out what you really need."

"I have already said. I have need of everything. Everything."

He had seen that expression on his son's face. He could understand exactly what Madame Duvoisin meant. The child had Michael's eyes, with their stealing hazel lights; she had the same colouring that he had had when he was little, although he couldn't see her hair properly because of the hat, but the set of her jaw was his, and her wide mouth, and her slightly crooked teeth.

My son, he thought, the wound fresh every time. *My boy*.

How often had Michael stood before him, just like this, all ablaze? *Diversionary tactics*, he remembered, *that's what used to do the trick*. "This is where we sleep," he unbolted the hatch, which was about two foot square, "It's very clever, look," he slid the catches on the inside of the hatch and two legs unfolded, "See, it turns into a table, which slots in–" he viewed the bag, "–just there."

In spite of herself, the child was intrigued by the cabin and she crawled inside. There were two miniature bunks with a gap the size of a wedge of cheese between them. She lay down on the one on the port side, testing it out. "There is no space," she observed.

Colin poked his head through the hatch. "When it's time to turn over, it's time to turn out, that's what Napoleon said. He was one of yours," he added. He had to reverse his way into the cabin because once he was inside there was no room to turn around. He flipped up the mattress to starboard, revealing a locker. "There's one on your side too, for your clothes."

He hunched himself up as the child leaned through the opening, undid her bag and started lifting things through. A couple of times she glanced combatively over her shoulder at him. Among the stacks of T-shirts and skirts (she hadn't got a single pair of shorts), he could make out a few paperback books (good), a smart phone (not so good), a pad and some felt tips, half a dozen pots of nail varnish, a kit for making beads from papier-mâché, a photo album, several comics and a soft toy that resembled a scrawny, lanky monkey with Velcro on its hands and feet.

"This is Amandine," she said, "She's from Madagascar."

"Well, clearly Amandine must stay, if she's come all the way from Madagascar," Colin attempted a smile, which got no response. "But I'm not sure that you're going to need the–" he counted them under his breath, "–eight skirts, are you?"

"But of course." She tried stuffing them into her locker, which was bulging already. She sat back on her haunches and huffed a sigh. "They are mine. I need them." She surveyed the scene, curling the hem of an orange dress with her toe. She scooped it up and inspected it, thoughtfully, then she tugged the dress on and pulled a skirt on over it, followed by two T-shirts and a pair of stripy cotton tights. She was reaching for a purple and turquoise pinafore, when Colin stretched across and stopped her.

"You're going to get awfully hot like that."

To his horror, the face she turned towards him was full of grief, buckling, brimming grief. Her arms were crammed with clothes and she buried her face in them. "I need... I need..."

The sight of it floored him. "Right," he nodded after a beat or two. By stooping low and easing himself onto her bunk, he was able to lift his mattress and open his own locker. He scrabbled about inside and chucked a couple of pairs of trousers, most of his shirts and his second-best pair of shorts onto the deck. "I've got far too much stuff, actually. Much too much. More than I'll ever wear." He tried another smile, a warmer one this time. At the bottom of his locker were his waterproofs and his best shorts, two pairs of pants, two pairs of socks and two T-shirts. "One to wear and one to wash," he said bracingly.

The child regarded him.

"Plenty of room now."

With her eyes still on his face, warily, she began to stuff things into his locker until it was so full they could barely fit the lid back on. In the end they lined the shelves under the mattresses with her tops and her fleeces, so that when they lay down to test out their living quarters, their faces were only a couple of feet from the ceiling. A curling little laugh escaped from her, but then she covered her mouth with her hand as if she had done something wrong.

They looked at one another.

THE DRAGONFLY

"Where is the kitchen?" she asked, as if to change a subject which had never been broached.

Colin pointed to the seat on the starboard side of the deck. He clambered out of the cabin and lifted it up. "Here." Inside was a Primus stove, three saucepans that fitted inside each other, a water carrier, some plastic cups and plates, some Tupperware boxes and two glass jars full of tea and coffee.

The child nodded. "And the bathroom?"

"Here." Beneath the bench on the port side was a portapotti and a bucket with a sponge in it.

She nodded again. "What's under there?" She pointed at the seat along the back of the boat.

"Everything else," Moving the handle of the outboard motor to one side, he lifted the seat to show her the jerry can, the mallet, the mooring stakes, the spare rope, his fishing tackle.

"Merde," she remarked, more admiringly this time, and he had to pretend that he didn't understand.

~~~

Next door to the *Dragonfly*, the owners of the gin palace were watching satellite television, unmindful of the way that Paris wrapped itself around the marina, the street lights and illuminated windows of apartment blocks enamelling the night. Craning his neck, Colin could just make out their faces in the blue blur of the TV. He contemplated their portly contentment, trying to picture how it might feel. Thirty years ago, when he was still a man with dreams, he had imagined such companionable oblivion for himself and Sally.

He pulled a wry face and shivered, for down at canal level the air was dark as felt, but no longer warm. He tried dragging his T-shirt over his elbows, already regretting the cavalier way

33

he had thrown most of his wardrobe out with the rubbish. The child had been so upset, so raw with all her sorrows. He leaned forward, peering into the cabin, for the curious experience of seeing her sleeping. She still had her hat on; although it was tipped back on her head and for the first time he could see her hair. He tilted the hurricane lamp so that he could study the different nuances of gold and brown, the corkscrew curls. She looked so vivid, even in her sleep. He half reached out, as if he just might touch her forehead. He tried to picture himself smoothing it with his hand, and how that would feel. With a sigh he scooped up Amandine, who had fallen out of the narrow bed. For some reason the sight of the monkey, with its fur thinning in places, one side of its head more worn than the other, moulded out of shape from too much loving, shook him right to the bone. Before he could contain it, something between a cough and a sob racked out of him, so that he had to press the creature against his chest to quiet himself.

Back on deck the night was cold. On impulse, he climbed onto the pontoon and made his way to the waste bins. Like some dispossessed old drunk he rooted through the rubbish bags until he found his own and yanked out a sweatshirt and jumper. He pulled them both on – a leaf out of the child's book – and thought he would have his one cigarette of the day before he turned in.

He smoked it standing up beside the cabin door so that he could look down any time he liked and see his granddaughter. Earlier on, thinking what on earth he was going to do with her, he went across to the Capitainerie and bought a navigation book for the French waterways. His original plan had been to sit tight in Paris so that he could be on hand to help his son build his case. He stared into the asphalt dark. Well, that didn't appear to be an option. He flicked his cigarette into the water, watching the fallout of bitter sparks. He knew that he couldn't spend six weeks knocking about in the Arsenal Marina with a nine-year-old girl who'd need entertaining and amusing. He wouldn't know where to begin. A trip would help him manufacture an adventure for her. Leaning down, he retrieved the navigation guide from the shelf above his bed and began leafing through charts showing mighty rivers like the Seine and the Yonne. He licked his lips. The *Dragonfly* had never been further than the Kennet and Avon canal – their finest hour to date had been a voyage to Avoncliff for a spot of fishing and a ploughman's at the Cross Guns pub. With a cautious finger he traced the line of the river through the untamed *banlieux* of Paris, wondering what lay ahead of them now, and whether he or his beautiful little boat would be up to the job.

CHAPTER FOUR

It was three-thirty in the morning and Michael couldn't sleep. Three-thirty in the morning didn't seem that different from three-thirty in the afternoon. Imprisonment didn't only mean the loss of freedom; it meant the loss of meaning: everything you did was just serving time and if you weren't careful, and Michael wasn't always careful, it would be easy to feel that nothing mattered anymore.

The bed was the wrong bed; the room was the wrong room. The morbid shadows that existed at night time in the corners of a prison cell unnerved him. They made him think of the first few nights away from home after his mother left his father, that same feeling of temporary exile that turned out to be not quite so temporary after all. He drew a breath in as he found himself back in the emigrant landscape of unfamiliar sheets and alien smells with the vulnerable little boy he had been all those years ago. It was like taking an elevator down into ancient history, to the point where all the trouble started, his stomach fluttering at the nauseous descent.

Down and down and down he went into the watery wash of light of a spring afternoon. The air was still damp with fallen rain and he and his Dad had come tumbling back from football in the park covered in mud and leaf mould. Bathwick

Wanderers (Dad) had been playing England (Michael) and had taken a thrashing. "Seven One, Seven One," he sang an anthemic chant all the way back to the house. "Can we play Top Trumps?" he asked, kicking off his trainers without undoing the laces.

"When you've had a shower…"

"*Dad…*"

"And given me your dirty clothes. I can't send you home to your mother in this state."

There was a catch of breath in his chest when his father said this: the dawning, the remembering. He couldn't work out who to love because loving them both as he did seemed to be out of the question.

"Go on, scram, or there won't be time."

While they played Top Trumps at the kitchen table, he kept darting glances at the clock, glances which became more frequent as his Dad cooked the lunch, a proper Sunday roast with all the trimmings just for the two of them. They had pancakes for pudding and his Dad was doing his party piece, tossing a pancake with one hand while flipping a coin with the other, when the doorbell rang. Michael was conscious of tidying up his smile and putting it away.

"Better get your things…"

He stared at the floor, feeling suddenly precarious.

"Hey…" his Dad ran a finger down Michael's cheek. "Who's my boy?"

"I'm your boy…" he whispered.

"*Who's* my boy?"

Michael couldn't answer.

"Seven One, eh? What about that?"

The bell sounded again.

"Time's up, old chap."

They walked together to the door; Michael measuring his footsteps, he already knew the number it would take. Colin reached for his hand and squeezed it.

"Chin up," he said gently.

Michael nodded.

His mother was standing huddled close to the front door, to keep out of the drizzle. All three of them tensed as his Dad opened it.

"How's he been?"

"He's been fine."

Michael hovered in the hallway, his school reading bag in his hand.

"I think he finds the changeover difficult," he heard his Dad observe in a quiet tone.

"Don't we all?" his Mum said. She stared unseeingly at the shrubs which lined the path. She studied her shoes. "I didn't really want to go into this, not right now." She looked at her watch. "but since you've raised the subject – can I come in for a moment?" She stepped into the hall. "Michael, go and sit in the car."

"He can watch a bit of telly if he wants."

"He can sit in the car."

They none of them moved though, and Michael started putting his books into his school reading bag with sad precision.

"He gets upset when he's leaving me as well, you know," his Mum pointed out, walking into the sitting room. "It works both ways."

"That only makes it worse, doesn't it?" his Dad said, following behind.

Michael watched them through the open door way. She swept her gaze over the shelves of books, then into the garden. "Is that a *boat* you're building?" she asked, diverted for a moment. He nodded.

"We can't go on like this." His mother's voice was smooth. "I'm thinking of applying to the court to suspend the visits for the time being."

Michael dropped his school bag. His mother looked over her shoulder at him, annoyed.

"Go and sit in the car, Michael. I'll be with you in a moment," she said, turning back to his father. "If these visits are upsetting him there's no point, is there?" she reasoned and Michael put his hands over his ears, to blot out the sound. "You could take him out for tea, that kind of thing, but no more overnights, until he seems more settled…"

"*What?*"

"You were saying that he gets upset. We have to put Michael's interests first…"

"But that's all I've ever wanted, that's what I've always tried to do: to put him first," his Dad protested.

~~~

Michael turned over in his prison bed. He lay on his back listening to the sound of Laroche breathing, trying to work out if he was awake or not. At the far end of the wing somebody was throwing a chair against a door with deadening monotony. The regular pulse of violence, the metronome tick of it, was everywhere.

Another memory surfaced of a Sunday visit – the overnights had finished months before – queasy from too many liquorice allsorts and blinking at the afternoon brightness, he and his father had come charging out of the cinema with the ululations of Africa sounding in their ears. Mufasa (Dad) led

Simba (Michael) safely through the Pridelands of Bath to a burger bar, where they hunted down two cheeseburgers and chips. Michael could have gone on being the young prince all afternoon. He drooped in his seat. He pushed his drink away.

"What's that? Over there!" said his Dad, nicking a chip as he craned his neck to see. "Gotcha! Come on then, you can track me through the Country and Western section of HMV if you like."

They continued the Big Game game to oblige each other, prowling from store to store, Michael coming in for the kill as his Dad immersed himself in the football results showing on the TV screens in one of the shop windows, but when they got home to the house all the golden prairie light ebbed away.

The doorbell rang. His mother was standing on the doorstep in a summer dress. She pushed her sunglasses back on her head, "Say thank you to Daddy and go and sit in the car. Now." She propelled Michael down the path. "I need to talk to you," he heard her say as she doubled back to his father. "It would have been easier to put this in a letter," she bit her lip. "The thing is, Étienne is going back to France. He's asked us to go with him."

His Mum was speaking in her irritated voice; the one she often used with him when he had done something to upset her but couldn't be quite sure what. "I want a divorce. We should have done it ages ago."

Michael leaned over, reached for the armrest and pulled the door shut. He thought he might like to live in the car for ever. Never come out. He sat for a while staring into his lap. There was an AA road map tucked into the pocket on the back of the driver's seat and he wondered about taking it out, leafing from page to page tracing the route until he had worked out how many miles it was from Bath to France.

Us: Mum, Étienne, me.

His parents were shouting.

"You can't do this to me. You can't do this to Michael."

So loud, he could hear them from the car. He thought he might feel better if he had a mint and as he leaned forward between the seats to pinch one from the packet on the dashboard he glanced instinctively to check if anyone was looking, just at that moment when his father swung back his arm to its full extent.

The blow sent his mother's head jerking sideways, the ferocity of it spreading out from the roots of her hair. Her sunglasses fell to the ground. As though in continuous motion, his father went veering away from her. She put the glasses on, a little crookedly because her hands were shaking. She turned and came rushing down the path, her hand pressed to her mouth. Michael sat back in his seat. He didn't really want the mint, not now.

He didn't know who to love, anymore.

~~~

In the pale prison light of the Paris dawn, he could hear the sound of stifled crying. He wiped his eyes on the sleeve of his tee shirt, but his T-shirt was dry. He tilted his head, trying to discern the strange topography of the man not sleeping in the bed against the far wall: Laroche with his head buried in his pillow, choking down furious sobs so that no one would hear.

CHAPTER FIVE

"Did you sail across the channel in him?" The child had finished her chocolate croissant and was halfway through the almond one he'd bought for Amandine.

"It's a her," said Colin, "She's a she." He glanced at her. She was sitting on the cabin roof, dangling her feet over the hatch. "Boats are feminine in English."

"In France they are men. *Le bateau*. Masculin."

"Is that so?

"And we are in France, non?"

"Have you finished with your plate?"

"So? Did you cross the channel in him?"

He so badly wanted to say yes, he so badly wanted to, that he almost committed himself to a *Little Ships of Dunkirk* moment, some fiction about setting off from Dover with a fair wind blowing, himself the hero of the tale, battling ferries the size of tower blocks and container ships all the way from Russia; he even took a breath to begin.

"I brought her over on a trailer on a ferry from Portsmouth. I parked up in the north of Paris."

The child picked a flake of pastry off her cheek and ate it.

"I sailed her down the Canal St Martin, though. We came through the tunnel under the Place de la Bastille, at the end over there…"

She wasn't listening. She swivelled round, bottomed her way along the cabin roof and slid down the sloping window at the front onto the bow. She slid down again, and again, not with joy, not with gales of laughter, but with great seriousness. Then she sat cross-legged just behind the flagpole – you couldn't call it a foredeck – and waited.

When everything was stowed away and the rope was loosened but not undone, he placed the navigation book on the bench at the back, anchored it from the wind with a pair of binoculars, made an excited, thumbs up sign at the child then busied himself with the outboard motor. He checked that it wasn't in gear, that the fuel switch was on and then let some air into the tank. He leaned in close, tinkering with the choke. The sun was shining and the heat was already collecting in thin folds just above the water. Satisfied with his preparations he gave one almighty yank on the starter cord.

There was a cracking sound and that slippery sense of a blow falling, of flesh splitting open. He spun round as the child screamed. She was splayed out on the deck at his feet, both hands covering her left eye. He had no idea that she had been standing right behind him. He dropped to his knees.

"It's alright, it's OK. Let me see. Let me have a look. It's OK."

Her mouth had that wide, breached look: the skin around it was stretched white and strings of spit ran from tooth to tooth. There was phlegm streaming from her nose and a red thread of blood running from under her fingers.

"Let me see," he whispered, holding her wrists gently.

"I won't hurt you–" *Holy God – as if he hadn't done that already.* "I just need to look at your eye, just a quick look." He peeled her hands apart. When she saw the blood, the child started sobbing, making her small frame judder. He put his arms round her, trying to collect her up and hold her to him, but she was uncontainable, punching and slapping in all directions, hitting him and hitting him,

"Laissez-moi, laissez-moi!"

He held her as best he could, though she kept slipping from his grip like a river fish. He held her until she was calm, until she had cried herself out. He was conscious of a knot of people gathering in that helpful way which boaters have. Cupping both her hands in one of his, he managed a brief inspection of her eye. His elbow must have caught her just on the line of her brow; there was a split about a centimetre long in her eyelid.

"It's nothing, it's just a scratch," he said, to put courage into both of them. He wasn't very good with blood. He clambered to his feet, holding the child in his arms. "Is there a doctor? A hospital?"

One of the boaters gestured up at the street on the other side of the marina. "There's a hospital in the Faubourg St Antoine. Là bas," she said. "You take a taxi," she managed in English at the end.

Colin nodded. Still holding the child, he clambered onto the pontoon. He glanced back at the *Dragonfly*, her hatch open, her rope not properly tied. No time for that; no time for anything. He half-ran towards the quay.

"Amandine! I cannot leave without Amandine. It is not possible."

He went racing back for the monkey and with his granddaughter half cradled, half slung over his shoulder, managed to shut the hatch and bolt it. There was blood and snot on his shirt, and his own sweat, and panic in the humid air. He climbed the steps to the street two or three at a time and ran along the boulevard and every taxi that he tried to flag down was occupied.

Finally, he succeeded in finding one and flung himself inside. The child lay in his lap, her stillness worse than all her screams. He felt rickety with age and remorse. He had barely caught his breath when they arrived at Accident and Emergency. He didn't understand the questions that they asked him. A nurse detached his granddaughter from him as if she were some kind of mollusc and sat her on the examination trolley, where she explained what had happened, her French fluid, expressive, and from time to time the nurse looked in his direction, nodded and wrote something down and he found that he could comprehend all of it, and none of it at all. The child had become the adult and he felt as powerless as a child.

"They say I must be knitted," she informed him.

"Stitched," he corrected her, automatically, and the child regarded him in baleful silence. "I'm sorry," he muttered, "I'm terribly sorry."

The doctor, when he arrived, read the nurse's notes noncommittally then studied Colin without speaking, sizing him up as a child protection risk, or so it felt. *They'll have the social workers on to me before you can say Jack Robinson. I haven't even had her for twenty-four hours.* He sighed and stared at the floor.

Lugubriously, the doctor turned back to the child, his manner suggesting Colin's dismissal. He was halfway to the door when a frightened little voice said, "Please don't leave me…" and he felt his heart rise to the surface of his chest.

~~~

It wasn't long before they were standing on the pavement outside the hospital. The doctor had glued the edges of Delphine's cut together as if she were an Airfix model. The swelling was spreading from her brow to her cheek bone and turning duck egg blue. ("To match the *Dragonfly*," Colin told her.)

"Where can we go?" she asked.

"We can go anywhere that you want."

"Anywhere?"

"Absolutely. My treat. To make up for–"

She shrugged, a Gallic shrug, so young, so young.

"I'm really sorry. I had no idea that you were standing there." He wasn't used to having people with him on the boat; that was the truth of the matter. The loneliness of the thought spread through every part of him. "I should have checked."

"De rien," she chirped. "Can we go to Gautier's?"

"Gautier's?"

"We used to go…" she tailed off, seeming to draw inwards, to grow smaller. "Before…"

He commandeered another taxi to take them to the ninth arrondissement and for a brief moment Colin felt like a young beau out on the town with his girl, not some old geezer minding a kid to whom he'd just done actual bodily harm. Her hand was lying next to his on the back seat, but he felt he didn't know her well enough to take it and give it a squeeze.

He wasn't sure what he was expecting, but it certainly wasn't a former soup kitchen from the Belle Époque, a vast dining hall with brass luggage racks above the tables. The child stood at the entrance, staring at the revolving door, her eyes enormous; she turned to him and he felt as if she was offering him her sadness and he had no idea how to take it from her.

"Amandine likes ice cream for dessert," she whispered.

"Does she, now?" he answered, shepherding her inside.

Fiercely, the waiter scrawled down their order – steak frites for Delphine and Toulouse sausage for him – on the paper tablecloth. His white apron had traces of gravy on it, or possibly, Colin thought, patron's blood.

"Papa always has sausages," she remarked.

It was the first time she had mentioned Michael. The chatter in the restaurant receded like the sea and for a moment he felt as if he was stranded on the shore of his son's life: Michael used to come here with his daughter and eat sausages. It was something to know about him, a glimpse afforded. Colin had to remember to breathe. *Papa always has sausages.* She used the present tense, as if Michael might come flickering through the revolving doors even now.

"And what about your mother, what did she have?" he asked with a dry mouth, walking on broken glass.

"Fish – I don't know the name in English – truite – with salad and a glass of white wine."

"It's the same."

"What?"

"In English – trout – it's practically the same word."

"Oh," she answered in retreat, as if she had already given away too much. He felt as if he had no option but to press on, now that they had started: there was nowhere else for him to go.

"How is… Papa? Have you heard from him?"

The child started to swing her legs under the table. She sat Amandine down between her knife and fork and began speaking to her in sing song baby talk French, as if she were explaining something complex to a two-year-old. It sounded very involved.

He wondered when the food would come.

"Amandine wants to know why you stopped talking to Papa," the child was staring at the Velcro on the monkey's paw.

"It's a long story." He reached for a piece of bread and broke the crust, holding the pieces in his fingers. "It's a bit complicated."

"So?"

He sensed her glancing at him. He pressed the sharpened edges of the crumbs down onto the table.

"I worked in an office," he cleared his throat, "A long time ago now, and we lived in England, your grandmother and your father and me."

"Where in England?" she whispered.

"In a town called Bath."

The slouch of her hat was obscuring most of her face, but he could just see the rim of the bruising.

"And your grandmother Sally taught in a university nearby."

"Sally…" the child echoed.

"She taught part-time and there was another teacher there–"

"What did she teach?"

"She taught something called Economics. There was another teacher there, a man, a French teacher, and they became… friends–"

"What was his name?"

Colin broke the bread in half and then in half again. "Étienne. His name was Étienne. He was from somewhere in the north of France, I don't remember now."

"Étienne."

"And he and your grandmother became very *good* friends and when his job in England finished and it was time for him to go home to France, he asked your grandmother if she would like to go with him."

The food arrived, complete with the kind of zinc covers you see in work canteens. The waiter removed them with a vindictive sweep.

"What did she say? Sally? What did she say?"

To the child it was simply a story, too remote from her own life to have resonance or meaning. He wished that it were so for him. Bitterness can become a way of life; he knew that now. "She said yes." He picked up his knife and fork. The sausages were covered in khaki lentils. He wondered what kind of man Michael had become – a man who ate this food, in this place, with this little girl and the woman he'd confessed to killing. "Do you want mustard with that?"

"Mayonnaise."

"Mayonnaise? With steak?"

"For les frites," she answered with her mouth full.

"You'd better ask for it."

"It's the same word." She propped Amandine against her water glass, placing a finger against her lips for her to be quiet. "You moved to France also – yes?" she asked, eating, not looking at him.

"I didn't go, no. Your grandmother went."

"And Papa?"

Colin felt very tired. The events of the morning were catching up with him. He wasn't used to all this... conversation.

"Yes," he breathed. The noise from the neighbouring tables was breaking like waves around them. "Yes, she took your father. She took Michael."

"And you didn't see him after that?" she asked with incredulity. "It is not possible?"

"Of course we saw each other, just not so often. As time goes by it's easy to lose touch."

The child nodded. She started swinging her legs under the table again. "Amandine is hungry for her ice cream," she said after a pause.

"What flavour does she like?"

"Chocolat!"

"And what about you?"

"I like vanilla and strawberry."

With help from her, he ordered more ice cream than a monkey could conceivably eat on its own, and paid the bill.

"I loved your father very much – love him," he corrected himself. "Like he loves you."

"Is it very easy?" she asked in a low voice, "To lose touch?"

It took him a while to frame his answer. "It's up to you," he said. "In the end, it's up to you."

~~~

"Stand well back," Colin glanced over his shoulder and grinned at his granddaughter. She was still out of breath from having run all the way round to the Capitainerie on the other side of the marina, to let them know that the *Dragonfly* wanted to pass down through the lock and out onto the Seine.

The outboard started first time with a brisk expectoration.

"OK, now the engine's running it's alright to cast off." He waited as she bundled the rope back through the cleat on the pontoon and dropped it like spaghetti on the deck. "Coil it up, that's right, like I showed you." He watched her busy little arms at work. "Ahoy there – and off we go!"

"What is ahoy?"

He shrugged, "It's something sailors say."

"But what does it mean?"

"I don't know – *hello*, I suppose, or *look out*."

"Ahoy," she called back at him, a note of mistrust in her voice; she sounded sceptical, miniscule French cynic that she was.

The *Dragonfly* swung out from her berth, shaking her tail as she went, her wash scattering opalescent water up into the air. He had to resist the temptation to put her through all her paces while they were still in the marina, but he wanted the child to be impressed. He throttled under the road bridge and into the open lock, halting neatly just next to the bollard at the lock side, and with a flick of his wrist looped the centre line over it. He put the engine into neutral.

"Look," he said. "I have to stay with the engine, so I need you to look after the rope from the middle of the boat, like this. You must keep it fairly taut so we stay close to the lock wall…"

The gates were closing automatically, sounding metallic sighs.

"…but not too close – see? You need to make sure that the fenders stop the boat from getting scratched." As the water began to sluice away, the rivery brickwork of the lock wall was revealed: slime and mucus in emerald and sage. "You might need to push her off a little bit."

"Ugh!" she pulled a face when he pressed his hand against the side to ease the boat out. "But it is all green." Reflexively she wiped her own clean hand on her T-shirt. "It is not *possible*."

"What's really important," Colin was getting into his stride now, "…is to make sure that the rope doesn't get caught – make sure it's taut, but free, like this. That way, as the water goes down, the boat can go down with it. D'you see?"

He could see that she kind of saw. She was frowning as much as her sore eye would permit, her mouth ruched up in concentration. *Too much information*, he thought as he handed her the line. He could manage the boat single-handed, but he wanted her to feel part of it.

Strands of weed and twigs and empty milk cartons eddied round as the gates creaked open. It was like the curtain rising at the theatre – before them, the Seine was revealed. He didn't rev the engine straight away, but sat there feeling the sort of wonderment that borders on gratitude. He was open-mouthed. "You can cast off now," he called to her, collecting himself, and he tooted the horn which made her jump and with a quick zip of the motor sped out onto the river.

There was a breeze blowing and the water was choppy, but the *Dragonfly* took it blithely. The child seemed a little less blithe: as the boat skimmed the waves she held onto the grab rails tightly and then a moment later slid along the bench to sit close to him.

"Are you alright?"

She didn't answer. Her eyes were enormous which meant, he was beginning to learn, that all was not well.

"Would you like to see Notre Dame?"

She swallowed.

Craftily, he tried another tack. "Amandine mentioned that she would really like to see Notre Dame," he began, "and the Louvre, and the Eiffel Tower."

She gave him a look of such reproof that it left him in no doubt he had trampled his way over some invisible line. "Amandine has already been up the Eiffel Tower," she responded with chill disdain.

"Hold on tight–" he advised, as a Bateau Mouche churned past them. She was called *Catherine Deneuve* and from their perch at the back of the *Dragonfly*, she seemed vast. The tourists on board waved and pointed as the wash from her sent the little boat skittering and toppling and Colin had to wrench at the tiller to keep them on an even keel.

Around the Île de la Cité was a complicated one-way system governed by traffic lights, which he had read up on the night before, which was just as well as the *Dragonfly* appeared to be fair game for the large pleasure craft – as they passed the cathedral, *Yves Montand* overtook them so fast it nearly sent them flying, cutting them up from behind by the banks of the Île Saint-Louis.

"It won't always be this rough," he exclaimed, struggling to keep them steady. The current was strong and the wind was blowing a force three, he reckoned: enough to tie a vessel twice the size of theirs into considerable knots. *Not quite like the Kennet and Avon Canal*, he thought, as they flew downstream under road bridges and rail bridges, stone bridges and steel bridges, bridges so gilded and ornate that they took his breath away.

"That must be the Louvre, over there behind you on the right," he called as they went speeding past, spray breaking over the bows and misting the cabin portholes. He was starting to enjoy himself, getting the measure of the river, his wonderful, expressive, responsive little boat nipping past houseboats and matching the police launches stroke for stroke.

The child was sitting tensely, her elbows and knees gripped at ninety degrees. He eased back on the throttle as it occurred to him that she might have been frightened, bounding along as they were, and just as he did so she arced back and then forward with astonishing grace and let loose a projectile stream of vomit.

The sick missed her own lap entirely, splashing his leg and filling his sandal as it fountained through the hatch and into the cabin.

"Don't worry. It's OK. Don't worry. Are you alright?" He couldn't put the engine into neutral, not with the *Dragonfly* pitching and dancing the way she was and so much river traffic all about. "I promise we'll stop as soon as we can. Just hold on a minute."

Her round, reproachful eyes regarded him.

"It couldn't matter less, honestly. There's nothing that won't wash," he tried again, but as he spoke the two of them caught sight of Amandine, supine on the bunk, plastered with puke from head to toe. The child's lower lip began to wobble, but with some effort, an acceptance of another affliction, she kept herself in check.

The spew was drying to a damp crust on his shin, but it was the dejected figure of the child, sitting with quiet, green dignity, which perplexed him. He looked at her doubtfully. He'd intended to do a quick circuit of the sights of central Paris to put her in the mood before heading south to the suburbs, but he knew from past experience that the thing about boating was never to make plans. As *Jeanne Moreau* went thundering past them, he leaned across and with a cautious hand he ruffled the child's hair. "It's OK, we'll soon get everything cleaned up and then you'll feel much better." He wasn't sure if it was his imagination, but for a second it seemed to him that she leaned her good cheek against him and he was conscious of the burden of the responsibility, the unanticipated obligation he'd acquired. "Perhaps we'd better head back to port. We can have a shower and I'll make us both a cup of tea."

"*Coca-Cola,*" she corrected him before he had finished his sentence.

"Of course, *Coca-Cola.* That's just what I was thinking," Keeping her as steady as could be, Colin turned the *Dragonfly* so that she was facing into the current and malodorously yet sedately, they began the journey back.

CHAPTER SIX

"It's legal, honest – you've got to try it."

Michael glimpsed a tiny plastic pouch held like a hidden cigarette between Laroche's fingers.

"S'called Benzo Roar."

He shuddered to think what orifice it had come from – or whose. "It's alright," he said, "it's not my thing. I'm not–"

"Like all the rest of us?" said Laroche with a smirk.

Christ, thought Michael. *The days are long here.*

"Everyone thinks that, when they come here. *I'm not like all the rest.* You wait. You'll see." He gave a smile that wasn't really a smile. "You sure?" he said, dangling the pouch between his thumb and finger. "Little ickle taste? You won't know until you try."

"No, I'm not interested." He picked up his book and started reading.

"If you change ya mind, you know where to find me, oink, oink."

He didn't like Laroche's laugh. He didn't like his… proximity. A sense of antipathy rose like heat inside him. For a moment everything he hated about his situation: the privation, the confinement – for fuck's sake, the grief – was made flesh in the figure of his cellmate sitting at the table, sprinkling some white powder into a Rizla, wrapping it with another and another, making a small paper bomb which he swallowed with a swig of water. Then he sat, holding on to the sides of the table, his eyes closed, waiting. Michael was transfixed by the veins standing out in his arms, the lunar whiteness of his knuckles with their bodged tattoos, L O V E   H A T E done with a needle and ink on another interminable afternoon in a cell just like this one.

Stop, he said to himself. *Laroche is right. I will end up* – he was going to say *like him*, but he corrected himself. *Full of hate.* Where had this whittled edge inside him come from? He was a designer. He was interested in function and form. He tried to make beautiful things. Everything had gone so wrong.

He started the paragraph he was reading over again.

Laroche began beating some insistent rhythm with his foot upon the floor. Michael went back to the beginning of the paragraph, trying to focus. Laroche kept beating his foot. Michael tried mouthing the words to himself to help him concentrate. Laroche introduced a counterpoint, tapping his fingers against the tabletop. With a single, flowing action, Michael could have thrown the book to the end of the bed to make a point; he could have thrown it across the floor perilously close to where the guy was sitting. He had it raised and ready. Then he remembered the guttural sound, the other night, of Laroche trying not to cry. He rested the book against his chest. He reminded himself of the man he had been, of the man he still wanted to be.

"You alright?" he said.

Laroche let his head fall back. "Too fucking right I am, ya Rosbif ponce."

~~~

"The number you have dialled is unavailable. The number you have dialled is unavailable. The number you have dialled–" For a moment, Michael understood why a man might throw a chair against a door time after time, or start a fight, or beat his head against the bricks, or sob into the private recess of the night. The disappointment was like a stain – blood, or some other bodily fluid, hard to erase. The whole fabric of the week was spoilt. "Please try again later." He listened as the dialling tone clicked in.

"Can I try again later?"

The kanga shook his head and then jerked it in the direction of the door.

"She's my daughter, please –"

The kanga shook his head.

"She's only nine."

"One call, that's the rule."

"But if she's got her phone switched off?"

"Not my rules. I don't make 'em. Shift yourself, now."

Michael followed him back to the cell, dragging his feet like a child. He remembered the race they used to have on sports day in primary school: see how slowly you can ride your bike without falling off. It was an art he was perfecting now: see how slowly you can do things – eating, reading, walking. See how slowly you can go, without falling.

Back in the cell he slumped on his bed with his head in his hands, something he regretted straightaway.

"Woss up, Rosbif?"

He sat up straight. He didn't answer. It was the only way he had to protect himself.

"I said, woss up?"

"Nothing."

"Louder – can't hear on the dark side over here."

"Nothing's wrong. Everything's fine. Everything's absofuckinglutely great. If you want to know."

"Alright, alright. Just asking."

"It was my phone call today. My daughter was out. That's all. I'm – sorry."

Laroche gave him a long, assessing stare, weighing something up. "I've got a daughter," he said.

Michael glanced at him, arrested for a moment.

"Yeah, yeah. Got a daughter. 'Nother kid on the way, woss more."

"I didn't know that."

"Zazie. Poncey name. I didn't pick it. I'd have called her Marianne, after me mum. She's four. *Zazie*, for Christ's sake." He shook his head.

"Mine's called Delphine. She's nine."

"Delphine, eh? That's a poncey name an' all."

Michael didn't answer.

"Different mothers, mine – obvs."

"Yes," he said. "I see."

"Wotch you need," said Laroche, leaning forward with a swift action, seeming to burrow inside his mattress, "is one of these little lovelies." He produced a cellphone which he threw into the air and caught in the heel of his hand, backwards.

"Where did you get that?" asked Michael, in astonishment.

"You can get whatever you like. Just need the contacts. And the notes. Chapot," he said darkly, "is taking deliveries by drone. An-y-thing."

Michael hadn't yet clocked who Chapot was. He didn't want to be seen to be looking.

"There's a lag in here, done for fraud, runs a business on his mobile buying and selling container ships he doesn't own. The world's yer oyster, mate."

"Could I...?" said Michael.

"It'll cost yer," said Laroche, twirling an invisible moustache.

"How much?"

"I'll think of something," he said with a leer. "You can be sure of that."

Michael hesitated. It would be another whole week before he could speak to her otherwise. "OK. Thanks."

It took three missed calls before she answered.

"Delphine?"

"Papa!"

Hearing her voice made her absence better and worse.

CHAPTER SEVEN

They set off the following morning with Amandine, who had been soaked overnight in a bucket of disinfectant, lashed to the flagpole to dry out, and her owner curled up in her sleeping bag in the cabin, turned away from her grandfather, staring into nothingness.

The evening before they had washed their clothes and their bedding and themselves, hosing down the deck and lockers just for good measure and now, as they crept back onto the Seine at a sober pace, Colin's nostrils were full of the ferrous smell of river water and the faint whiff of Gauloises that was always in the air.

The child was holding her grey tweed hat in both hands, pressing it to her mouth, breathing in and out through the material. Her hair strayed over the pillow in brittle curls. Wordlessly, she'd declined the croissant that he'd bought her for breakfast.

"You won't be sick again today, I promise. The wind's dropped, it's as quiet as a millpond out there and we're going where no Bateau Mouche would dare to go…"

She didn't answer.

"Would you like some orange juice? Or some tea?" *I can't give her Coca-Cola at half-past eight in the morning*, he thought. "Or some *Coca-Cola?*"

At all his patient little offerings, she shook her head.

As the *Dragonfly* followed a judicious course south towards Ivry, he maintained a running commentary, to cheer himself up as much as her.

"We're just going under the Pont d'Austerlitz," he called to her, "Austerlitz was one of Napoleon's biggest battles – did you know that?"

Nothing.

"Do you know why French bread is the shape that it is? So Napoleon's soldiers could tuck it into their boots as they rode along. It says so in the guidebook…"

In the face of her overwhelming indifference, he looked hectically round for more inspiration. The river frontage was changing: the opulent constructions of empire and ambition drawn aside to reveal the workings beneath. The plate glass office blocks and the broken glass of decaying quayside warehouses; angular cranes like mechanical birds; pallets and containers; the blue flank of a passing barge; the strenuous arches of a railway bridge; a couple sitting on the embankment next to an empty pushchair, the man holding a baby on his knee, the woman looking away; the exhalation of a slender chimney stack; a streak of graffiti and stretches of concrete, intersecting; a vapour trail high in the wistful sky. From the corner of his eye he could see a gravel barge coming up behind them, shouldering through the water. As it drew abreast of them, the river billowed and then flattened. There was a Renault Mégane mounted on the rear deck. The bargee gave a desultory nod of his head as he went past.

Colin decided that they would find somewhere to tie up for lunch, to give them both a break. He wanted to walk to the nearest bakery with the child. He wanted to point things out to her. He wanted to buy her a cake in the shape of a swan and bet her a euro that she couldn't finish it. He wanted everything to be simple and straightforward.

She wouldn't come with him though, in spite of all his persuasion, so he went to a Petit Casino on his own to buy the bread. Cake-wise all that was on offer were some madeleines, sealed up in cellophane bags, which looked as if they'd bounce if you dropped them, so he didn't bother.

When he proffered a ham baguette she regarded him with watchful eyes.

"You've got to eat something."

She shrugged.

"And eventually you're going to have to say something, too."

"I don't want to be on this boat. There."

"Look, I know that we didn't get off to the best possible start, but we're on our way now and once we get out of Paris—" he broke off, a thought occurring to him. "Actually, I'm going to need your help this afternoon." He flipped up the seat at the stern and rummaged around in the everything locker. "It's a VHF radio," he explained when he found what he was searching for. "There's a lock coming up fairly soon, a bit of a whopper actually, and we need to radio the lock keeper to ask him when we can pass through. The barges have priority, but hopefully he'll be able to squeeze us in at the back."

The child took the radio and turned it over in her hand. She ran her thumb over the brand name and pushed a button or two, then turned it over in her hand again.

"The trouble is, I can't speak French…"

She held the radio up to her ear.

"It switches on at the top," Colin said. "Then you turn this knob here to tune it to the channel that you want…"

The hiss and whisper of the VHF sounded between them. Technologically nimble, the child's fingers moved over the keys.

"It's channel ten for the lock. You might be able to speak to other barges, too. You press the button at the side to talk and you let it go to listen."

A voice squawked so loudly she almost dropped the handset. She swung her legs over the edge of her bunk and wriggled her way out of the cabin, a sly grin playing around her mouth.

"Press to talk, let go to listen?"

He nodded.

Reaching for the baguette, and groping for Amandine until she remembered she was tied to the flagpole, the child fired up the VHF. "Bonjour? Allo?"

A push-tow barge was grinding down the centre of the river. Divided into two separate craft, the container at the front was rammed full with building rubble, while doing the hard work at the rear was the engine section, topped off by the living quarters. There was a battered Citroën Xantia at the stern, with a hoist for lifting it on to dry land; squeezed in next to that was a washing machine apparently going through the spin cycle and in front of the cockpit was a playpen the size of a small British semi. The boat was called *Calista*.

The child was talking with her mouth full, wolfing down unintelligible syllables and sentences, scattering crumbs, her chatter voluble and artless. She started waving her baguette in the air as if to attract attention. "Au secours," she said as she signed off. "Au secours!" With a flick of the switch to turn the handset off, she flashed Colin a beguiling smile.

"Did you speak to the lock keeper?"

"I talk with Denis. We must be quick." She began tugging at the rope. "We need to throw off the boat, hurry, hurry."

"Denis?" queried Colin, starting the engine. "It's cast off. Cast – not throw. Is Denis the lock keeper?"

"Denis is Mister *Calista*," she gestured with the remains of her lunch at the disappearing push-tow.

Obligingly, at such short notice, the *Dragonfly* made her way up river in the wake of the massive barge. Colin viewed his granddaughter through narrow eyes. She preened at him – like a small bird, she settled her feathers. If there had been more space on deck, she would have strutted up and down. Coming under a road bridge, he could see the entrance to the lock on the left bank. The gravel barge was already tied up and the *Calista* was docking alongside her.

"But this is your lock," Delphine nodded at the sign by the entrance.

He squinted up at it. Port à l'Anglais.

It was an up lock and from their vantage point nearly three metres down, tucked in behind the churning sterns of the two barges, the quayside seemed unreachably high. The distant bollards were spaced for two hundred foot vessels, not small fry like the *Dragonfly*. Colin manoeuvred close to a ladder set into the wall and grabbed onto it with a boathook, which he passed to the child.

"Hold tight, now."

He was in the process of looping the line round the ladder and keeping an eye on the little girl, when a voice called down from above.

"It is Denis!" Delphine whooped, letting go of the boathook to wave. Colin lunged at the ladder as a bargee in a nylon singlet, sporting much armpit hair, frowned down on them. Not for the first time, he felt as if he were under scrutiny as a child protection risk. The lock was filling and inch by inch the boats were rising. When he and Mister *Calista* were nose to knee, the man began speaking. Colin couldn't understand much of what he was saying, he could pick out one or two words – kidnap, for instance, which like trout and mayonnaise were the same in English – and gendarme, he got that one, too. He turned to Delphine.

"Am I right in thinking what I'm thinking?" he asked her. "Am I fully up to speed with this?"

His granddaughter was making a detailed study of the hoist on the back of the barge, as though she might sketch it later, from memory.

"Perhaps you could put me more fully in the picture? What exactly did you tell our friend here?"

She didn't look at him directly, but her eyes flicked sideways. "I said to him that I am on this boat against my will. Which is true," she added defiantly. "I say the same to you, non?"

A complicated inflection escaped from Colin. "You did say that, yes. Although that is *slightly* different from…"

"I didn't think that he would call the police," she said in a small voice.

"Has he called the police?"

The bargee took a long hard look at the darkening bruise around the child's eye and switched his gaze to Colin. With a hand the size of an Alsace ham he cleaned out the contents of one ear, wiping his finger on his trouser leg.

"He says you must give a satisfactory account, or–"

"I'm her *grand-père*," he began, while the man cleaned out his other ear. When assistance with translation was not forthcoming from his granddaughter, he said in a louder voice,

"Vacances… grand-père… Angleterre." He smiled and nodded and then for good measure he attempted a Gallic shrug.

Denis was unimpressed. With ostentatious slowness, he craned his head to look at the back of their boat, where the *Dragonfly's* name and registration number were emblazoned in a deeper shade of blue. He appeared to be making ponderous mental notes.

In a moment of inspiration Colin whipped his mobile phone out of his pocket and began thumbing through his list of contacts, "You can talk to her grandmother, if you like. She will explain."

This was an eventuality that Delphine hadn't costed into her escape plan. "Pas nécessaire," she said swiftly to Denis. "I make a joke, une petite blague. Amusante, non?"

Ahead of them the lock gates were opening. Mister *Calista* said something to the child, then muscling up his shoulders he stared at Colin. He jabbed two fingers at him. The meaning was clear in any language: *I'll be watching you.*

"And bon voyage to you, too," retorted Colin, while the child, who appeared to have shrunk to about half her size, fiddled with the VHF for a moment and then put it quietly back in the locker.

~~~

They continued on their way in circumspect silence, with the reticence of those who sense they must be mindful of one another, without being certain how.

"Where are we going?" asked Delphine dully, at one point.

"South," he answered, hedging his bets.

"South where?"

"I'm not exactly sure," he said. "South until the butter melts, I suppose."

A little while later she tried again. "What is a dragonfly?"

If Colin heard, he didn't answer, and after this their efforts petered out, their unfamiliarity with each other too awkward to overcome.

The opening to the marina where they were to stay the night was screened by branches. The mooring consisted of a municipal leisure centre with harbour attached, full of fatigued yachts covered in plastic sheeting spattered with bird shit, houseboats undergoing a kind of Forth Bridge-style renovation that would never be completed, and bumptious little motor cruisers. They tied up near a jetty where two lads were attempting to deflate an inflatable canoe and cram it into an unfeasibly small holdall. The child regarded them with critical interest as they flattened and rolled and then lay on the canoe, to no avail.

"It's a flying insect, actually." Colin set a saucepan of water on the Primus stove. "A dragonfly. They look like little brown bi-planes. And there are damselflies as well. You see them all the time on the river, as blue as an August sky. If you sit very quietly sometimes they'll settle on your hand."

"The *Dragonfly*," The child scrutinised her own small palm, rolling the dirt out of the creases with her thumb; "It's a pretty name."

"Some people call them the devil's darning needle. There's a legend that if you fall asleep by a stream the *Dragonfly* will sew your eyelids shut."

"Like me," she piped up, "I had my eyelid sewed!"

"Glued—"

"It's the same thing," she countered. She went back to studying her hand, flexing it, then cupping it and holding it out, tilting it this way and that. "I have a pretty name too," she remarked, "but you never call me by it."

He stiffened. The saucepan was coming to the boil and he turned off the gas. "Don't I?"

She shook her head, "Never."

He didn't have to make a mental inventory, or check, or ask himself why. He sat there, watching splinters of lime scale spiral through the water to the bottom of the pan, contemplating the sadness which was like a shadow of himself: it rose in the morning when he rose, and moved through the day with him, and settled down with him at night.

"Pourquoi pas?"

He wondered whether it was easier for her to ask difficult questions in words that were more familiar to her.

"I don't know why..." he answered, untruthfully. He thought of all the years of habitual denial, when her name had been unspoken. *I don't have a son anymore and he doesn't have a daughter. I no longer have a wife. I am nothing and have no one.* It was easier like that. It ruled out the prospect of further loss. He chewed on his lip, then opened his mouth as if now, prompted and put on the spot, it might be possible to speak. His mouth closed of its own accord. He was frightened of naming her. It would be an admission of something. It would acknowledge too much. "I suppose I'm scared of messing things up," he muttered, as if that would explain it. "Grown-ups are hopeless at getting things wrong."

She was taut beside him.

"You're right, it is a pretty name," he managed, hunching his shoulders forward. He found he didn't want to let her down. He didn't want to fall short. He cleared his throat in preparation, straightening his back.

She put a finger to her lips, but he was past noticing.

"Delphine," he began; it was like learning a new word in a foreign language, he was trying to make sense of it in his mouth. "Delphine…"

"See?" she whispered, hardly hearing him. "See?"

The sound of her name spoken aloud took him almost to the brink and for an instant he thought that all his unhappiness would come tumbling out; he blinked and swallowed, aware of a congestion deep inside him. When he had got a grip on himself, he followed her gaze and saw that two damselflies, quivering blue, were coupling on her grimy hand.

CHAPTER EIGHT

It's funny how the past can trip you up and send you sprawling. Michael sat with Laroche's cellphone in his lap, the gnawing absence of his daughter twisted up with the guilt that never left him into a hard knot, a knot that had tightened as he'd listened to her talking; she was breathless with news. She told him that she was on a boat with her grand-père. It took him a moment to realise she meant his father, and the *Dragonfly*. He felt a twinge of jealousy at the thought of the two of them together, even though he'd agreed to it in principle. How dare he turn up, just like that, after – as if–?

"Do you mind if I make another call?"

Laroche pursed his lips together. He rubbed his thumb against his fingers, implying payment that Michael wasn't going to think about.

"Just a short one. To my mother-in-law."

"Conversations with mothers-in-law are never short."

He dialled Lisette's number, ready to take her to task for letting Delphine go without consulting him, full of the righteous indignation that any father would feel.

"Allo."

She sounded just like Charlotte. Any sense of righteousness that he might have had, evaporated. He hung up.

"That was bloody quick."

Michael studied the blank screen of the phone in his hand. "It was a mistake," he said. "I shouldn't have called." He leaned across and passed the handset back to Laroche. "Thanks, though. Thank you. I owe you one."

"Two," Laroche pointed out.

"Yes," Michael said absently. There were too many voices – Lisette's, Delphine's and, whisper her name, Charlotte's – sounding in his head. He replayed the conversation with his daughter to drown the others out. After telling him about the *Dragonfly* she clammed up. He remembered the difficult diplomacy that children of separated parents have to acquire: who you can tell what. It was a learning curve with a sharpened edge. Attempting to get any other information from her was like extracting teeth. He tried asking her how she was feeling.

"OK."

"How's – grandpa?"

"OK."

"Are you having a nice time?"

"It's OK."

With mounting desperation, Michael asked her about Amandine instead.

"She's been eating ice cream at Gautier's and had some stitching done."

Gautier's. He bit his lip. It was Charlotte's favourite restaurant. She was a regular there. The maître d' always kissed her on the cheek when she arrived and showed her to a table in the window. For a moment, from wherever she was, she seemed to gaze back at him over her shoulder. *Perhaps I was wrong about you after all*, he wanted that look to say, and he could feel the smoulder of her which used to burn him so. "Poor old monkey always in the wars," he said, swallowing. The realisation that for him, Delphine's life would be lived at one remove came with a bitter taste. "Shall I ring you next week?"

"OK…"

~~~

"Wotcha thinking?"

At the sound of Laroche's voice, Michael jumped. "What?"

With Charlotte's backward glance still filling his thoughts he was unarmoured. "I was thinking about my partner."

"The one you done in?"

He nodded.

"Woss the story, morning glory?"

"It's not a story," he said tersely.

"It's always a story," replied Laroche.

He didn't answer that. "I loved her very much."

"Yeah, right."

"She was older than me, and wiser. And very beautiful, at least I thought so. And unpredictable. And undependable." He took refuge in silence for a moment and sensing he was onto something, Laroche gave him the benefit of the doubt and said nothing. "And unfaithful," he said, with the merest lift of his shoulders, not a shrug, a small flinch of incomprehension.

The bell for recreation sounded.

Michael dreamt about Charlotte that night. He thought it was Charlotte, but could have been his Mum, he wasn't sure. She was carrying lots of china – plates and stuff – and she wouldn't let him take them from her, even though she knew she couldn't hold them on her own.

CHAPTER NINE

When Colin surfaced the next morning, she was gone.

He was lying in his berth, his dreamy half-sleep infused with the scent of cut grass, and the cabin washed with the unspoilt sunshine of early morning, when he opened his eyes, saw her empty bed, sat upright in a panic and cracked his head on the roof.

Holy God! He scrambled into his shorts, rubbing his forehead with one frantic palm, buttoning his flies, scootching on his sandals, remembering to tug on a T-shirt and realising too late that it was inside out. The hatch was already open and he lurched onto the deck, scanning the leafy port.

"Delphine?" he yelled, with none of the inhibitions of the previous day. He couldn't see her anywhere. He leapt up onto the mooring, leaving the startled *Dragonfly* to right itself, the wooden planks crashing under his feet as he ran from one boardwalk to another. He could hear the creak and rasp of ropes as the boats he passed responded to his alarm, heaving forward and then falling back; he could hear the creak and rasp of his own lungs as he called for her time after time.

He skidded to a halt and stopped an oversized man with a newspaper and a baguette under one arm. "Fille?" gasped Colin. "Jeune fille?" An image of her slight body floating in the river filled his thoughts. If she wasn't face down in the Seine, past saving, she'd be on the loose somewhere between Ivry and Paris trying to make her way home, crazy child who no longer had a proper home to go to. "Have you seen a girl, about nine years old, wearing a hat, with a—" He should have taken proper care of her, he'd injured her, he'd made her sick; whichever way you looked at it, he'd loused up.

"Jah!" Beads of sweat were breaking on the man's upper lip.

"Where?" asked Colin, "Where is she?"

"Over there—" the man pointed to the far end of the enclosure where a row of neglected live-aboards sidled together.

Colin hacked his way across the marina. He heard his granddaughter before he saw her, and slowed to a lope, following the splash and ripple of her laughter to an overgrown corner of the port, where broad reeds stirred the slacking river, the planks of the pontoon were split from too much sunshine and wild flowers in pale throngs filled every gap.

Irritation and relief went coursing through him indecipherably. She was slinging chunks of yesterday's bread into the water, leaning way back to give traction to her throw, which promised much in terms of effort, but seemed to deliver very little, the bread landing only a few feet from her. She was giving a running commentary and as he drew closer he could see the tiny figure of Amandine propped haphazardly, gazing with fortitude at her own knees. He couldn't pick out a word that the child – that *Delphine* – was saying, but he understood the music of her conversation, the tone of wonder, the different pitches of delight, and amusement, and hardly-daring-to-believe…

He hung back, trying to catch his breath, while insects scatted through the air. After a moment, he shoved his hands into his pockets and wandered up, as if he were on his way somewhere and just happened to be passing.

"Morning," he managed.

"Colin! Colin! Look, oh look–" She clapped her hands together, sending a spray of bread crumbs everywhere. "I don't know the word – c'est des loutres – regardez!"

Twisting through the current, turning and weaving amber and gold, were two otters. His granddaughter snapped off a piece of bread and passed it to him, without taking her eyes off them. The crust felt rough between his fingers and he held it for a moment, hesitating.

"They like this so much," she whispered and to encourage him she lobbed a stale chunk in their direction. With lazy grace, the smallest otter fielded it, rolled over onto his back, held it to its mouth with scratty claws and started chewing at one corner. Colin stared at its white staccato teeth. His granddaughter gazed up at him and a warm contagion began to melt his anger and his panic, and grinning back at her he pretended to spit on the bread and polish it on his shorts, before bowling it into the air, a perfect Yorker, which the largest otter caught at the boundary, before diving down and away, until he was out of their sight. With a flip and a slip the other one disappeared.

Delphine stood staring at the last of the ripples.

"Let's walk to the shops and get some breakfast, shall we?" he said, as the wrinkled water spread and settled.

She broke up the last of the bread and threw it with unreliable aim at a pair of geese. She was still smiling and in that instant, Colin found himself wondering if he would ever dare to let himself love her like he had loved her father, and felt stricken at the thought.

~~~

"No, not like that, hold it up a bit – that's it."

They were sitting almost knee to knee in the freckled sunshine, while Delphine held his shaving mirror at an angle which reflected the fenders on the boat behind them and Colin tried to shave himself in the brief seconds when he caught sight of his chin. He dipped his razor into the bucket and rifts of foam swirled round the blade.

She was watching him intently, making a study of him and every time she regarded him from a different angle, the mirror moved.

"You've missed a bit."

He pulled the skin along his jaw line taut and shaved where she had indicated. She nodded in a tolerant way that suggested she would have made a better job of it herself.

"And there—"

He scraped away at his upper lip, under her scrutiny. "If you could hold the mirror still for a moment…"

"Don't you have an electric razor?"

"No."

"Papa has an electric razor."

"Does he?" Colin schooled himself to be casual. It wouldn't do to allow his heart into his mouth every time Michael was mentioned. At the same time, he found it strange to think of him as a man who shaved, who had a job, a wife, a life in Paris which he knew nothing of, when he was fixed always and forever in his thoughts at about the age of ten, before the family exploded into smithereens. His stomach knotted at the thought of all that Sally had taken from him. He cleaned his razor in the water once again.

"Yes. And one day he was late for work so he took it with him in the car and the battery ran out and he went into a meeting with half a – what is it?"

"Beard."

"Beard," she repeated. "In French it is *barbe*," she told him in an informative, important little voice.

"Le barbe?"

"Non, non, c'est feminine – la barbe."

"French is a crazy language." He rinsed his face in the bucket and patted it dry. "How do I look?"

"Old," she answered, unsparingly.

"That's OK, I am old."

A breath of sadness flickered across her face. Her hand reached subconsciously for Amandine, who had been left sitting in the cabin with the phone on her lap. The child contemplated herself in the mirror, staring into her own eyes as if there was something she couldn't quite understand.

"What happened to Sally?" she asked without looking at him.

Colin was emptying the bucket over the side. He watched the stream and tumble of the dirty water. "She died of breast cancer the year after you were born."

Delphine, who seemed to be disappearing inside herself, didn't answer. He shook the drips from the bucket and wiped it round with his towel. After the horror of the divorce, Sally's death had caused a secondary grief to spread insidiously through his system, settling in his organs, eating at the vital parts of him. He put the bucket back in the locker, closing the lid quietly. The towel was damp in his lap. He folded it in half and then in half again, his watch strap catching on a thread. He yanked the loose thread taut and snapped it off, turning to his granddaughter – Sally's grandchild too. She was wiping her arm across her face and the very thought that she might be smudging away a tear had him on his knees beside her, "Are you alright?"

She nodded.

After a moment or two she shook her head.

Then she nodded once more.

"Where are we going today?" she asked shortly.

"South," he said.

"But of course–" she didn't smile, although for a moment she looked as though she might.

"Until the butter melts," they said together, making a raggedy chorus, a tattered pledge of good intent. She jumped up and put her arms around his waist which momentarily flummoxed him, and then she gave him a wheedling grin,

"And is it possible for me to drive?"

~~~

He did let her drive; some of the way, on the straight bits when there was no traffic. She had two speeds: fast, and heart-stoppingly fast.

"Where are the brakes?" she squealed as two Canada geese streaked past the *Dragonfly's* bows, heading helter-skelter for the bank.

"There are no brakes."

Beneath his seat the crockery shivered in its locker, the vibrations changing key as the child accelerated.

"Look at me!" she crowed.

"You put it into reverse if you want to stop…"

"Like this?"

"Careful–" There was a smell of burning metal and the *Dragonfly* jack-knifed gracefully through blue smoke. The river settled as close as silk, shimmering and spun. "A bit like that," Colin said weakly. "Shall I take her for a while?"

They changed places and Delphine wriggled round in her seat so that she could dangle her feet over the side, her toes letting small slits of sunlight into the green water where the weeds bubbled under the surface, paddling which kept her amused all the way to the outskirts of Melun, where the Seine started to seem less like a motorway and more like an A road. There was a provincial feel to it: the depth was shallower and the current wasn't bustling quite so busily. In the centre of the town it wound its way around an island. Colin had prepared himself for this.

On the island was a prison.

Delphine stared up at the implacably high walls, with Amandine peering out from underneath her chin; the expression on the child's face as impenetrable as the jail itself. He kept looking straight ahead, as though, just now, their passage required particular concentration, but from time to time he risked a glance in her direction.

"There's the prison," he said shortly.

"I can see."

"How is Papa…?"

She said something in French to Amandine, something disparaging, he thought. "Are we nearly south?" she asked him a few minutes later, with a flicker in her gaze.

"We're on our way…"

"Good. When will we arrive there?"

He didn't answer.

She spent the rest of the afternoon reading a comic in the cabin – it was as far away as she could get from him while still remaining on the boat. Eventually, she poked her head out of the hatch. "Where shall we rest tonight?" He noticed that her speech sometimes had a kind of quaint formality; her brittleness untranslatable.

"I think we shall rest at Samois-sur-Seine, if it pleases you Mademoiselle."

"It pleases me," she replied and he wasn't sure who was humouring whom, but he was relieved that once again both of them were trying. "Je serai ravie. I will be ravished," she added graciously.

Even in July, with the lime trees sighing in the heat, turning the evening air syrupy with sap, a town with a closed funfair is a melancholy sight. The main square and the scribble of streets leading from it were lined with sideshows which had their lurid shutters up; the chrome ranks of the dodgems stared glassily into the middle distance and the arms of the rocket ride reared up at gawky angles. Like a soundtrack of dismay the generators kept up their enervating hum. The supermarket was closed; the library was closed,

"Everything's always shut in France. It's shut because it's a Monday, or it's shut because it is lunchtime, or it's shut because there's a fair in town, but then the fair's shut too. It's a miracle that anybody makes a living here at all."

"The bar is open over there…"

"I can't take you into a bar – you're nine."

The owner wore a white vest and had braces holding up his serge trousers and the only other customer wore a white vest and had a belt holding up his serge trousers, his style statement personalised by the addition of a greasy canvas cap. The cracks in the mosaic floor were filled with what looked like coffee grounds and they couldn't find a table that didn't wobble when they put their drinks upon it. Colin ordered her a *Coke*, but the delivery wasn't due till Thursday, so she had to make do with *Orangina* and Amandine was not amused.

Delphine slurped through her straw. Colin plotted the line of the rivulets running through the condensation on his glass.

The room was divided by a brick arch which still had Christmas decorations pinned to it. The man in the cap turned the page of his newspaper. Delphine drummed her heels and Colin had to fight the urge to ask her not to. The owner wiped down the counter with a fraying piece of rag and as an afterthought cleaned a circular orange tray with something of a flourish. A bee flew in through the open window and then realising the error of its ways, straight away flew out again.

A summer evening, a French village, stifled expectation, the lamenting heat...

Colin swirled the beer around his glass and drank a mouthful, making it last.

"Who was Albert Dreyfus?"

A page was turned, a tray clattered, Colin swallowed his beer.

"Why do you ask?"

"I saw a sign on a building back there."

He craned his head to see, frowning. There was a commemorative plaque high up on the side of the house at the end of the street opposite. "I can't see."

Her mouth made small whisperings as she repeated, "In this house lived Fernand Labori, the lawyer who defended Albert Dreyfus and Émile Zola."

"It was a cause célèbre, I seem to remember" he answered, keen to show off his grasp of French history, "At least, I think it was. Dreyfus was accused of something that he didn't do – was it treason? I'm not sure – but because he was Jewish and there was a lot of prejudice about in those days, nobody believed that he was innocent."

The bottle of *Orangina*, with its flakes of orange pressed to the occluded glass, was halfway to her mouth. She stared at the dulled surface of the table, not drinking. She set the bottle down.

"What happened to him?"

"He went to prison, as far as I recall." He banished a fleeting picture of the pale, repelling walls in Melun. "Old Fernand can't have been much cop as a lawyer, plaque or no plaque..." he went chuntering on, covering for both of them, until it became impossible not to acknowledge the change in atmosphere: hot air touching cooler air, currents shifting.

Delphine put both elbows on the table. "Samois-sur-Seine is a very boring place and I feel sorry for anyone who ever had to live here," she announced.

Colin surveyed her with some surprise, "That's not very nice," he said placidly.

"Very sorry for them," she persisted.

"Are you going to finish that?"

"I don't like it here, I don't like *Orangina* and I don't like–" A huge manufacture of emotion was under way. She scraped her chair back as he reached for her drink and took a swig.

"I wish I was–" the lack of anything to wish for – her home, her mother, her father, her old life – only seemed to make things worse. She grabbed Amandine and bolted for the door, knocking into the furniture, making a chair topple and leaving him open-mouthed. He glanced at the men in vests, who looked away. The owner wiped down the counter; the man in the cap folded his paper in half and cleared his throat.

Colin eyed a beer mat on the table. He touched the corner of it with his finger, conscious of the contained turbulence which seemed to sit so oddly with Delphine's playfulness; of what near neighbours her laughter and her brooding silences were turning out to be. As he groped in his pocket for some change, he wondered which one of them was most out of their depth. He paid the bill, reminding himself that he was the grown-up, that right now he was all she had.

As he hurried back through the little town, the funfair was beginning to strut its tawdry stuff and the air smelt of candyfloss and diesel and hot rubber. The bakery was open and he doubled back, scanning the yellow cellophaned glass for a cake in the shape of a swan among the tired fruit tarts and the cracked meringues. Nothing doing, but he spied a frog made of green marzipan and chocolate and dashed in to buy her one of those instead. In the window of the newsagent's was a display in homage to another local boy made good – the musician Django Reinhardt. He bought an ancient CD housed in cloudy plastic and then hurried back to the port.

He spotted her sitting on the quayside clasping her knees and for a moment her neat outline with its stilled angles seemed unimaginably familiar to him. He speeded up, waving the baguette above his head in salute and then, his joints making faint protest, lowered himself down beside her. He could feel the warmth of the stone through his shorts.

"Was it talking about the trial and Dreyfus going to prison that upset you?" he asked without preamble.

"Yes."

They looked at one another, each of them momentarily disarmed by their own candour.

"I thought so," Colin said after a pause. In the distance he could hear the spangled music of the funfair and for a while he sat listening to the fragmented chords. "Because of Papa...?"

She didn't answer.

"I thought you might like this," he slid the paper bag containing the marzipan frog towards her. She glanced at it, then rested her chin on her knees.

"Because of his trial...?" he tried again.

She sketched a shrug, a slight shifting of muscle, nothing more.

"We can't not talk about it, you and me."

He thought he saw her expression harden, but it was the hardness that comes from shouldering a burden: there was effort and stress and pain written in her face, though she said nothing.

"The reason we can't not talk about it is that we both love him, we care about him, we mind what happens to him."

She started picking at the bald patch on the side of Amandine's head, running her fingernail along the thinning weft of the material. She didn't utter a word.

"Are you angry with him?"

She stared at him in brief astonishment and shook her head.

"For what he's done?"

A thread was coming loose in the tight black darning of Amandine's nose and she rolled the end of it between her finger and thumb with renewed absorption.

Given half a chance Colin would have retraced his steps to the bar and ordered himself a drink considerably stiffer than the lightweight French beer he'd had earlier – a cognac perhaps, or a Calvados. At difficult moments his default response had always been to walk away: to potter in his shed, to wash the car, to build a boat… He gnawed at his lip, "If you don't talk about something, if you can't bring yourself to talk about it, then you run the risk that it becomes bigger than it needs to be," he went on, doggedly.

Delphine looked at him with strange compassion, as if she could see that he was floundering because she was floundering too. "It is not possible…" she said haltingly and he couldn't tell what wasn't possible – for them to talk, or for the horrible, shitty mess that Michael had made to be any bigger than it was.

High above them an arc of wild geese slung themselves homewards across the sky and Colin lost himself in the whirred telegraphy of their wings and the whisper of the lime tree leaves which shed their scent like rain. "Do you like marzipan?" He lifted the frog out of the bag and wagging it from side to side he croaked, "Hello Delphine," and then answered on her behalf, "Hello Mr Frog." It was the best that he could do.

She took the frog and to oblige him she bit off its chocolate-coated toes.

"Good." He climbed onto the *Dragonfly* and helped her down beside him. "Tonight I'm going to give you your first one pot cooking lesson. We'll make risotto and when we've eaten we'll drink *Coca-Cola* by the light of the moon."

Delphine chopped garlic, onion and mushrooms somewhat erratically, while Colin put his new Django Reinhardt CD on the CD player. He didn't just cook, he acted out the cooking with extravagant gestures, tossing the vegetables up into the air and catching some of them in the pan, while the rest bounced over the side and into the river. As they sizzled in the hot oil, he started tapping along to the music with a wooden spoon on the edge of the frying pan, then the outboard motor, the cleats and Delphine's grey tweed hat, so that in the end she couldn't not laugh.

He put up the cabin door table and sat her down at it, spreading the drying up cloth over her knees as if it were the finest damask. With a sweep of his hand, he presented the can of *Coke* to her,

"Mademoiselle…" he said in a cod French accent, "I zink you find zis is a ferry good year, non?" He ripped the ring pull off with a bow. "You waunt to taste?"

Delphine tasted; she gave him a bashful glance.

THE DRAGONFLY

"Might I recommend ze risotto for zis evening? Ze onion I have plucked myself from ze shelves of *Leclerc* and ze mushrooms zey are waild…"

He clowned for both of them and when he slumped back in his seat after the meal was over and smoked his one cigarette of the day and their merriment threatened to fold up into something small and disposable, he turned the volume on the CD player to full and towed her up onto the quayside and the two of them danced chaotically to Reinhardt's indefatigable rhythms until the night was so black that they couldn't dance anymore.

CHAPTER TEN

For one hour in the twenty-four they were allowed outside their cells. They could visit the library, they could watch TV (in the vegetable patch, where all the vegetables sat in rows) or go to Miami Beach (the gym). Michael chose to walk round the prison yard to inhale the different, diesel scent of the air, the fumes of Paris as potent as the sounds of the world outside: sirens and alarms, the chime of a church bell, a motorbike accelerating. He'd worked out who Chapot was; a middle-management baron who managed to procure a decent haircut for himself and through some dark deed had earned the privilege of wearing unobtrusively well-cut clothes. There was nothing intimidating about Chapot until you realised that he ran the money, he was the banker to the big guys. That was instructive in itself.

Joubert had yet to reveal himself.

As Michael walked up and down the yard he kept expecting to see Dustin Hoffman shuffling along beside him, going quietly mad behind his round Dega spectacles. He'd watched *Papillon* with Charlotte in their early days – it might even have been their first date. One of his favourite films had morphed into the story of his own life and now the person going quietly mad was him.

~~~

The heat made everybody restless. Later that day the prison was put on lock down because some head banger tried to start a fire in the chapel by setting light to a pile of hymnbooks. As the evening drew in Michael could hear the sound of laughter in the dark – not the kind that might make him think of summer nights with Charlotte; the reckless, nothing-to-lose kind. The unkind kind.

"Whyja do it, then?"

He had been looking at his watch approximately every twelve minutes for the last two hours and there was still ages to go before lights out. There was something physical about the slow passing of time, the muscle burn of every hour, the cramp and spasm of a single minute. He felt riven with it. He could have groaned aloud – perhaps he did, because Laroche sent the same curveball question his way again.

"Whyja top her? Yer missis?"

He made a study of his watch. It had a red second hand, to draw the eye of those who might otherwise overlook the rhythmic sloth of its tick. He examined the white face, the black rubber strap, the buckle. He unfastened it and laid it on the table, pressing it flat.

"I didn't mean to," he said, finally.

"Tell that to the jury, oink oink." Laroche leaned back in his chair and put his feet upon the table, close to Michael's watch, far too close, within easy breaking distance.

"I met her when I was sixteen and she was in her late twenties. She was a projectionist at the local cinema and I got a holiday job, tearing tickets. She'd wanted to be a film editor, originally, but it didn't work out. When the lights went down, I'd glance up at the box and there she'd be, silvery and silhouetted, like a ghost. Sometimes, once the film had started, I'd go up to the box and stand at the back. I told her it was so I could watch the movie, but it was so that I could watch her, which of course she knew. She kind of – took me under her wing."

A derisive *oink* came from Laroche's direction. "That's one way," he said, "of putting it."

Thinking back, breaking the rule that he had made for himself, offered a bitter release. "She always wore blood red lipstick. Everything else was black – clothes, nail varnish, everything. She was terminally sophisticated. There was something… guarded about her," he said to mend the breach that he had made in his forgetting.

Laroche curled his lip. He had a way of registering contempt that was economical.

"Being with her was totally crazy, that's why I loved it."

Laroche made an idle wanking motion with one hand. "You didn't answer the bleedin' question," he observed, regarding him speculatively. "Devious little sod, aren't you?"

"I'm not the one," he answered, touched on the raw, "who blubs into his pillow when the lights are out."

CHAPTER ELEVEN

They raced the weather all the way to Moret-sur-Loing. Small squalls of wind whipped loose along the riverbank and the molten afternoon was stretched to breaking point. On the horizon, clouds accumulated, darkly.

"It's going to be lively tonight." Increasing the revs, Colin glanced at his watch and checked the book on the seat beside him. Along the right bank, the trees in the Forest of Fontainebleau closed ranks and the light in the wooded inlets turned to shadow. Birds fretted in the branches and a cormorant, impatient with drying its wings on one of the mooring posts in the river, took flight.

Saint-Mammès was a blowsy village at the conjunction of the Seine, the River Loing and the Canal du Centre. It was a commercial port and already the great black slabs of barges were tied up one after another, vast bulwarks against the coming storm.

They sped past the embankment on the approach to the town, looking to right and left, but even the smallest berths were crammed with tenders or dinghies. There was nothing for it – they would have to seek shelter on the Loing, though it wasn't on their route.

"You'd better put your anorak on," Colin called to Delphine as the first fat drop of rain splattered over the deck. The wind stopped making sly jabs and thrusts and started a full on assault, and as they picked up speed and the landscape went slicing past them on either side, the strain on the engine shook the boat until Colin thought his teeth would rattle. Caught between the mauve river and the violet sky, he almost missed the opening to the narrow tributary and found himself swerving through the gap. He slewed the *Dragonfly* into reverse and the rain came juddering down on them.

Delphine was crouched at the entrance to the cabin, quiet and white.

Through the pelting torrent – he wiped his eyes on the sleeve of his jacket and straight away had to wipe them again – he could see that the Loing was lined with houseboats and faded yachts. An unsecured tarpaulin whined; a terracotta pot of herbs went flying from someone's deck into the water; he could hear the fibrillation of ropes beating in the wind, of fastenings working loose. *We're never going to be able to moor in this, even if we can find a place*, he thought to himself, though out loud he shouted at Delphine, "Close the cabin door and try to keep yourself dry," adding as an afterthought, "And put on Amandine's anorak…" to give her encouragement.

"But Amandine hasn't got an–"

Her objection was lost as he battled his jumpy little craft along the first kilometre of the river, as far as the lock which marked the start of the Canal, where the Loing veered off un-navigably towards Moret. It was too shallow for the big boats, but at that moment, to Colin, shallow sounded good. He thrashed his way past the *Pas d'Amarrage* sign with the raindrops flying like bullets round his head. He was so intent on finding a space that he hadn't even thought *how* he would moor, and he was about to point the bows straight at the bank and hope for the best, when a figure, bent double as though streaking through enemy territory, came skidding into view.

"Throw me your rope—"

Clutching the slippery tiller in one hand, Colin reached for the rope and threw.

"Have you got some kind of a stake?" the figure shouted through the perforating rain. Slipping sideways, Colin slammed the locker open, groped for the mooring stake and lobbed it onto the bank. The mallet followed.

The water was falling around them in sheets and it was hard to tell what was river and what was not. Hunched in a strange contortion to ward off the worst of it, Colin watched as the figure – a woman with cropped hair, wearing shorts and a singlet so wet that it had turned translucent – hammered and looped and tied in double quick time.

"This should hold you for a while, until it slacks off a bit—" she shouted, then skidded back the way she had come.

Colin shrugged himself out of his wet anorak and through the hatch into the cabin in a single action. He was panting from the exertion and it was as if some of the storm entered with him. He rammed the hatch shut.

"Phew!"

He sat on the edge of his bunk. More contortions followed as he tried to remove the wettest of his clothes as modestly as possible. The *Dragonfly* keened, hurling herself from side to side and Delphine rolled up into a tight ball, gripping her disconsolate monkey.

"First things first," hunting high and low, Colin produced two carrier bags, some *Sellotape* and a pair of scissors. "Foul weather gear for Amandine…" He began the design, but before long his granddaughter uncurled herself to watch and after a little while she took the scissors from him and started cutting shapes from the plastic bags.

"We could use the off cuts for wadding, to keep her warm." While the child busied herself making a passable life jacket and a sou'wester, heavily padded, the seams held together with *Sellotape*, Colin forced himself to face the prospect of foraging for their supper.

"I am just going outside and may be some time…"

In fact, he shot out and back in a matter of seconds, bringing with him a motley assortment of celeriac salad, tinned mackerel, a packet of unmade jelly, one Babybel cheese and some pistachio nuts.

"Marvellous – we'll live like kings."

They sat side by side in the storm, eating with their fingers, which they wiped on their clothes – "That's what T-shirts are for," he remarked with a grin. He didn't want to seem too solicitous, for her to know that he was worried she might be worried, though he could see the fear in her huge round eyes.

A shaft of lightning split the air.

"Perhaps we should have an early night…?"

With no teeth cleaning, no hair brushing, they bundled themselves into their beds. Aggrieved now, for the tempest was beyond a joke, the *Dragonfly* rolled and hauled against her rope.

"Night, night," said Colin.

"Bonne nuit," replied a high little voice. A moment later a small hand reached across the gap between their bunks. Gruffly, he took it in his big paw and held it until she fell asleep.

~~~

Colin had given up all pretence at being a good sleeper years ago, back when he and Sally – well, back in the dim and distant past. His ploy these days was not to crave the sleep he couldn't have, but to enjoy to the utmost the rest which came his way. As the detonations of the storm grew fainter, he slipped into provisional slumber, helped by the swim and slip of the *Dragonfly* trying to outwit the current. While the weather gnashed at the outside of the boat, he nested deeper into his sleeping bag, basking in the feeling of being sheltered, of warmth and languor. Half-thoughts drew him back to the surface and then let him go; he was caught and then released. He pressed his head deeper into the pillow, no longer able to distinguish the drowse of the river from the drifts of sleep which ensnared him: drowsing and drifting, drifting and drowsing.

Drifting?

He levered himself upright. The porthole was steamed over and he wiped it clear. Through the darkness he could see the anthracite lights of the river scudding past. *Holy God, she's broken free of her mooring.* For a moment he wanted to curl up and hide his face beneath the pillow. He looked again and saw the kaleidoscope of riverbank and slanting trees. A broken branch went cracking past them. There was a jolt as the *Dragonfly* hit something – Colin flung himself to the other side of the cabin and peered out – a rowing boat – and Delphine woke with a scream.

"It's alright, it's nothing," he knew that he was shouting, trying to out-pitch her, but he couldn't help himself, he couldn't stay calm. "The mooring's come loose. It'll be fine. I just have to start the engine. We'll be tied up again in a jiffy, I promise you."

As he yanked open the hatch and the rain came spilling into the cabin, Delphine started to cry. He held her hand for a moment. "It'll be fine."

They were twenty metres from the shore, the *Dragonfly* flailing and confused. The only thought in Colin's head was to fire up the motor, to regain control. He ripped at the starter cord, but the handle was wet and it went shooting from his grip; he ripped at it again.

Wheezing disagreeably, the engine started. The tiller was all over the place and they went shearing off to starboard and he nearly toppled over on the dancing deck. It felt like a kind of madness: for a moment he was overcome with a crazy elation, at the mercy of the persecuting rain. He swung her round as best he could, his wilful little boat skittering sideways. He pulled hard to straighten her and for a moment it seemed as if she would fall into line, but then he heard a thud thud thud against the keel, a whining sound so sharp it almost drew blood and the motor cut out.

Colin hung over the stern. "Get me the torch," he yelled at Delphine. "Put your life jacket on, then get me the torch."

"I cannot find—" her words came wobbling out; she couldn't make her fingers work.

"It's OK, it's fine. Just concentrate on getting your life jacket on. One thing at a time. Good girl. I'll get the torch."

He tore the everything locker apart and found the torch. He hung over the stern as far as he could reach, into the weir of the night; he tried to lift the outboard engine clear of the water, tugging at it, then heaving with all his might, but it was stuck fast. He smacked his forehead. The mooring line was caught round the propeller. Cardinal Rule Number One, never start the engine with a rope in the water. "Fuck!" and then, turning in contrition to the terrified little girl, "I'm sorry, I'm so sorry. It'll all be alright."

He stared at the indigo water that coiled and uncoiled itself around the boat. "Right," he took a deep breath, trying to keep the shakiness from his voice. "I'm going to have to go into the river and have a look underneath her – it's OK," he said to pre-empt her, "It'll take me two minutes at the most."

Her face had that breached look he remembered from when he hurt her eye: her mouth stretched and twisted; a mix of misery and fright that he could not bring himself to see. "It'll be fine." Dimly, he thought it might help her if she had something to do, something to focus on. "I want you to be in charge of the torch. I'm going to need some light down there. Can you manage that?"

She raised her head. Her face was rinsed clean with the rain. "I ca–"

"Excellent," he replied as she faltered. "Now, I want my Swiss Army knife and a shoe lace."

"Grandpa–?" She never called him that; not voluntarily.

He looked at her in her pyjamas and life jacket, with Michael's lavender tweed hat clamped to her head, the rain water cascading from its brim, "Courage," he said it the French way, "*Courage.*" She bit her lip and nodded. He busied himself unthreading one of his trainers and lashing his pen knife to his wrist. Then he knotted a sturdy line around his waist and tied it to the cleat.

"I won't be long," he shouted and jumped into the river.

The water wasn't as deep as he had expected – he could feel its icy grip around his chest and his feet touched the rocky bottom before they were ripped from under him by the current. He was hurled to the length of the rope and he hauled himself back along it, hand over hand. Through the darkness he could see the outline of the *Dragonfly*, her duck egg paint wan in the half light of the hidden moon. With one hand he caught hold of her side.

"Torch!" he called up to his granddaughter and with a guttering little sob, she found the torch and held it out towards him.

"I can't take it – I want you to shine it down into the water near the propeller."

Delphine nodded, her lips as blue as if she were in the river with him. The trembling beam shone down.

"Excellent–" he shouted, struggling to open the knife while holding onto the boat with one hand as the current tried to claw him away. "Can you tilt it at an angle? That's it, well done, as close as you can get. Good girl."

Without warning he ducked beneath the surface. He could feel his scalp contracting with the cold, tiny bubbles streaming close to his skin and the lick of weed. He tried to find a footing on the stones beneath him but his feet went skating sideways as the *Dragonfly* veered, then seemed to change her mind and spun back the way she had come.

Clinging to his lifeline, Colin groped for the propeller shaft and clutching his knife, fingered his way down until he found the knuckle of rope bound around the blade. He swiped at it once, twice, while the blood seemed to drain from his head and fill his lungs instead. He thrashed to the surface, gasped, swallowed water, choked, gasped again, so intent on trying to get his breath that the lifeline began to slither through his fingers.

"Grandpa–!" She flashed the torch into his face and he could see the red stitching of the veins behind his eyes illuminated as he blinked.

"Nearly there," he shouted, coughing and spitting. He gripped the line, hauled himself close to the boat and dived again. He could feel the raindrops inverting themselves as they landed in the water all around him and the river pressed into his ears. He grasped the propeller shaft and slashed at the rope one more time. If he could cut through it, they could lift the motor and untangle the propeller from the boat. He let go of his lifeline to saw at it better, knowing that in seconds he'd be sent lassoing far into the current. He cut and cut. He could feel the strands splitting apart in his fingers. His chest burned him. He sawed and pulled and the severing of the rope sent him flying to the surface, all akimbo, releasing him into the air.

He made it to the boat and hooked his elbows over the side. "Done it," he panted. He tried to lever himself on board but the *Dragonfly* lurched and Delphine gave a terrified yelp as she lost her balance. He dropped down into the water. "Hold on tight, I'm going to try again–" This time he hooked his leg over the side and thrust himself upwards with all his strength, his ageing muscles cold in the glimmer of the night.

He held out his hand for Delphine. "Pull – help me – pull!" She grabbed him and started ratcheting him upwards, his splayed body awkward as a crab. She dragged at him, bumping him over the locker one rib at a time, until he had enough purchase to deliver himself, shoulders first, onto the deck.

They stared at one another like wide-eyed opponents, each uncertain of the other's next move.

"I'm going to get us moored so tight to the riverbank–"

Her teeth were chattering; her body gave a little spasm, she nodded as if she wanted to believe him.

"We'll get ourselves dried off in a jiffy and before you know it you'll be warm as toast," he was extravagant with his promises, but what the heck. "It's better than being on a beach somewhere like Benidorm, eh?" he asked uncertainly. "At least we're having an adventure…"

"Is it so far to get to Benidorm?" was all she said.

~~~

The following morning Colin woke to the sound of rain. He listened to the drumming on the roof with a sinking heart. Across the way from him, Delphine snoozed, her face pressed into her damp tweed hat, with Amandine, dressed as a north sea trawler man, clutched to her neck.

In the confined space he struggled to put on his least wet clothes without disturbing her. He crept out of the cabin and retrieved his fishing umbrella from the everything locker, ramming it into the bracket where the red ensign usually flew. It covered the entire deck area; in fact, he had designed the deck specifically to fit beneath the umbrella. Sheltered now, he set about rigging up the Primus stove and put on a saucepan for some coffee.

That done, he went and checked the mooring and then surveyed the scene. In the middle of the night with the river in full spate it felt as if they had travelled the length of the Amazon, but in truth they were about three hundred yards from where they had first tied up. He shook his head. The saucepan was coming to the boil. He climbed back on board and made himself some coffee.

"Colin–?" Delphine's scrunchled little face appeared out of the cabin, still creased with sleep.

"Morning."

She glanced upwards at the umbrella. He followed her gaze. "Try to think of it as some kind of conservatory."

"Is it still raining?"

"Just a tad. Do you want some coffee?"

"Breakfast?" she asked him hopefully.

"I'll have to go into the village."

She yawned and then tasted her mouth with her tongue and swallowed.

"You were very brave last night," he spoke quietly, staring into his mug because he didn't want to embarrass her, or himself. "Very brave."

"Pfff." She leaned right out of the cabin, reached for his mug and took a swig. "Pas de sucre!" She pulled an appalled face, "No sugar – bleeugh." She crawled over to the side and spat.

"That's a little extreme…"

Delphine remained hanging over the edge of the *Dragonfly*, but for a moment all impetus left her body. She became very still. "Colin…" She didn't turn to look at him.

"Hmm?"

"It would have been more simple to cut the rope from here, non?"

His mouth was full of coffee. He gulped it down too quickly and could feel it scalding his gullet. "What do you mean?"

"Well, it was attached to this – what do you call it–?"

"–Cleat–" with a sinking heart he saw where she was heading.

"–this cleat – yes – it was attached here, non? So you could have just…" She didn't finish the sentence. She didn't have to say it.

His throat was still hot. He swallowed. "Leaned over and cut it from there?"

She nodded. He saw her catch her lip between her teeth. She looked as if she wished she had never brought the subject up, as if the last thing she wanted was to see his fallibility.

On the far side of the river a family of ducks was walking tidily along the bank. The drake brought them all to a halt and then stood by as one by one they jumped onto a tethered rowing boat. Colin watched them as they arranged themselves along the central seat, shuffling into line and then sitting in unison. He had never felt so abject.

"I suppose I could have," a sense of his own idiocy settled heavily on him. "It was dark – I couldn't…" the possibility had never occurred to him. All he could think of was that the propeller was clamped under the water and needed to be cut free. "I should have done, you're right. That's what I should have done. Just leaned over – just–" he made a cutting motion. He swore bitterly inside his head, so that she couldn't hear. His hand fell to his side. "I am very sorry, Delphine. More sorry than I can say. You were very brave and I was very stupid, incredibly stupid–"

"De rien," she chirped, "It's nothing. If you had cut the rope just like that–" she tugged at his sweat shirt for emphasis, to get his attention, to make up for everything, "–then we wouldn't have had an adventure, would we?"

He saw the narrative that she was offering him. "No…" he dragged his answer into several uneasy syllables.

"Well, then."

"No, we wouldn't have."

"Otherwise, we go to Benidorm, non?"

He gave an uncertain smile "If you say so."

Across the river the ducks stared glumly through the rain.

"I say so."

"OK," he nodded.

"Good."

"That settles that, then." He gave an extended sigh.

"Breakfast?" she piped.

I am a very foolish, fond old man, he thought to himself. Out loud, he said, "I'll have to go to the village. I need to find a launderette where we can dry our clothes. Do you want to come?"

"I must write a postcard to my grand-mère," she answered piously, glancing out from under the umbrella at the rain, "And today is my day for talking to Papa…"

"Will you be alright on your own?"

"There is Amandine. She is always with me."

"I won't be long. I've already checked the line's secure." He hesitated, not wishing to be too obvious in his attempts at bribery and corruption. "Is there anything in particular that you'd like?"

Delphine had anticipated this. "Tiger prawns, please," she said as she ducked back into the cabin, "and îles flottantes – Maman used to buy them in a little pot at the supermarket – and maybe a crêpe, too?"

"Hmmm," he answered, "Maybe…"

She dismissed him with a little wave.

~~~

The charms of Moret-sur-Loing were lost on Colin as he zipped under the mediaeval gateway and went careering down the ancient high street with a bin liner full of sopping clothes clutched in his arms. Once, the walls of the town were fortified with twenty towers; Thomas Becket had consecrated the church; there were associations with the Three Musketeers. All of it passed him by – the war memorial with its desperate lists of names, the arthritic old buildings, the civic floral arrangements that shed their petals in the stupefying rain.

He hurtled into the launderette, stuffed the clothes into the dryer, realised he hadn't got the right money, legged it back to the square where the only shop open was a florist and because he didn't know how to ask for change he had to buy a bunch of something which looked like daisies but cost a fortune, hoofed his way back to the launderette, bought tokens from a machine screwed to the wall but only just, shoved them into the dryer and slumped down onto a white formica bench to collect himself.

He was soaked to the skin. When he had caught his breath, he peeled off his anorak and his sweat shirt and, as an afterthought, his socks, and added them to the drying clothes. He sat clammily, contemplating the shoe prints all over the wet floor, the general air of grime. Through the steam and the cigarette smoke he could make out what appeared to be an extended family on an outing to do the week's wash: grandmother, several sons all talking on their mobiles, a young woman with a baby in a push chair. They spread and settled and conducted their business – the men kept darting out into the road to shout loudly into their handsets. The young woman stared out of the window, or smoked, or chewed at the broken skin round her fingernails. Briefly, Colin wondered what their home must be like, if the launderette on a rainy day was a better bet. He tried in vain to picture himself and Sally trundling off for a day at the washeteria with Michael. Eyeing the sprawling family, he thought of the compensations of poverty – time together, which they probably didn't want, but which to him, bereft of his son and his wife, seemed beyond value. He wouldn't have minded an afternoon doing the laundry, with his son for company.

How did it go so wrong? It was a question he had spent years both asking and avoiding. He knew the end point of it all: the fracturing afternoon in Charlotte's office – *that* afternoon – when things were said that could not be retracted and lives were ripped apart as easily as tearing paper.

THE DRAGONFLY

He watched the young woman hoist the baby onto her lap and clean his chocolatey fingers one at a time by putting them in her mouth.

For years he chose to console himself with the thought that the rot set in when Michael first met Charlotte. It was a narrative he could tell to colleagues and friends almost without flinching. *Kids! You do your best for them and then—!*

He remembered the phone call from Sally: the first intimation of catastrophe. He was in his office, the windows were open and a summer breeze was batting the vertical blinds against each other. He was halfway to the filing cabinet when the phone rang and he picked up the receiver absently, riffling through the files with his free hand.

Colin?

He remembered the sight of his hand resting on the drawer as if he had momentarily forgotten what he was looking for. He remembered the glint of the links in his watch strap, the pores of the skin on the back of his hand, and somewhere in outer space, the click of the blinds. He remembered fixing on detail after detail, searching for something that was safe and ordinary, that wouldn't give way.

It's me.

He hadn't heard her voice for years. He could almost have believed she was calling from home to ask him to stop off at the supermarket and pick up something for their supper.

Are you there?

He couldn't bear it. He clicked the receiver off and managed to get himself back to his chair before the phone rang again.

I need to talk to you about Michael.

He was incapable of answering her.

Colin?

OK then, talk.

105

He wants to give up college.

Was that it? The news was everything and nothing.

But he's only just started.

I know.

Why?

He remembered the engulfing pause as she appeared to weigh things up, before she dropped her bombshell.

The thing is, Charlotte is pregnant.

The dryer slowed and the clothes fluttered to the bottom of the drum. He fished out his sweatshirt, shaking it to cool it, and put it on; the zip on his anorak burnt his neck. He put his socks back on, wobbling as he stood on one leg, then he filled the bin liner with the roasting clothes. He was halfway to the door when he remembered the daisies. He turned and went back for them. The listless young woman was feeding potato crisps to the toddler to keep it quiet, blowing smoke over its head.

"Madame?" Colin hesitated; he held out the flowers. She stared at him, taking the measure of his gift. She accepted them with an embarrassed smile, looking sideways to the street outside.

~~~

He arrived back at the boat with a tub of prawn cocktail and a packet of plasticky crêpes (none of that pudding which came in pots, no swan-shaped cake) to find that Delphine was entertaining.

"Colin! Colin! This is Tyler. She is an artist from America." She was delighted with the crêpes.

The woman who had helped them moor stood up to introduce herself, catching her head on the spokes of the umbrella. "I came by to check on your granddaughter…"

He inspected her remark for signs of reproof, but found none: only an un-English kind of neighbourliness. "I just popped into town–" he hefted the bag in his arms, "–to dry our clothes."

"You travelled quite a distance overnight…" The woman looked back along the river, "That was probably my fault. I guess I should've tied you to a tree or something."

Colin shrugged. He fiddled with the bin liner, making much of ensuring the clothes were comprehensively covered by the plastic.

"Though then your line would have been across the path and that is not allowed. Have you noticed how the French do everything by the book? I mean – two hours for lunch? Who ever heard of that?"

He nodded, as if the matter were deserving of serious thought. She nodded also, but to a brisker tempo, then to restart the conversation she said, "I just wondered if your granddaughter–"

"Delphine," interjected Delphine, her mouth full of crêpe.

The woman smiled. "I wondered if Delphine might want to come in out of the rain. My boat's up near the lock. But she was very clear that she should stay here till you got back. But hey, you're getting wet…"

Colin was conscious that if he joined them on the *Dragonfly*, with the drying, one of them would be obliged to sit practically in his lap. "It's OK," he shrugged. "I think it's slacking off a bit." He peered up at the unremitting sky. He could feel raindrops trickling down his legs, there was grit on his shins from where he had sped along the riverbank.

Tyler switched her glance from one to the other. For a moment nobody said anything. "Well, like I said, I just wanted to say hello to Delphine here. She's French – I guessed you would be too, but you're a Brit. Will you listen to that rain…?"

Politely, all three of them listened to the orchestration of rain on the umbrella.

"I'll be getting along now…" As she stepped onto what passed for dry land, drops of water splashing into her eyes and making her blink, Colin saw her features in close-up: they were sparely drawn, she had a dreamer's face, a faraway face, as if she were an uncertain participant in the here and now.

"If you guys want to visit with me later…" she flipped her hood up over her hair; he noticed its cropped blackness had a silvery weave, like shot silk. "…my boat's the one with all the pictures up, back that way. I make a good cup of coffee. You'd be very welcome." She broke into a run, then turned to wave, running backwards, grimacing and pointing at the sky. "Can you believe it?"

Colin climbed down on to the *Dragonfly* and dodged under the umbrella. After he had dropped the bin liner onto the deck, on a reflex he stuck his head back out and watched with interest her long-limbed, athletic figure skipping the largest puddles, outdistancing the rain.

CHAPTER TWELVE

"Oi, Rosbif! Come over here," snapped Laroche with a jerk of his head, indicating his side of the cell. The boundary line between them was curiously drawn: Laroche could put his feet on Michael's bed, but Michael had to be invited to sit beside him at the table. The evolution of these laws was touchy and intuitive.

"It's payback time."

Michael was a long way down. He had been trying to stop himself from thinking about the flight of stairs at home, the vertiginous distance from the first floor to the ground, the endless loop of Charlotte, falling. He'd been trying to stop himself from thinking about the coat that she was wearing – it was purple, and she only ever dressed in black. He'd been trying not to wonder what that signified, if it signified anything at all: a change of heart, for sure. He'd been trying not to think about that instant of lunacy: the physical strength in a pair of outstretched hands, the swift brutality of a single shove.

There was a storm coming. He stared through the slit of window at the blackened sky outside, where sudden shafts of sunlight glanced against grievous clouds. He remembered telling Delphine the rays were the souls of the dead flying up to heaven, before he knew better.

"Payback?" he said with a shiver, conscious that his voice struck a higher note than usual.

He was stalling for time.

"One good turn deserves another," said Laroche. "Two phone calls, as I recall. Oink, oink."

From some crevice hollowed out in the overflow behind the basin, he produced a cellphone, a different one from before. "My new kid was born last week, more than three weeks 'overdue', though there was no talk of inducing it," he said with a grunt, "not that anyone told me about, leastways." He stared at the phone before holding it out to Michael, who was conscious of a simmer in the air. "I want you to text my wife and tell her that she might think I'm fucking stupid, but the sums don't quite add up on that one, and even I can work that out. Alright?" he said. "I want you to let her know loud and clear IN CAPS that I am so on to her, that I have been on to her for months and I know just what she's up to, and while you're at it you can say–"

"I don't think I can do that."

"I'm *sorry?*"

"I'm not comfortable–"

"Comfortable? Yer 'aving a laugh, mate."

"–with the kind of things you want me to say. I wouldn't feel–"

"No such word as *can't*. Isn't that what they tell you? In school? Not that I would know, oink, oink, 'cos I – didn't – go – to – school–"

"I can't get involved," said Michael.

"Well, you are *involved*, mate. You owe me for two. Remember?" Without warning, he reached across and with one stringy forearm he pressed Michael's neck against the wall, leaning into it until he couldn't breathe. The swift brutality of a single shove. "You're so fucking up yourself, you pussy," he hissed before he let him go.

There were paisley lights before Michael's eyes "Why don't you write it yourself?" he said when he'd recovered his breath. He felt sick.

"Why do you think?" Laroche sneered at him.

"I think you don't know how."

"Tick. Go to the top of the class."

He swallowed and half-swallowed, "I wouldn't feel right," he said, "writing that sort of thing for you." His throat felt mashed.

"Well, la-di-fucking-da!" Laroche growled. "You're taking the piss, ain't you? Telling me what I can and can't say to my woman, when you topped your own." For a moment he glowered in his direction, then the steam seemed to go out of him. "The sums don't add up," he said. "Even I can work that out."

"Can't you read or write at all?" asked Michael.

Boot-faced, Laroche shrugged.

"I'll teach you, if you like," said Michael, cautiously. "to write it yourself."

Laroche held out the phone again. There was no arguing with him. "I must only of been inside for a month when she said she was pregnant," he said. "But I'm not stupid."

Michael took the cellphone from him. "I just owe you for one, after this."

Laroche nodded. "Now you can tell that bitch that I'm on to her, that I've been on to her for months, and if she thinks–"

He started to text.

I h o p e y o u a n d t h e b a b y a r e d o i n g o k. "There," he said clicking Send and passing the handset back. He looked out at the black horizon where the sun's rays still shone, but he could see no sign of Charlotte's soul, flying high into the sky.

~~~

He grew used to the daily routine and began to feel better. One of the kangas had told him he'd been made Bicycle Repair Man – cue fanfare and drum roll. He considered it to be overdue recognition of his former life in industrial design. He had a sneaking suspicion there was once a Monty Python sketch that he used to watch with his father called Bicycle Repair Man. It was a privilege granted to prisoners on remand and he knew he shouldn't look a gift horse in the mouth, although on reflection he would have preferred a Trojan horse in his current circumstances.

All the bikes left at all the tips in Paris were brought to the prison to be overhauled, and then they were auctioned off for charity. The idea was that it would be rehabilitation for both the bicycles and for VN1692F – Michael– though it would take more than some WD-40 and a squirt of oil to put him right.

He'd be starting on Monday. He felt like a person again, almost a man.

CHAPTER THIRTEEN

In between the straitlaced, righteous little towns the countryside flashed green: the tired, maternal green of fields in high summer, the chemical green of abandoned quarries full of standing water, the munificent green of hedgerows. River rolled into river and Colin and Delphine stood to attention and saluted the statue of Napoleon, as he lorded it over the point where the Yonne branched off from the Seine.

The rain petered out, leaving the sky moist and discoloured like skin when you rip away a plaster; the weather remained queasy and convalescent. When the umbrella had dried out, Colin took it down and put it in the locker and the world seemed brighter in the revealed light. The effect of it was lost on Delphine, who seemed heavy limbed; he could sense the melodrama of her boredom, the slump and flop of it.

He handed her the guide book. "Tell me something about Sens," he suggested.

She fell forward, crashing her head onto her knees as if the prospect of reading aloud would kill her. "Sens is in the Department of the Yonne in Burgundy, North Central France," she began pulverising the words, making dust of them. "The town saw the trial of Peter Abelard; Pope Alexander III stayed there, as did Thomas Becket and..."

"…Colin Aylesford and his granddaughter," he went on as she gave up. "That's where we're headed. Should be there by four-ish. Do you want to drive?"

No joy there.

"The Cathedral is well worth a visit."

She groaned, mightily.

"It's very old. One of the oldest in France," he shrugged. "It's all part of your education."

"Don't make me," she gave a blistering sigh, but she perked up a bit when he told her how Peter Abelard had been castrated for the love of Héloïse. "It is not possible?"

"It happened."

"Cut right off?" she asked, with lemon juice eyes.

He nodded.

"Merde…"

"You probably shouldn't be saying that, should you?" he ventured mildly. "Not too often, at any rate."

She scowled at him and then began to subside with boredom once again. He watched her shoulders droop and splay.

"We've got a lock in a moment, but after that, why don't you make those beads…?"

"What beads?" she asked in tones of biblical doom.

"That set you brought. Papier-mâché. You could make some necklaces and earrings and sell them on the quayside when we get to Sens."

She swung round and regarded him with interest. He made her take the tiller while he hunted round and found an old edition of *Practical Boat Owner*. "There you go," he said encouragingly. Before long, streamers of torn up magazine were escaping in the wind and Colin put on a brave face as she mixed glue in one of the mugs, dripping it down the side of the locker and over the deck. The kit involved moulds and a brush which shed its hair and small pots of poster paint with flip top lids.

"Mind you don't knock tha–" he fished a handkerchief from his pocket and started mopping up some unfeasibly yellow goo. "It's fine – don't worry – look, it's almost gone."

A kind of Sunday afternoon peace descended: Delphine cut up paper and glued and stuck with such absorption that she looked like someone at work, rather than a child at play: her movements had their own awkward economy; she was both intent and inexact. When she held up a row of knobbly spheres, tilting them this way and that in critical inspection, the concentration on her face filled him with a twinge of sadness and he glanced down, wondering how on earth her mother could have considered walking away from such a little scrap of hope and promise.

He stared at the shifting landscape, indifferent to his concerns. A motor cruiser went past them, heading northwards. The *Dragonfly* toyed with its wash. He hardly felt the movement of the boat when they were sailing, but sometimes, when they were on dry land, the ground would shelve away without any warning.

~~~

His mind kept wandering back to Charlotte.

The first time he'd seen her was at the top of the stairs coming down from the platform at Bath station. The light was behind her and other passengers were shovelling past him and he was so consumed with a hunger to see his son that he didn't fully take her in at first.

It was Michael's Christmas-time visit, which came after the main event – was it the day before New Year's Eve, or the day before that? Such details had once seemed so important, so territorial. Michael had been eighteen the previous July and Colin went over to Paris on the Eurostar and took him out to lunch. He didn't stay over, though Michael protested, "If I'd known that you wanted to I would have…" without specifying what, exactly.

He came lolloping down the stairs, against the flow of stragglers hurrying to catch the train. He was wearing a rucksack and held his arms above his head, to avoid bumping into people, or being bumped, but the effect was to make him look as if he were wading into water which would soon be beyond his depth.

"Hi Dad."

Between them they fumbled the pass – they failed to kiss, they didn't quite manage to slap each other on the back because of the rucksack and ended holding each other by the forearms, until they let go.

"Happy Christmas, son. Well, I suppose it's happy New Year now, but – well, happy – whatever! Happy holidays! That's what the Americans say, isn't it? Covers a multitude of sins. How was your journey? Here – let me take that–" He kept on talking, knowing that as long as he did, it was OK, it would seem quite natural, for him to gaze at Michael. He began to pull at the rucksack. "Let me give you a hand," and he kept holding on to the strap of the bag and making his offer of help, of slavish, I'll-do-anything devotion, in any number of ways, "You must be worn out… why don't I just… let me help you down the… let me… why don't you let me…" until he became conscious that Michael was actually fending him off.

"You haven't met Charlotte."

He swung round as if he'd been caught red-handed. "Charlo–" The greeting died somewhere in his throat.

She was a woman in her thirties, and he'd been expecting a girl. She was dark, with fine hair that was not her best feature, asymmetrically cut, when, for some reason, he'd been expecting someone fair, someone fleet, someone else.

She looked as if she rarely saw the light of day. Her skin was on the blue side of white, and there was violet pigmentation round her eyes. She was lost in the first exhalation of a cigarette, her gaze blurred, her thinness accentuated as she breathed out. Colin could tell, without her saying anything, that she was here under sufferance. He could tell from the way she took another drag at her cigarette, from the way she lined her gloves up before putting them in her bag, from the way she hefted her suitcase and reckoned the distance down the stairs, from the way she sighed and began to pick her way down one step at a time, that she didn't want to be in England, or in Bath, or with him. She was a study in ennui.

"Hello there, why don't you let me take that for you?"

He supposed there was a kind of glamour to her: her pillar box red mouth, her pallor, her slanty little hat – who in England wore a hat like that? Who in France, come to that? She had too many rings on her fingers: big, silver, statement rings. Her hands were mottled with the cold. He could feel how freezing they were when, prompted by Michael, "Dad, this is Charlotte…" they shook hands with each other.

"Let me take your…"

Apparently out of reserve, but more to stake a claim to his son, to demonstrate ownership, she handed her case to Michael. They whispered to one another as they walked towards the car, while Colin led the way empty-handed, disbelieving.

Charlotte rarely seemed to eat, she drank litres of water every day and all her energy and focus went on smoking. She smoothed the packet ceaselessly, she felt the flint of the lighter with her thumb, she studied each cigarette before she lit it, feeling the balance of it between her fingers. She breathed smoke from her mouth like a spell, as if she were exhaling her own essence. *Smoke signals*, Colin thought. Her studied sophistication and her interest in a teenager didn't quite add up although looking back now, he saw his own craving for Sally in Michael's obsession with her. He could almost understand.

"Colin – regardez!" Delphine demanded of him, holding up a single bead with some plaited twine attached.

"That's very good – what is it?"

"A key ring, for Papa," she said with considerable pride.

~~~

In sleepy, Sunday Sens, disaster struck. They had moored up on the town quay, looping the forward line through a rusted ring that Delphine could hardly lift on her own. All the rubbish bins were full and there were bottles piled up round them. They dropped the rear line in some dog shit and while he rinsed it in the river with distaste, she laid out her wares.

With the rope clean and his hands scrubbed until you could see the marks of the brush on his skin, Colin put the saucepan on to boil.

There was no gas.

A catastrophe of unimaginable scale: *no gas*. No gas meant *no tea* and no tea was an unimaginable deprivation.

He swallowed.

In a tone which sought to minimise the impact of what he was saying, for his own benefit as much as for hers, he tried to explain the situation to her. "I'm afraid we've run out of gas." Put like that, it didn't sound so bad. "The bottle's empty," as he went on, he contrived to keep the tremor from his voice. "We'll have to find a garage…"

Delphine was unperturbed.

"It means there won't be any tea–" he said in a rush, before he could compose himself "–for the moment."

"There's always *Coca-Cola*," said his granddaughter, quick to spot an opportunity.

"That's not the point," he unclenched his jaw. After a moment he rallied himself. "We just have to find a garage."

The two of them trailed round Sens, dragging Colin's folding trolley behind them. The offending empty bottle rattled and bumped down kerb and over cobble stone. A plastic chain closed off the entrance to the first garage that they found; the second one was open for petrol sales but nothing else, although full bottles of gas in all sizes stood in a metal cage on the forecourt. Colin hooked his fingers between the bars and then let go. He licked his lips, searching for the truant taste of finest Ceylon. They struck out into the suburbs, right to the edge of town. There was a garage with a pick-up truck blocking the entrance to the kiosk, then another one with a closed sign up and the shutters down.

"We'll have to buy a cup of tea…" he couldn't keep the glumness out of his voice.

"And a *Coca-Cola*…"

"…in a café." Images of not-quite-boiling water with the tea bag on the side came unbidden into his head. Warmed milk? He couldn't even go there.

But in the whole of Sens there was not a cup of tea, with warmed milk or otherwise, to be had. There was a kebab shop open in a side street leading up to the cathedral (one of the oldest in France – oh sod the cathedral) and that was all.

He kept a grip on himself long enough to buy Delphine her *Coca-Cola* from the kebab shop and get them both back to the boat. Jittery with disappointment, he put the dismembered Primus stove back in the locker and shut the saucepan away.

"I'll teach you Spit." It was a kind of racing patience and he was wired and manic enough to keep slapping his hand down on the smallest pile of cards without ever giving her a chance. "You put the jack on the ten like that–" *slap* "–you can turn a couple more cards over so you always have five showing–" *slap* "–if I don't have a cup of tea soon I'm going to go stark raving mad–" *slap*.

"Colin–" his granddaughter complained as he won the second game.

"It's no good–" he stood up and rooted about in the locker. With jumbled hands he filled the saucepan from the water bottle and went steaming off down the quay. There were three or four boats spread out between the *Dragonfly* and the bridge and each one of them was locked up, their owners off exploring the town.

Well, good luck to 'em.

He stalked back and set the saucepan down beside the uneven rows of Delphine's beads: two key rings, a bracelet, a pendant and a necklace, together with a small heap that she had lost interest in. Their imperfections pinked at his heart and for a little while he managed not to simmer or thirst. He taught her Damn It (like whist but with betting) and made a game of stealing her *Coke* when she was sorting through her cards.

When a small peniche appeared on the horizon, the two of them climbed ashore and did a Robinson Crusoe caper of deliverance. Delphine wasn't interested in the prospect of tea, but she liked doing the dance. They lined themselves up, ready to assist the new arrival with their ropes.

"It's Tyler," called Delphine, waving. "Bonjour Tyler! Hello!"

Colin stayed long enough to help with the mooring before hurrying off to find his saucepan.

"We've run out of gas – would you mind?"

Tyler hesitated for a moment, contemplating the saucepan he was holding. "You could come and have coffee with me…"

"Tea–" he said, before he could stop himself.

"You Brits are all the same. What is it with you and tea? Sure, you can have tea, or coffee, or–" She glanced speculatively at the sky, crinkling her face in the late afternoon sun, "I could fix you a drink…"

"Tea would be fine."

She lowered a ladder bolted to some plywood towards him and Colin set one end on the ground. "My attempt at a gang plank," she grinned. "Welcome aboard."

Tyler showed them to seats on a small shaded deck at the stern, with that enviably frank, uncomplicated, easy manner that Americans have made their own. Except, Colin noticed, she wasn't that uncomplicated. She had a smile which spread, then somehow faltered; a stammer of a smile, which lacked the courage of its convictions. From time to time she would inspect her fingers, examining them singly as if looking for calluses, before wiping her hands on her shorts. As he peered round her, trying to see down into the galley and check on the kettle's progress, she said uncertainly,

"I don't really do much entertaining, as such. You folks are… well. You know…" She hooked her right arm behind her head and then, after some reflection, let it fall. "I don't really… I haven't… not anymore."

Delphine had given up listening long ago. "Are those your pictures?"

"Those–?" Tyler swung round inquiringly, as if it were possible that some other artist might be exhibiting on her boat. "Oh, those…"

In his parched and weakened state, Colin could see that in every window of the cabin there was a picture, framed and hung so that it faced outwards. As he rose to take a closer look, the saucepan still in his hand, she turned away, and he noticed that her movements took up more space than would normally be required, in spite of her efforts to confine herself. She made her way down the steps into the cabin as if she were putting on a cardigan that was too small for her.

"The kettle!" she called behind her, by way of explanation.

Delphine was grimacing at the artwork. "They are affreuses – these images."

"Affreuses?"

"Terrible. I could paint these pictures. With my left hand, I could paint them."

"Keep your voice down…"

"But it is true, non?"

"Well…"

It was true; the pictures were not very good: well-meaning watercolours in doubtful shades, the perspectives all awry. He moved from one which depicted what could just conceivably be a group of Charolais cattle coming down to the waterside to drink, to another which showed a woeful vase of hydrangeas, and then on to a townscape and beyond that, something which looked like a small London bus, but must be a boat, pulling up in a lock. He and Delphine exchanged a glance.

"Tea!" Tyler, holding a tray high against her chest, made her way back onto the deck. "Oh, you're looking at my *work*." She put a reverential emphasis on the word.

"Yes…"

"I'm just… you know… well." She handed him a mug of hot water and said, with a little more conviction, "I have a selection of teas, actually. Roiboos, green tea, just plain ordinary old English breakfast, rosehip, fennel…"

"Plain ordinary old English breakfast sounds just the ticket," he answered, contemplating the hot water with a sense of hope which had been compromised, but not extinguished.

She handed him a sealed sachet. "I'm not really, you know… I've only just begun my life as an artist. Oh Lord of Lord City, I haven't warmed the milk–"

"It's fine," cried Colin, keeping a tight grip on his mug. "Cold milk's just great."

She hooked her arm around the back of her head. "So what do you think of my pictures, then?"

"Your pictures are just great," he answered, not looking at Delphine as he assembled the component parts of his tea.

"I'm an artist too," announced his granddaughter, drily. "I make papier-mâché beads." She took little persuading to go and fetch a sample of her wares.

"I'm really loving what you are doing here with this necklace – it's so… expressive."

"You can buy it if you like," Delphine offered, with an eye to the main chance. "They're all for sale."

"I do like. I really like. Does this bracelet go with it?" Tyler asked, picking up a string of softly collapsing paper balls.

Colin sipped his tea with a brief premonition of the watercolours he might soon be involved in purchasing on a reciprocal basis.

"Yes – and the key ring."

"Oh, I am so in need of a key ring."

"It is possible you need earrings too?"

"You know, you're right there – I do." The proffered earrings were drooping greyly. "They'd make a wonderful... present. For someone." She patted the pockets of her shorts. "Am I going to be able to afford all this? I need to lay my hands on some ready money here."

In spite of the intensity of his telegraphed warnings, Delphine stated a hugely over-inflated price and to her great credit, Tyler paid up without hesitation; she even let her keep the change.

"It's cool, the exchange rate's working in my favour at the moment." She made Delphine, who was richer than she could have believed possible and newly enslaved, tie the necklace round her neck. "Am I going to be just *the* most chic woman in this goddam town, or what?"

The kind of peace which comes late on Sunday afternoons settled round them. In the distance they could hear the affronted barking of a dog; beneath the surface some perch shimmered and then disappeared. Colin could feel the breath of the evening on the back of his neck, warm and benign.

"Can I fix you that drink?"

He shivered as if he had been roused from sleep. "Sorry, I was miles away."

Tyler inclined her head, and the silence rippled round them as green and gold as the river.

"What's the name of your boat?" he asked, to make conversation.

"*Sabrina Fair.*"

"Wasn't that a film by Billy Wilder?"

"Yay!" She made an odd gesture, like doing a high-five on her own, her palm meeting thin air. "It's about an American girl who's been to Paris. She has this great line: she says she wants to be at the centre of things, not standing on the sidelines watching, and that's how I'd like to be but I'm not, because that's exactly what I do: I stand aside and watch. And paint, sometimes," she added as an afterthought, catching at her lip. "Can I fix you a drink?" she asked, altering the emphasis this time, changing the inflection, making it into a whole new question.

Colin's eyes slid to his granddaughter, who looked as if she would soon be crashing her head to her knees with boredom once again.

"I've got satellite TV," said Tyler following his gaze. "In case that makes a difference—"

It did make a good deal of difference. Delphine settled down to watch *The Simpsons* in the cabin, with her cash and another *Coke*, her face suffused with reflected yellow rapture. As the distant traffic droned and an ancient pedestrian walked along the quay and two teenagers kissed on the parapet of the bridge and the river licked and lapped at the boat, Tyler, drink by drink, told him all the things that she wasn't.

"I'm not really a people person, you see. I thought I was, but it turns out that I'm not... I'm not married now – I got my *get out of jail free* card a couple of years back... I'm not into having a relationship any more. Once bitten would be OK, once bitten would be fine, but if you've been swallowed whole and then spat out... To tell you the truth, I'm not that good at painting, but God I just adore doing it... Don't get me wrong Colin, if I'm being overly negative here, I love my life and I wouldn't change anything about it..."

Listening and sipping his glass of wine, he thought it would be easy to repay these tumbling confidences with his own list of all the things he'd failed to be, but it seemed to him that what mattered more was who and where he was now – an old geezer, high on the sweet river air, drifting through France.

"What will you guys do for food this evening? With no gas?"

Colin shrugged. "Get a kebab. Delphine's probably sick of my cooking by now."

"You'd be very welcome…"

He was aware of her tentative face beside him, conscious of her anxious kindness, the breeze of her, the outdoorsiness of her brown arms.

"How do you manage the boat all on your own?" he responded, wondering if he sounded evasive, when he didn't mean to be, entirely.

"I'm good. I'm really good. I'm nimble and I'm organised and I don't mind asking for help. And I love doing it."

He nodded.

"What about you? How do you manage?"

"The *Dragonfly* is so small she practically fits in my pocket. And I've got Delphine to help me."

They looked away from one another, in opposite directions. The night air was so warm Colin felt as if he could lean against it and it would take his weight. He hardly realised he had sighed.

"I suppose I ought to…"

"Yes, well…"

"…take my granddaughter…"

"Perhaps another time…"

"…and get that kebab."

"She's a great kid."

"Another time – yes, maybe."

"Yes. Yes, maybe."

"Well, then…"

They took their leave. Ahead of him, Delphine went dancing down the gang plank on her tip toes with her arms outstretched. She jumped hard, near the bottom, trying to overbalance him. After he had recovered himself, the two of them set off along the quay and the flapping of her flip-flops sounding like birds' wings taking flight.

The sun distilled to darkness in the sky.

"I really like Tyler," the child said, with an arch note in her voice. "She's so kind. She has such… good taste. And maybe I am wrong about her pictures. It is possible. Maybe they are not so affreuses, not all of them. Maybe she needs to practice a little bit, that's all."

Colin switched his saucepan and the small electric ring that Tyler had lent them into his other hand. "What will you do with your ten euros?"

"Buy a video camera, to make movies," she answered without hesitation. She flashed a smile his way, and he was struck by the scope of her dreams, their randomness, and the fact that they remained unbroken.

"That's my girl." He peered at her through the gathering dark. "You're right, Tyler is kind." He craned his neck to look back. On the deck of *Sabrina Fair* a figure was just discernible in the dusk. He saw her raise her hand and the paler skin of her forearm gleamed for a moment in the light of the rising moon, as she touched the papier-mâché beads around her neck.

CHAPTER FOURTEEN

"*Aw man!*" said Laroche plaintively. "Alright then. Teach me something useful. None of that *the cat sat on the mat crap*. Teach me to write *I'll punch your fucking lights in*. That'd be cool. And *twat* and *wanker* and perhaps *Wotch you looking at?* Or how about *Woss your problem, dickhead?* You could teach me to write *dickhead*. That'd be sweet. An' *tosser*."

"How about *bellend*?" asked Michael dryly.

"Yeah, that an' all. *Pillock, bollocks, knobber.* Yer getting me interested now."

Michael drew up a list of the foulest language he could think of and added every conceivable insult under the sun, some of them Shakespearean, for good measure. That covered most of the letters of the alphabet.

"I'll write something down, we'll read it together, then you copy it out afterwards."

Laroche yawned. He unwound his spine one vertebra at a time until his head was resting on the table.

Michael smoothed the sheet of paper and began to write. A whistling breath came out of Laroche's open mouth.

"OK, then…" After a little bit of trial and error, involving reading cards with individual words on them amongst other things, Michael tore up sheets of paper into little squares and wrote a single letter on each. Grudgingly, his head tipped back and his jaw slack, hardly looking at what he was doing, Laroche assembled his first autonomous word : C O K S U C E R.

It was a breakthrough.

Within days he was making phrases. I'M BLADDERED. ARE YOO FUKING ME OVA? CACK OF YOU GITE. One day, when Michael came back from rec, thirty five minutes outside in the greasy drizzle before they were herded indoors again, he found a note on his pillow.

I MEBE DICLECKSICK BUT LOOK AT ME DOING THE RITIN, GOBSHITE.

He glanced over. Laroche was lying on his back, his arms folded behind his head and his ankles crossed with loose nonchalance. His eyes were closed. He was fake sleeping, but his tight little mouth was twitching at one corner and an aura of supreme self-satisfaction was exuding from every pore. Michael regarded him for a moment with something he could have dismissed as grudging admiration, but it felt more humbling than that.

COULD DO BETTER, DOUCHEBAG, he wrote back in reply.

~~~

Michael's first morning in what was known locally as the hobbit shop because only hobbits would work for fifty cents a day started unremarkably enough. The workshop was a skinflint construction with walls a single brick thick and ancient aluminium windows that had the permanent glitter of condensation on them. Looking up at the exposed ducts and piping under the pitched roof, lit unforgivingly by fluorescent lights which dangled from long chains, he thought the place was probably bristling with asbestos. The best spots – by the stove in the corner as far as possible from the door – were already taken by the regulars, but he squeezed into the middle of a row of sullen mechanics, where a dilapidated old bicycle upended and balancing on its saddle was waiting for him. On the bench was some WD-40, a hank of wire wool, a selection of allen keys on a ring and the kind of villainous wrench you wouldn't expect to see in a high security prison.

The word *Rosbif* flittered round the room in audible whispers. It felt a little like being handled: it was deliberately intrusive. Michael examined the bike. It was a Bertin, or had been once. There was no chain. The rust of decades obscured most of the paintwork and the nuts and bolts holding the frame together were so corroded that they couldn't be undone. He gave a quick blast with the WD-40 then set to work with the wire wool, rubbing away with specific, detailed movements.

Rosbif... Rosbif... Rosbif.

He worked at the nuts that were holding the front wheel in place, flecks of oxidised steel like gold leaf coming loose and adhering to his skin. At length, he was able to release the wheel and he turned his attention to the rear. He wiped his palms on his jeans, but the rust held tight to the lines in his hands. He started rubbing with the wire wool, causing infinitesimal erosions in the metal.

Rosbif... Rosbif... Rosbif.

The words were so persistent that he couldn't be sure if they were still being mouthed, or whether they had lodged themselves in his ears and were eating away at his brain. He craned his head around, searching for one of the kangas. There were two guards at the far end of the shed, chatting, chewing gum. One of them caught his eye and held it, his gaze sustained, as corrosive as rust. The man scratched his chin and turned back to his conversation.

When Michael had used up his supply of wire wool he crossed over to the bank of cupboards on the far wall as he had seen others do.

"Oi! Rosbif!"

He glanced around then wished he hadn't. All the men were studiously working on their bicycles. He tore off a length of wire wool from a huge bag full in the cupboard and went back to his place. The ring of allen keys was gone from his bench. He rolled the wool into a pad between his fingers, folding in the fraying ends. There was a threat in the air like the coming of rain: invisible, suggestive. He crouched down and resumed scratching away at the bike, concentrating on what he was doing. He removed the rear wheel. The pedals were next, but they were jammed on tight and he needed an allen key to release them.

"Can I borrow your allen keys, mate?" he said to the man next to him, a jowly bloke with a hanging lower lip.

"Use your own," the man mumbled.

Michael looked at the bench. His keys were back where they had been before. He stared at them for a moment. "Thanks, mate," he said, after a beat.

It was a hard way to earn his fifty cents. The day was filled with an accumulation of inflicted setbacks. Minor hitches: things spilt, or removed, or bent out of shape. *Rosbif… Rosbif… Rosbif.* Someone tripped him up when he went back to the supply cupboard and he knocked a bicycle over as he tried to stop himself from falling. *Rosbif.* The guy mending the bicycle had him by the ear and swung him round in a half circle before the kangas could intervene. He got twenty-four hours in the punishment block for fighting and as he was marched away by two officers a voice from behind him called out, "Oi Rosbif! It was me wot fucked yer wife."

A day later, when Michael was returned to his cell, he found Laroche sitting at the table writing, his breathing heavy and laborious. He was working on a new list of words. BOOK PAGE SHELF TABLE LEND BORROW READ READING TALKING QUIET RETURN OVERDUE STAMP.

"I'm gonna get me a job in the library," he said without looking up. "No point in poncing about in the hobbit shop. Only a BAMPOT would do that."

"Bampot?" said Michael, strangely pleased to be home. "That's a new one on me."

CHAPTER FIFTEEN

"I'm not coming. I won't come. It's too hot for Amandine and it's too hot for me."

"Now look here—"

The two of them were not quite shouting at each other: Delphine was not quite shouting in a way that suggested she very soon would be and Colin was not quite shouting with the tested patience that comes from long practice.

"I don't want to see the town. I've seen plenty of towns. I don't want to come. I want to stay here."

"But I need to get some petrol."

"I don't want to get petrol. You can get petrol without me."

"But Joigny's supposed to be nice."

"Sens was supposed to be nice," she answered darkly, as if that settled the matter.

High in the ozone, in the blue air, a helicopter hacked in lumbering circles, each one lower than the last. Colin shaded his eyes. "It's coming in to land, I think."

From the far side of the river an important little launch was skimming towards them carrying two men in evening dress, although it was only mid-afternoon. Delphine picked at a scab on her elbow as they tied up behind the *Dragonfly*, but as they started unloading a length of red carpet, she swivelled round to watch.

"Ah, Colin…"

He was briefly charmed by the way that, with her French accent, she could turn his name into the bars of a song; he liked the lilt and swoop of the syllables as she spoke them, "*Colin…*" For a moment he was entranced to be her reference point, the person she showed things to and shared them with. All the fight about fetching the petrol went out of him.

"There's a restaurant over there–" he jerked his head at the other bank. "A famous one. People come from far and wide…"

The noise of the helicopter was raining down on them. Delphine covered her ears and squealed, "I think it must be the President. Or maybe Daniel Radcliffe or Lady Gaga." The downdraught flattened Michael's lavender tweed hat against her hair. "Do you think it is possible?"

The two immaculate men were rolling the red carpet from the launch up the river bank. One of them was not happy with the lie of it and half rolled it up in order to perfect the angle in relation to the launch. When they spread it out a second time he seemed painfully unconvinced. He brushed some dried grass from the pile with a morose sweep of his fingers and then shot his cuffs as if to have done with it. The two of them processed to the end and Colin had to physically restrain Delphine from jumping ashore and running after them.

"I think it is the Mayor of Joigny and his deputy and they are here to meet Robert Pattinson," she declared breathlessly.

"I think they're waiters, actually. Very smart ones," he replied, conscious of the oil on his shorts and the fact that he had been wearing the same T-shirt for three days now.

As the two helicopter passengers, clad in expensive shades of camel and bent low because of the churning wind, came scuttling across the field, his granddaughter scrambled up onto the cabin roof and started waving Amandine high in the air.

"Bonjour! Bienvenue! Welcome to Joigny, Robert! My name is Delphine and this is my boat and we are making a grand voyage south until the butter melts!"

The couple sped along the red carpet without so much as a glance in their direction. Delphine slid back down onto the deck trailing Amandine loosely behind her.

"I don't think it was Robert," she sighed as the launch pulled away with its precious cargo, "Robert would have waved. He would have said hello at least. He probably would have come on board for a *Coca-Cola* and signed an autograph for Amandine. She collects them, you know."

Colin tweaked her cap. "I'm going to get that petrol."

"He probably would have," her lower lip was jutting out and without thinking he nudged it back into place with the knuckle of his finger.

"What about you?"

She leaned against him for a moment, a negligible gift of tenderness, and as she fiddled with a loose thread on the monkey's little snout, he was conscious of the careless warmth of her arm against his shirt. A quick twist of an emotion that he couldn't name spiralled inside him.

"Why don't I set you up with a fishing rod?" If I'm getting the petrol, you ought to be doing something productive – it's only fair."

"I cannot do fishing – it is not possible."

"It's easy…" He dug the bag with his fishing tackle out of the everything locker. "I used to go fishing with your dad when he was about your age; he had his own rod and everything…"

Delphine ran the monkey's paw across her cheek ruminatively as she watched him assemble the fishing tackle.

"It screws together like this; you put that bit on there and thread the line through here…"

"Did Papa like fishing?"

He broke off from what he was doing, flooded with the memory of the two of them sitting damply under an umbrella by the canal, a flask of warm tea and their sandwiches wrapped in waxed paper on the grass between them, with Michael ticking off everything they caught in his I-Spy book of river fish.

"Yeah, he did like it. He was very good at it, what's more."

He finished assembling the fishing rod. "You're very like him, you know," he said to his granddaughter, after a pause; he found himself wishing that she would lean against him one more time, but she was scanning the middle distance, her eyes darting this way and that as if she had mislaid something. "To look at. You've got his hair, and his colouring."

"Papa's going thin on top. That's why he wears a hat." Her voice sounded terse, as if she were correcting him, as if this was something she had gone over with him many times, but her eyes were still searching, on and on, trying to locate all that she had lost.

"That hat?"

She chose not to answer. He could see she was brimful with something, something which darkened her gaze further, which caused her to fold her lips tight and rest her chin on Amandine's head, something which made her draw in a breath and look at him acutely, and then say nothing.

"And you laugh exactly the same way that he does, with your mouth curled up a bit at the side. That was one of the first things I noticed – the way you laugh."

"OK, I'll do the fishing. I'll do it. If that's what you want," she shouted to shut him up.

He blinked in astonishment. He laid the rod along the locker, taking his time as he digested the sour taste of victory. "You don't have to…"

Delphine rolled her eyes to the heavens.

"Not if you don't want to…"

"I've said I'll do it."

"I just thought that it might—"

"Colin," she shouted, then she clapped her hands over her ears and started making *la la la-la la* sounds at full teenager volume, although she was only nine.

"OK, OK," he looked up and down the mooring, smiling and nodding at the one or two boaters watching them with interest. "Let's hit the rewind button. Do you want to do some fishing while I go and find the petrol?"

"No."

"OK."

"But I will."

Reflecting on the weird way in which you can win an argument and still feel you haven't got what you wanted, he showed her how to bait the hook with a bit of old bacon and how to reel the line in. He cast the rod for her.

"Amandine goes fishing often," she observed dispassionately. "She catches sharks and everything. In Brittany, when we go on holiday."

"Well, let's see what she can do with the Yonne." He peered down into the river and then passed her the rod. "I won't be long. Don't talk to strange men and don't leave the boat under any circumstances. Understood?"

She gave him a withering glance. When he reached the end of the pontoon and turned to look back at her, she was up on the cabin roof with her headphones and sunglasses on, doing a kind of lying-down dance, the fishing rod with its line snagging in the water abandoned on the deck below.

~~~

To calm himself down, he had his one cigarette of the day over a furtive beer in a bar in the main square. 24/7 childcare! Not for the fainthearted, or the recently retired except in very small doses when there was a parent on hand to bundle the child back to. He stubbed his cigarette out half-smoked and checked his watch.

The route back to the mooring was downhill, thank God, and the streets were laid out in a thousand year-old grid designed to keep out as much of the sunlight as possible, but still the mediaeval houses, their walls the colour of scorched earth, seemed to glimmer and shift in the glare.

He paused on the bridge to catch his breath, his eyes seeking the *Dragonfly*. In the distance he could just make it out, lazing in its berth, moving with wide-hipped indolence from side to side as the current went swaying past. He took his hat off, wiped his forehead on his arm and fanned himself. Beneath him, the reflection of the town lay like oil upon the water and it was bliss, for a moment, to lean against the cool stone and gazing down, to lose himself in the marbling of clouds, the inflections of blue shot through with river green.

Beyond the port de plaisance was a recreation ground and he smiled to himself to hear children squealing and calling, their vaulting laughter the soundtrack of a summer's day, picturing the games of chase, the terrible pleasure of a dare, the hide and seek, the racing to catch up, the always out of reach –

He hesitated, his hat motionless in his hand, the heat collecting round its brim. The clamour, dispersing through the air, changed tone, drawing out into a single cry of anguish. He strained to place it, tilting his head to hear more clearly. It wasn't coming from the rec. He crammed his hat back on to his head and heaving the jerry can into both arms, he started to run.

Sprinting with twenty litres of fuel sloshing against his chest was impossible to sustain for long. He reached the end of the bridge, panting, and set the container down to rest for a moment. When he picked it up again it seemed twice as heavy, but he staggered on for another fifty metres before he had to stop again. He rested with his hands against his knees, weighed down with the recognition of that cry. *To hell with the fuel!* He left the can there in the middle of the path and dragging more breath into his lungs, he started to run in real earnest, conscious of the epilepsy of the tall trees flashing past and the panic rising inside him.

A crowd of boaters had gathered round the *Dragonfly* and he charged through them scattering them to right and left.

"I'm her grandfather – let me through – excuse me please–"

He didn't know what he expected to find. He just knew that he couldn't stand the swollen, shrilling sound of Delphine's screams.

There was a woman standing next to her, her arm encircling the space around the child, as if comforting her without actually having to make contact.

"I'm her grandfather–" he cried, and the boaters took a few steps back. "What is it? What's happened?"

Delphine was incapable of stopping herself from sobbing; the hawser sounds of her crying kept coming and coming. Her head was hanging and in her hand she held the mallet, glistening silver with gore.

Colin dropped to his knees beside her. "Tell me what's happened?" Her hair had fallen forward, hiding her face and when he tried looping it back so that he could see her better, he could feel that it was stiff with… matter. She had a trail of greasy blood down one cheek; it was all over both her hands and the mallet, the palest blood imaginable: a smear of platelets and scales.

He took the hammer from her and laid it on the pontoon. He held her against him, lacking practice, and she pressed her face into his T-shirt and all her tears and sticky fishiness washed over him.

"I killed it. I didn't know what to do. It wouldn't keep still and I couldn't hold it. I couldn't get the hook out of its mouth. It kept moving. It kept twisting. I tried to get the hook out and I couldn't, and I couldn't throw it back into the river with the hook still there, so I found the mallet in the locker and I hit it and it kept moving and I hit it. I hit it and hit it." She looked at him with bleary eyes. "It wouldn't stop moving…"

Colin sat back on his heels. He had thought the chances of her catching something with a ratty old bit of bacon were about a million to one. He extracted a handkerchief from his pocket and held it out. "Here, spit on this."

Delphine spat halfheartedly and he wiped away the blood from her cheek. She burrowed back into his T-shirt when he had finished and she huddled close as if she had been washed ashore there, limp and spent.

"Why don't you show me what you caught?"

He could feel the muffled shaking of her head between the crook of his neck and his collarbone, but he clambered upright, lurching a little under her weight and she clung to his top with a barnacle grip.

THE DRAGONFLY

One of the helpful boaters had retrieved the jerry can and placed it on the pontoon with a nod. He thanked the man silently and the small knot of people loosened and began to disband.

He set her back on her feet, keeping a tentative hand on her shoulder. "Why don't you show me…?"

She answered by curling herself closer into the harbour of his chest.

"Well, let's get cleaned up a bit, shall we?" With her still attached to him, he rinsed the mallet in the river and then knelt her down and made her wash her hands and arms, the scales of the fish silvering the surface of the water. "Come along now…"

She hardly seemed to know what she was doing. He led her like a child – she was a child, something that it was somehow easy to forget – back along the pontoon to the *Dragonfly*.

Lying on the deck amongst its own weeping viscera was a big fat catfish, a double figure warrior. "Delphine, you are an absolute marvel! I'd kill to land a catch like that. How on earth did you do it? You are extraordinary!"

Still she pressed her face against him; he could feel her wet breath and her wet tears seeping through his clothing. "I'm not," she gulped.

He crouched so that he was level with her. The world looked different from this preteen angle. "You are to me," he said.

"I'm a not nice person."

"Don't be ridiculous, of course you are."

"You don't know me."

He scratched the back of his head. "I'm getting to know you…" His knees were seizing and he wanted to stand up, so he said in rather a rush, "You're sunny and you're brave and you make me laugh."

She shook her head, her eyes downcast, not meeting his gaze, and her tears coursed and then dripped onto his shorts. He made one or two attempts at mopping her cheeks, then he levered himself up, climbed onto the boat, wrapped up the catfish in a carrier bag and opened a *Coke* for the two of them to share. He sat himself next to her and to his delight she leant against him.

"I tell you what we'll do: we'll sail the *Dragonfly* across the river to that famous restaurant, where we can probably only afford one crisp between us, and we will take your fish with us and ask the chef to cook it for your supper. How does that sound?"

She managed a watery smile which had him wondering if his attempts at kindness made things worse. The smile faded and for a moment she had an orphaned look about her that he didn't like to see.

"You can wear your best dress and I will find a pair of shorts that doesn't have oil on them and put on a clean T-shirt for the occasion. Maybe we should ring them up and ask them to come and fetch us in their launch. Why don't we? That's what we'll do – we'll call them."

She gave an almost imperceptible nod and wiped her eyes with the back of her hand; she straightened her spine. It was bad enough seeing her upset, but even harder to see her being brave. "That's my girl," he said gruffly. He ruffled her hair. "The only thing is – you'll have to do the talking."

~~~

Delphine put on a bit of everything: an orange skirt, some grey leggings, a long-sleeved blue T-shirt and something green and floaty over the top of that. She twisted up her hair under the lavender tweed hat and painted her nails in different colours.

All of this was done privately, and without joy. Colin watched from the corner of his eye as he shaved and washed his hair in the bucket. He towelled himself dry, shaking his head like a dog coming out of the sea, scattering drops everywhere.

"Colin! Now I will have to do my nail all over again. It is not possible—"

"Are you ready?"

"I have to paint again – this nail, and that one. Mer—"

"Let's get going."

"—de."

They couldn't find a phone number for the restaurant. No launch, no red carpet, but they set off through the rec, over the bridge and along the quay on the other side, as irritably as an old married couple.

An immaculately dressed waiter met them at the entrance.

"Poisson – jeune fille – rivière—" With no help from his granddaughter, Colin made catching motions, the carrier bag swirling with dangerous scents. "Ou est le—?"

The maître d' appeared, and Colin tried again.

"Poisson—" He started to unwrap the fish, and the piscatorial scent immediately intensified. Delphine, with an existential sigh, made a minute examination of a vase of lilies every bit as tall as her, standing by the reception desk like angels clustered at the gates to heaven. "Jeune fille—" He clapped his hands together as if catching something: flies, catfish, moonbeams?

"May I help Monsieur?" asked the maître d' in impeccable English.

Arrested mid-mime, Colin replied with a courtesy that matched his. "My granddaughter," he gestured in her direction; if Delphine could have climbed into the vase of flowers, she would have done, "Caught her first fish this afternoon. In your river. It is an extraordinarily fine specimen, and deserves the finest cooking."

Accepting the compliment while at the same time keeping to a safe distance, the maître d' humbly inclined his head.

"Which is why we have come here."

"It is not ordinary for Chef to prepare something he has not sourced himself," came the murmured deprecation.

"It is no ordinary fish," said Colin. "Well, actually, it's a little bit... damaged... in places, you can see it put up a very good fight."

The head of service took the carrier bag and finessed it onwards to the waiter at the speed of light. "We will ask the kitchen..." Anticipating Colin's thanks, he humbly inclined his head once more and Colin, in turn, inclined his just a fraction further. "Would Monsieur et Mademoiselle care to enjoy a cocktail...?" His glance passed over the terminally embarrassed Delphine. "On the terrace, perhaps, where it is quieter?" he suggested, diplomatically.

Colin wetted his lips with his beer and gazed at the river; through the limestone balustrade he glimpsed the duck egg blue prow of the *Dragonfly* and his chest welled at the sight. *What would you think if you could see us now?* he said silently to Sally. As he stared at the child sitting opposite him, he had the vaguest notion that all the hurt which had dogged him for so many, many years might somehow be cleansed by her. She was drinking noisily from a tall glass containing a symphony of juices that was a fruit salad – almost a meal in itself. She was swinging her legs, but he didn't say anything. He rolled the beer around the inside of his glass and smiled inexpertly across at her; she made a slurping sound back at him and he knocked about one pound fifty's worth of beer down in a single gulp.

THE DRAGONFLY

A man in chef's whites with chequerboard trousers approached their table. "Mademoiselle," he began. "Is it true that you caught so magnificent a fish from the river this afternoon?"

Delphine's eyes rounded. With the straw still in her mouth, she nodded.

"I propose a preparation très simple, I will grill your fish myself and serve him with a bitter almond emulsion, perhaps une salade verte on the side and some potato frites."

"With mayonnaise?"

The chef smiled at her. "That was my thought precisely. It would be a pleasure."

He went gliding back to the kitchen and Delphine finished her cocktail and wiped her mouth on her sleeve. She leaned over the table and held her hand out to him. He took it a little diffidently, and the two of them sat there companionably, while she picked the dirt out from underneath his fingernails, and the sun went tumbling through the clouds casting comet's colours across the sky.

CHAPTER SIXTEEN

Michael dialled Delphine's number, conscious of the breathing presence of the kanga a few paces behind him.

"Hi Kiddo!"

"Papa! It's me!"

He felt a kind of limpness, a physical sweetness at the sound of Delphine's voice.

"I cannot speak for the while because Colin is letting me drive but before I go–" she gasped.

"You're driving *what*?"

"Le bateau. Colin showed me how to do fishing and I caught one that was enorme – I do not know the name – and we went to a restaurant and I saw Robert Pattinson, or it could have been Daniel Radcliffe I'm not sure, in a helicopter, but I couldn't get his autograph. You can speak to Colin now because I must do some steering–"

He was thinking of why it should cut him so, the idea of them fishing together. It brought back memories he thought he'd finished with and for a second or two he was so immersed in them that he was unaware of a disturbance on the line and then he heard a man clearing his throat at the other end. He felt a swift contraction of the heart.

"*Dad–?*" In the background he could hear the thrum of a motor and the swish of water. "Is that you?"

"Michael. This isn't… it probably isn't the right–"

"Is she OK? Delphine? Is everything alright?"

"She's fine."

"Where are you?"

"We're both fine. On the canals… heading south. It's all alright."

"Time's up," said the kanga from somewhere unexpectedly close to him. Recalled to his prison life, Michael gave a little shiver.

"Got to go," he said, hanging up. He stood there stricken when the call was over, staring at the handset, the sound of his father's voice a reminder of everything he'd loved and lost.

~~~

"Sixteen… seventeen… Woss the snag, Rosbif? Eighteen… nineteen…" Laroche was doing press ups on the floor beside his bed, the macho kind with a clap midair between each one.

"What?" said Michael, as if from a great distance, as if from a boat on a river that he couldn't picture.

"Twenty…!" Laroche snapped out of the press ups and onto his haunches, panting. "Woss your damage?"

"Damage?"

"Problem. Woss your problem?"

"I haven't got a problem," Michael pulled out a chair at the table and lowered himself onto it. Then, as an afterthought, as Laroche showed signs of embarking on another set of exercises, he said, "Something weird just happened."

Half way through some flex or other involving some muscle or other, Laroche's head swung round. "Yeah?"

"I just spoke to my Dad."

"I haven't got a dad. Must of done once. They're an accessory you can do without – after the fact oink oink."

"Will you please stop doing your bloody exercises? I can't–" Michael clapped his hands over his ears to block out the perpetual... evidence... of his own lack of privacy, of Laroche's endless, endless presence, of the grinding sameness of it all. "I can't hear myself think! Please!"

There was a pause, an injured silence, during which Laroche picked himself up and smoothed down his trackie bottoms. "No need to go all section eight on me," he said. "You could just ask."

"I'm asking."

"I'm sitting still now," said Laroche. "Look at me. Completely still. Not moving a muscle. See?"

"Yeah," said Michael, staring at his shoes.

"What's with you and your ol' man then? Must be some bad shit there."

"There is," said Michael.

"So?" said Laroche.

"Stuff happened," he said, wishing he'd never brought the subject up.

"I get that."

"My mum told my father that Charlotte – she's my partner–"
"Was."

"She was my partner," said Michael, barely missing a breath, "My mum told my father that Charlotte was pregnant and he wasn't very happy about it and–"

"And?" said Laroche encouragingly.

Michael became aware of the weight of his gaze upon him, although his cellmate, true to his word, hadn't moved an inch. It took him a long time to answer. "There was an argument," he said in the end. "My father... well, he offered Charlotte money to get an abortion."

Laroche whistled. "Way to go, Daddy!"

"She wouldn't speak to him, she was so angry."

"And you?"

"I saw him once after that, when Delphine was born, and we haven't spoken to each other since."

"Is that *it*?" said Laroche dubiously, cracking his knuckles. He shook his head. "If that's it, you gotta man up, Rosbif. Mind if I do me sit ups now?"

CHAPTER SEVENTEEN

They moored out in the wild the following night, a guilty economy on Colin's part, which in no way compensated for the insane extravagance of their three star supper. Forests of silver birch flickered right down to the river bank and they had a job to tie up amongst all the reeds and nettles.

Even tinned cassoulet for two, a couple of bruised pears and the end of a baguette managed to seem like a feast. They ate in a scattering of shade to the subtle song of unseen insects, with the salt smell of a distant bonfire in their nostrils and a pencil line of wood smoke tracing across the sky.

Colin extracted his one cigarette of the day from its flattened packet. It had snapped just below the filter, but he lit it anyway. "Fancy a game of cards?" he asked out of the corner of his mouth.

Delphine pulled a *maybe, but preferably not* face, then she stared at him, waiting to see if he could do better.

"Hangman?" he asked doubtfully.

She shook her head.

A thought occurred to him. He contemplated her through a grey exhalation – without the filter, the cigarette burnt his throat. "Why don't you show me your album?"

"What?"

He started coughing. "The photos…" he prompted wheezily, "In your photograph album." He chucked the dog end into the river. With a hiss it was extinguished. "Why don't you show me?"

"Oh, those…" she answered dismissively, leaning over the side of the boat, watching a hundred minnows swarm towards the cigarette and then, in disappointment, swarm away. The surface of the water looked like grazed silk and she cupped her chin in her hands and gazed at it.

They spoke at the same time.

"I'd really like to see them." / "What is hangman?"

"Is it on the shelf above your bed?" He persisted, stooping down and peering into the cabin.

"Oh, Colin," she said with exasperation, as if her patience was being tried by a small and very stupid child. She grabbed the photo album before he could reach it and clasped it to her chest. Plonking herself down on the bathroom locker, she opened the album a crack. "There–" she flashed a page at him and then snapped it shut and rested it on her knees.

The album's see-through plastic cover was spangled with light from the low-slung sun. When Colin blinked, he could still make out its golden shape. He perched himself beside her, waiting to see.

Delphine frowned and shot him a look. She opened another page by about thirty degrees. "That's me."

He caught a glimpse of her face in close-up, sucking on a long string of spaghetti, moustachioed with bright red sauce.

"And that's me." She was ice skating in the open air in front of some palatial Parisian building, one stubby leg stuck precariously out behind her. He thought he could see Michael's figure gliding out of the frame.

"And that's me in Brittany," she remarked, warming to her theme. This time she opened the page completely and laid it flat on her lap. "Where we went camping." He could see a whole sequence of images of Delphine aged about three playing by a rock pool, squatting, gesturing, reaching out, totally absorbed. On her face was the expression he often noticed when she was talking to Amandine, although Amandine was nowhere to be seen.

"Who's that lady?" He nodded at a fair-skinned woman in the act of kicking sand at the photographer, the whitened grains curling upwards like spray, her laughter caught at that moment just before breaking. She was wrapped in a sarong and he was fascinated by the orange and red and cream colours.

"Maman, of course."

Of course. He studied the picture, seeing what Michael, presumably the photographer, saw: her hair streaming blackly in the breeze, longer than he remembered, her face as pale as he recalled. The next photo, taken seconds later, showed her bending forward, as if hilarity had overcome her. Her head was twisted round towards the camera, the last notes of laughter fading to blue.

Delphine flipped the page over. "That's me in the swimming pool." *Flip*. "That's me on my bike." *Flip*. "That's me asleep in the tent. I like that one." *Flip*. "That's Maman." *Fl–*

"Let me see," with his finger, Colin stopped the page from turning. The picture had been taken on long exposure, at night time, in what looked like the entrance to the tent. Charlotte was sitting at a folding table, one arm resting on the melamine surface, the other supporting her head. A gas lamp must have been lit just out of shot – he could almost hear the faint roar of the gauzy bulb burning and in the cadmium flare of the light that it cast, her face was soft and uncertain, as though she were about to suggest something, as though she still might. She seemed smiley, pliable, she could have been a little tipsy, the strap of her camisole had slipped down her arm, sleepily.

She looked loving and lovely. He hadn't expected that. He hadn't expected to see in her the kind of tenderness that melts and flows. He leaned in to stare at her face more closely just as Delphine let the page fall shut.

"That's enough now," she said, hugging the album to her and he could see that she was right; it was enough, for both of them. Enough for now. She put the album on the seat and sat on it. "We play cards, OK?"

"OK. What do you want to play? Snap, or Damn It? Or shall I teach you Gin Rummy?"

"Teach me Gin Rummy," she demanded, and they sat up late cheating at cards until the glitter went out of the river and night fell.

~~~

"Colin! Colin!"

"Eh?" He flailed his way up from the depths of sleep. Delphine was shaking his arm. "What is it?"

"Something has happened!"

"What time is it?" He squinted at his watch, wincing at the earliness of the hour and then pulled his sleeping bag over his head.

"Look–"

"Go back to sleep…"

She leaned across and with her finger and thumb forced his right eyelid open. He started up, blinking.

"Careful – you'll have my eye out." He rubbed it with his knuckle and shouldered his sleeping bag around him with disgruntled movements.

"Look outside–"

"It'll be a miracle if I can see anything at all," he grumbled, "Ever again," then following her pointing finger, he said "I can't! I can't see anything."

"That is what I am trying to tell to you – doh." In frustration she smacked her forehead with her hand.

Crustily, Colin tried to wipe the porthole clear with his finger and when that failed, with his sleeve. It remained thickly smeared with white. He regarded Delphine. "Hmmm."

Shrugging a sweatshirt on, he looked at his watch once more, allowing his granddaughter plenty of opportunity to apprehend his sense of injury at the time it told, before he began opening the hatch.

She barged her way out before him. "Regardez…!" she breathed.

The mist lay in skeins on the surface of the water. The *Dragonfly* was buried deep beneath its fondant folds and when Delphine stood up, only her head and shoulders could be seen. Colin surfaced beside her. It was like entering a world of make-believe and the two of them stood blinking as if they'd just stepped through a wardrobe or fallen down a rabbit hole.

Delphine began to giggle. "It's meringue!" She tried scooping the mist into her mouth but the vapour went slipping through her fingers. The bright, white lightness of it made him think that, like shaving foam, he could put blobs on her nose and chin, but although their hands chased and swerved, the fallen cloud could neither be caught nor contained and the two of them stood laughing in the whitewashed world that the dawn had revealed.

"You're soaked through," Colin observed, as the skin around her mouth turned blue. "We'd better get you warmed up."

As they dived down to find the entrance to the cabin an unearthly noise stopped them in their tracks. It was a carnal sound, rhythmic and urgent, a breathless sound of pursuit, questing, thrashing, reverberating.

A hundred metres down river, through the mist and up into the sky, rose a swan, its muscular arc curving just above their heads. They could see, feather by feather, the line of its neck, ending with the strange hieroglyphic of its beak. Close to, its feet looked murderously black and the vast sweep of its wings seemed to violate the air.

Colin tilted his head back and then further back, watching the fearful mechanics of its flight as the swan went straining higher and higher. He could feel the downdraught fierce against his face.

"Merde…" breathed his granddaughter and he didn't correct her.

It was a moment of weightlessness, of disorientation, of perfect delight. On and on went the mighty bird, wisps of mist spilling from its plumage as it claimed the whole wide river for itself. They listened until the leathery rasping of its wings was no more than a sigh in the distance and its white shape was absorbed into the sky. After a second or two, Colin bowed his head; his neck was stiff from looking upwards and he felt chilly now the spell was broken and the swan was gone. Delphine shivered beside him.

"Turn round," he said, "and I'll give you a hot potato."

"Quoi?" She stared at him, unable to keep the suspicion from her face. She turned around, craning her neck so that she could keep an eye on him.

He breathed out hard between her shoulder blades then rubbed the warm air through her pyjamas and into her frozen muscles. "Can you feel that?"

She nodded. "Do it again."

He did it again, and then again. "Better now?"

She grinned at him. "Much better. Shall I give you a – what do you call it – a hot potato?"

She turned him around and huffed and puffed into the small of his back and pummelled at his T-shirt, so that he was aware of a small patch of warmth seeping into his creaky bones.

"Thank you," he said after a moment, conscious that these days he bruised more easily than he used to. "Thank you very much."

Temporarily restored, the two of them stayed on deck a while longer, watching the mist dissolve, but as the morning was disclosed in all its purity, he couldn't help remembering the pictures of Charlotte, laughing and luminous, and he was suddenly afraid of what they might reveal.

CHAPTER EIGHTEEN

Michael couldn't stop thinking about the sound of his father's voice. He couldn't quite believe that they'd spoken. He couldn't get over how simple it was just to say hello, to start a conversation.

Since then, he'd been trying *not* to mind that his Dad was with Delphine and he wasn't. Trying *not* to mind was a skill he had made his own. He had tried *not* to mind that his father let Étienne steal Mum from them. He had tried *not* to mind about all the things his father should have said and done, such as asking that Michael stay with him instead of going to France. His father had never once said that. He had never once put up a fight. Maybe he thought he should take it as read, but you can't, when you're a kid, read those kind of things. You don't have the vocabulary.

Laroche's vocabulary was coming on no end, however. He'd read one whole paragraph today, from some paranormal gothic fantasy called *The Monstrumologist*, which had surely put his skills to the test.

"You should sign up with Education for an adult literacy course," he said and Laroche looked at him as if he were something he'd trodden in.

CHAPTER NINETEEN

They caught up with Tyler in Auxerre; or rather she caught up with them, since the *Dragonfly* skimmed along the Yonne as quickly as her namesake. Scenting shops behind the city's exquisite mediaeval facade, Delphine announced that she absolutely must have new clothes as she had worn everything she owned and Colin pointed out that there wasn't a millimetre of space left on the boat and as the two of them staked out their negotiating positions, the scarlet prow of *Sabrina Fair* came gliding towards the quay.

"OK, I'll admit that you could do with some shorts."

"Shorts?" Delphine couldn't believe her ears. "Colin, I am in rags and you are talking to me of *shorts*."

"It's Tyler!" he called to distract her. "Let's go and help with the ropes…"

She wasn't going to be diverted that easily. As he went hurrying towards the space where Tyler was manoeuvring (with impressive skill, he noted) Delphine cantered along beside him, "If we are going south until the butter melts, then I am definitely going to need a dress for the sun – with shoulder straps, not like this – in this I will boil–"

"One pair of shorts and that's my final offer," he lunged for the line which Tyler flung in his direction.

"It is not possible…" she wailed.

"Here, tie this off while I grab the other rope."

She tied and he grabbed and Tyler lowered her gangplank.

"Wait a minute…" Colin went dashing back to the *Dragonfly* to retrieve the electric ring that she had lent them. "Thanks so much for this. It was a lifesaver – really, it was."

"Cool."

She was standing with the light behind her and staring into the sun he couldn't clearly see her face, although from the easy tilt of her head he sensed that she was smiling.

"So are you going to give it back to me?"

"Oh yes – yes, of course." Collecting himself, he leaned up and passed it to her. "I'm sorry; I thought we might have bumped into you sooner. I didn't mean to hang on to it for so long. I hope you haven't needed it."

"I stayed over in Sens. I wanted to do an interior of the cathedral."

"Yes," he glanced over at Delphine. She was throwing gravel into the river, sowing gritty patterns over the surface. "We didn't quite make it as far as the cathedral."

"It's horses for courses, I guess."

"I guess," he echoed.

He could have left then. He could have said something about needing to buy Delphine some shorts, although God knows he didn't fancy trailing round the shops in the heat, but he didn't. Instead, he shoved his hands into his pockets. "The cathedral here looks pretty special too, now you come to mention it…" He shaded his eyes and gazed across at the imperious outline which dominated the far bank, its pale buttresses casting themselves upwards in the name of God's good grace.

"There's the abbey as well…" Tyler nodded in the other direction where, like a matching bookend, the abbey sheltered from the sunshine under its terracotta roof. "Spoilt for choice," she gave a gleeful shrug, "I'll need to stay here for days."

"We're not in any hurry either, as it happens…" he answered, as if the thought had just occurred to him. He stared upstream in the direction of their notional departure. When she didn't answer, he found himself filling the silence, "That's the beauty of it – the freedom. Being able to go with whatever takes your–" he cleared his throat, "With whatever interests you…"

"The open river, instead of the open road."

"Yeah – the open…" he found that he didn't know how to finish, or possibly where to start. He glanced at his granddaughter. She was evidently bored with filling the Yonne with gravel.

"I need to get this child a pair of shorts…" he excused himself. Delphine shot him a look suggestive of deferred retribution. "Child!" she protested in a whisper which warned *and don't get me started on the shorts.*

"The town's beautiful – real beautiful," Tyler said in a flurry as he was turning to go. "Well worth a look round."

He hesitated, peering up at her. Her smile switched on and off like faulty neon. She had a now you see it/now you don't kind of shyness.

"It does get a good write-up in the book," he answered circumspectly, aware of his own instinct for caution. *Because of Delphine,* he told himself. "Do you know it, then?"

"I've been here a couple of times. On my travels…" Casually, she stretched up and began tugging at the dead heads of flowers in a window box on the wheelhouse roof, dropping them one by one over the side into the river. Colin watched the dying petals saturate and slowly retreat downstream. He looked sideways at her and could see the weather in her face, her skin faintly scored by sun and wind and rain.

Delphine tugged at his hand and then with a quick twist of irritation, she made as if to load him onto her back and carry him away with her, nearly flooring the two of them in the process.

"It's a great place to buy shorts, that's for sure," she observed as he staggered and then recovered himself.

"*Col–in!*" urged his granddaughter, her eyes pinned wide with terrifying messages.

"Youguysfancymeetingupthisevening?" asked Tyler with such rapidity that neither of them could be sure what she had said and she had to repeat it, making her sunburn blush.

"This evening? Well, that sounds…" He deliberately avoided Delphine's eye. "It must be our turn. Why don't you–? What about – supper? And perhaps a drink first? With us?"

All three of them turned to contemplate the *Dragonfly*, which bobbed like a bath toy beside the gin palaces and barges moored along the quay.

"Do you have enough…?"

"Space?" supplied Colin, "Plenty. Well, just about. We'll manage."

"If you guys are sure…" Tyler addressed her equivocation to Delphine, who appeared to be blowing imaginary smoke rings into the air. The child glanced speculatively at her over the end of her invisible cigarette, then looked away.

"We'll do a barbecue," he said brightly, pleased with the idea.

"*Now* can we go into town?" implored Delphine and started pulling him away.

~~~

The barbecue and the Primus stove were perched on dry land and Colin, Tyler and Delphine were bunched up together on the *Dragonfly* with their knees crammed under the cabin door table. Tyler had brought a vast salad with several different types of lettuce, endive, artichoke hearts, roasted peppers, ribbons of carrot, crumbled goat's cheese, pine nuts and torn basil all slathered in a home-made herb mayonnaise – *I'm not much of a cook* – which took up most of the available space.

"I really like that dress you have on, it's so cute. Did you tie those straps yourself, or are they stitched that way?"

"They're stitched, I think," Delphine squinted down at her sundress.

"It's a great effect. That shade of… what is it, fuchsia…? really is your colour."

Importantly, as one who has no time for idle chatter, Delphine stretched right across Tyler and turned the chicken legs over on the barbecue, just as her grandfather had shown her. She then put the tongs down in the dirt on the quay as an added touch, on her own account. Colin said nothing. He was struggling to peel the potatoes by the flimsy light of a solar lamp dangling from the flagpole. From time to time a lick of wind blew the red ensign over it, causing a tiny power cut.

On the other side of the river the avenue of trees lining the bank was spangled with fairy lights. They could hear the murmur of conversation coming from a hotel boat moored close to the footbridge, the attacking sound of cutlery on china plates. The kitchen faced outwards and they could see the white shadows of the chefs moving in greasy intimacy, in a space that was almost as small as their own.

"Blast!" Colin dropped the knife and held his thumb up to the lamp; a rind of skin was hanging loose. "It's nothing," he tried not to look at the small punctuations of blood that were already rising to the surface of the wound. "I'm so cack-handed."

"Let me see, let me see," Delphine yanked his hand towards her, "Yuck – that is dégôutant."

"It's nothing, really," he said whitely, thankful he was sitting down. He was about to dunk his hand over the side into the river,

"DON'T do that," cried Tyler, "Have you had your tetanus?" He pulled a face.

"Hold your hand above your head," she gestured with her own hand, as if to show him how.

A trickle of blood wound round his thumb and onto his palm, following his lifeline, or the line of his heart, or the other one, he couldn't remember what it was called. He looked away woozily.

"I'm not very good with blood…"

"That's OK – blood is my forte. I'm fantastic with it. I really come into my own when there's blood around. Have you got a first aid kit?"

"It's in the everything locker. We're sitting on it."

They had to take the table down in order for them all to stand up, which involved putting the huge bowl of salad on the quay.

"Keep your hand above your head," Tyler ordered. "I didn't know you were a fisherman," she said, slinging the tackle onto the ground next to the growing pile of barbecue, stove and salad until she found the first aid kit.

"I'm just an amateur, Delphine is the professional."

While she swabbed the cut he made Delphine tell her about the three-star catfish, the double figure warrior.

"Wow – is that so?" Tyler applied sticking plaster to his thumb, smoothing the ends down. "There. I think you'll live."

"The chicken!" yelped Delphine, clambering over her grandfather and reaching for the tongs. The leg she inspected was charred and blackened and sprinkled with ash.

"Guess we'd better hurry along with those potatoes," drawled Tyler. "Though we sure could do with more light..."

They all stood up again, precariously close to one another, while Colin hunted for candles in the everything locker until he remembered that he kept them on the shelf above his bed.

"There!" Lined up along the quay, the tiny flames glimmered, tremulous in the night air.

"Why don't you let me–" with her complicated smile, Tyler took over the cooking of the potatoes.

"I was going to do mash," he explained, wondering if she would notice that the spuds were getting a bit wrinkled and rooty, *much like him, much like him.*

As she swung into action, organising Delphine to cook some sausages to eke out the burnt chicken, he leaned back into the shadowy limits of the light from the candles and watched her. Even at the maximum possible distance, they were so close that the cuff of her shorts skimmed his leg as she moved; she smelt of sunshine overlaid with soap and he found himself wanting to press his nose against her skin as if she were a flower, and inhale. He felt a pricking of emotion at the prospect, pensive at the thought of all the years now fled, when he could have had a new life instead of grieving for the old one he had lost. Not that he hadn't tried to make a fresh start, or at least gone through the motions: there'd been a woman called Ruth he met through work who liked photography and country walks and doubtless had a good sense of humour, but the gap between who she actually was and who he wanted her to be yawned wide and he suspected that the same had been true for her as well. In a moment of absurd optimism, he'd even joined a dating agency. He groaned aloud at the thought. Looking back, he'd let circumstances get the better of him, and then blamed his failure upon Sally. *Well, it was too late now.*

"Cheer up – it may never happen!" Tyler was pounding the potatoes into submission.

Quite.

He stole another glance at her. She wiped her forehead on her wrist, on the inside where the veins cast blue shadows on her skin. It was warm still, even in the darkness. Perhaps she was conscious of his eyes upon her, because for a moment her mouth looked as if it might waver into a smile – that ambiguous flare he'd noticed before – but she banged the fork on the side of the pan as if she'd thought better of it, and he wondered if this was intended as a rebuke, as if he'd gone too far, although he hadn't moved at all, hadn't done anything to suggest – *Never mind my second childhood, I'm having my second adolescence here.* In his confusion he turned to say something to Delphine, anything, when Tyler announced with a flourish, "Dinner is served."

They all stood up so that he could retrieve the crockery and cutlery from the kitchen locker and as he set forks and plates on the cabin door table, he felt obscurely irritated with himself.

"Why France?" he asked. He could have sworn he heard his granddaughter say on a breath *Why France?* and was tempted to kick her under the table.

He steeled himself, "Salad?" and handed her the enormous bowl.

Salad? came the faintest whisper.

"Distance, mainly. I wanted to put distance between myself and – just about everything, to tell you the truth. Distance and the Impressionists…"

"I saw a fantastic exhibition of Van Gogh in London…"

I saw a fantastic exhibition…

He turned round and stared hard at his granddaughter for several seconds; there was a derisory edge to the innocent expression on her face.

"And the wine, of course," said Tyler a little tensely.

"And the scenery," added Colin.

"These chicken legs are just great. You are the neatest cook," she said to Delphine.

At this, Delphine slowly unfurled herself; it was as if she came into bloom and Colin later remembered her sitting upright and smiling with gratification or maybe, in retrospect, with malice.

"Would you pass me the potato?" she asked sweetly. She took the pan he handed to her and sniffed at it, and sniffed at it again. "Does it smell strange to you, grand-père?"

She never called him grand-père; he should have been alerted. He took the pan back and sniffed it, shaking his head.

"It smells fine to me."

Wide-eyed, Delphine turned to Tyler, "What do you think? It smells a little… Je ne sais quoi?"

Tyler shrugged. "I didn't put anything out of the ordinary in it," but to oblige the child she leaned forward to sniff and as she did so, Delphine rammed the whole pan of mash right into her face.

CHAPTER TWENTY

Living in a state of permanent anticipation was grinding Michael down, he felt as if he was trying to second guess his own second guesses. The hobbit shop was the worst: the whispering, the sudden noise to act as a diversion, the sleight of hand – what he had mended, broken; what he had lost, found; tires slashed, air released, rags stolen, washers missing. It was unrelenting. He couldn't believe that Belfiore, his loose-lipped, heavy-limbed colleague on the bench, could be that adroit. He ended up suspecting everyone, even the kangas, who seemed to enjoy the sport. He didn't think he'd get a single bicycle stripped down and rebuilt. He'd be repairing his own repairs until the end of time.

"Fight back. Show 'em who's boss." Laroche was ruling pencil lines on a plain sheet of paper. "You don't have to suck it up," he looked at him darkly. "Unless of course you want to…"

"I don't want to."

"… maybe that's your style."

"I don't have a – style."

"'xactly. That's your problem. Dunno how you're going to manage when I'm gone."

"You're no help. You're not there."

"The Lord moves in a mysterious way."

"Are you going?" Michael asked with a pang of anxiety.

"Trial coming up. All good things come to an end, Rosbif."

"I wish," he said, "I wish."

After a moment, Laroche put his pencil and ruler down. He folded his arms and regarded Michael with a sardonic gaze that travelled the whole length of him. "I don't think you did it."

"Did what?"

"Killed your missis wot you miss so much. Don't think you did. Don't think you've got the cojones. That's c-o-j-o-n-e-s, but the j is silent – am I right?"

Tension jerked through Michael, the quick yank of it in every tendon. "You are right. The j is silent."

"You haven't got the 'nads, the family jewels…"

"It was a – a single moment. A loss of–"

"The bean bags… the walnuts… the dangly bits… the spunk bunkers."

"Shut up, Laroche!"

"Have you?"

"Look, this is none of your fucking business."

"I said the moment I saw you, you wouldn't – hurt – a – fly."

Michael took a breath but before he could protest, something was released inside him and he stopped anticipating, or trying to appease. Instead, he grabbed Laroche by the shoulders and hauled him upright. He didn't hit him. He wanted to, but he didn't. He shook him once, with all his might, and threw him back into the chair.

"Enough," he said.

The room was full of compressed air. You could have heard a pin drop.

Laroche was the first to exhale. "That's how you do it," he said wryly as he set himself straight, "Like that, but rougher, yeah?" He tugged his sweatshirt back into place, then picked up the ruler that had fallen on the floor. "Could try harder, but at least it's a start."

~~~

There was a peculiar truce between them. The tiny space in their cell became prairie wide, the sparse furniture distant hides.

"I don't want to talk," said Michael, when Laroche opened his mouth to speak, "I've got nothing to say."

Laroche wouldn't be deflected. "D'you think we'll stay in touch?" he mused, "When I cross over to the other side? Postcards? That kind of thing. Letters home?"

Straight away Michael thought of Étienne. Looking back, he could see that Étienne realised he couldn't have his mother without him, but then he didn't know what to do with him once he'd got him. They dropped each other pretty bloody quickly after his Mum died. He remembered saying goodbye to him after her funeral, and that weird embarrassment as both of them realised that they no longer had to give a toss about each other. They didn't even send Christmas cards, after that.

"Cross over?" he asked, to thaw the frost.

"To the other side."

"You might get off."

"No chance."

"You might go back to the big wide world."

"No chance," said Laroche.

CHAPTER TWENTY-ONE

"I will deal with you later," Colin contained his anger as best he could, which was quite well in the circumstances. "Don't even think of finishing your supper," he said as his granddaughter reached for a chicken leg, moving with that tired languor which sulkiness can inspire. She froze at his words, holding the chicken leg in mid-air, before she let it drop from some height onto her plate.

"It was a joke."

"I am going to apologise to Tyler and when I come back I expect to find you in your bed."

"It was just a joke, a trick," her eyes, downcast, narrowed for a moment. "A trick that Papa taught me..."

For once, he was unmoved. "She was our guest."

"I thought at least you could take a joke."

"After she bought those beads, as well. I can't think what got into you."

With small, punishing gestures Delphine wiped her sticky fingers one at a time on her new dress, losing herself in the damage she was doing.

Colin gritted his teeth. "I'm going to say sorry to Tyler. I'm going to do that first. And you are going to go to bed. We can talk about this in the morning, when both of us have had a chance to think about it." He climbed off the boat, never a dignified operation even at the best of times. "I can't imagine what got into you," he repeated, too busy mastering his indignation to take in the riptide of unhappiness that flooded her face and then bleakly drained away.

~~~

As Colin made his way along the quayside, his footsteps became slower and slower. The night air was alert to the instinctive arcs of starlings coming to roost in the branches of the chestnut trees which lined the river, and a sallow moon hung low above the city lending a nicotine stain to the sky. It made him think that he would give anything to have his one cigarette of the day to fortify himself against the scene which lay ahead. He felt for the packet squashed inside his pocket, then glanced back at the *Dragonfly*. The candles they had lit along the quay were guttering and going out; Delphine's porthole was in darkness; the promise of the evening was quite extinguished. He sighed. Ahead of him the red prow of *Sabrina Fair* drowsed on the current. Stepping over the mooring line, he peered in at the nearest window.

Tyler was wearing a different T-shirt. She was combing out her fringe, holding the hair close to the roots and tugging; uneven runnels of water coursed down her neck and over the private pallor of the skin behind her ear. When he tapped on the glass she jumped and then laughed to cover her sudden fright. It was an anxious laugh, as if she already knew she had revealed something of herself, more than she would have wished, without knowing exactly what. She chucked the comb onto the table and ran up the stairs, disappearing from one frame and appearing in another as she emerged onto the deck.

"I'm sorry–"

"I'm sorry–"

As synchronised as the starlings still zinging overhead, they started and stopped at the same time.

"No, no, I'm really–"

"I didn't mean to take–"

"You go first–"

She ran her fingers through her damp hair as if the thought of combing it had only just occurred to her. "I didn't mean to take so long…"

"I'm really sorry…"

"… but the potato seemed to get everywhere…"

"I was worried that it might have burnt your face…"

"… and in the end I thought it was simpler to wash it out properly – it didn't burn me – and then I couldn't find a clean T-shirt."

"It must have been scalding hot."

"No, not really – I took so long mashing it!"

"I can't think what got into her – into Delphine."

"It was nothing. A childish prank – rather a good one, I must remember it."

"She's just not like that–" Colin broke off, struck by the realisation that he didn't know what she was like, not really. He knew her, and he didn't know her at all: she was Michael's child; her advent into his life a compensation for all that he had lost.

"I was going to come back, but by the time I had found a T-shirt…"

"Oh, I wouldn't have blamed you–"

"… it seemed a little after the event. I thought you probably would have finished."

He craned his neck upwards. While they were talking the yellowing clouds wreathed themselves around the restless moon. The chestnut trees were hectic with skirmishing birds. "We never got started."

"I'm sorry," Tyler was examining her hands, polishing the calluses on one of them with the tip of her finger as though this was an operation which required precision.

"I sent her to bed," he grimaced. "Without any supper." With a twinge of guilt, he contemplated going back to his little boat and scooping the child up so that he could apologise for everything, for the whole damn lot, though he would hardly know where to begin. "I probably shouldn't have done that."

Tyler shrugged, "Well, you know best…"

He pulled a groaning kind of face, straining all the muscles of sadness and uncertainty.

"I think you're great with her." She was about to examine her hands again, but then she changed her mind. "So no one's eaten that chicken?"

He shook his head and then before he could stop himself, from some dark and ungovernable pit deep within, he blurted out, "Her mother died. A couple of months ago–"

"Oh my God! I am *so* sorry to hear that."

He regretted it immediately, the need to explain.

"I had no idea. I'm so sorry. So you've lost your – daughter?"

"My son," he answered shortly. "My son is Delphine's father."

"I had no idea," she apologised.

"You weren't to know – look, I could really do with a drink, I don't know about you."

"To be honest, I could really do with some of that chicken and a bit of salad–"

"Your salad!" he exclaimed, reminded of the wreckage of the evening.

"But a drink would be cool too."

They looked at one another, weighing up the odds. "I could go and fetch some of the food. I'd ask you over to the *Dragonfly*, but…"

"No, no, no. You fetch the food, that's fine. I'll open a bottle. Do you want red or white?" Tyler spoke in a rush, careful not to step on any conversational cracks which might appear.

Minutes later, Colin edged his way up the gang plank balancing the huge bowl of salad and two plates of burnt chicken and undercooked sausages, with a baguette tucked under his arm. "I thought you probably wouldn't want any potato…"

"Mash is definitely off the menu," she struck a pose to hide her self-consciousness, then immediately felt embarrassed. "Shall we have it on deck? Or do you think…?"

"On deck is fine."

She looked at him keenly. "You don't think that it might get… cold?"

The bowls and plates weighed heavily in his arms. "You can always put on a jumper–"

She nodded, as if that hadn't occurred to her. She seemed fiercely preoccupied.

He eased his arms into a more comfortable position, making the edges of the plates scrape together.

"Lord of Lord City, let me help you. Look at you, standing there carrying everything still. What kind of a hostess am I?" She tried to take one of the plates, but they were balanced in such a way that she almost sent the whole supper crashing into the river. "I am such a klutz! I am so sorry!"

He made it to the aft deck, just, and delivered the meal hugger mugger onto the table; some of the sausages falling to the floor and rolling beyond reach into the shadows.

THE DRAGONFLY

"I'll have them for my lunch tomorrow." She sat down warily and gestured for him to do the same. As soon as they had perched themselves at opposite ends of the bench, she jumped up and disappeared down the steps into the saloon.

"The wine!" She reappeared with the bottle held like a trophy in both hands. "It's an unpretentious little – I don't know what!" Some of it found its way into his glass. She chased the drips across the label with her finger, which she wiped on her shorts. "It's Burgundy, at any rate," and before he could prepare himself she flopped back down, picked up her knife and fork and asked, "How did she die? Delphine's mom? Is it OK for me to ask?"

Some insects were going crazy around the candle on the table. He wondered if they were biters. Mosquitoes loved him; he always got bitten. He remembered shining a thousand watt torch up into the sky to reveal to Michael the night world of tiny winged things. He sat with his mouth half open ready to speak.

"You don't have to tell me. I don't mean to…"

"No, it's fine. It was an accident." Rapidly, he filled his mouth with sharp-edged pieces of black chicken, allowing time for his words to settle and register with them both.

Tyler's face was suffused with sympathy.

"She tripped." He tackled the salad, forking up endive, an artichoke heart, some roasted pepper, a few ribbons of carrot, whatever he could find. "On the stairs. She was carrying a heavy bag…" He tailed off, contemplating the casual tragedy of his narrative, a version which would let Michael off the hook, wishing with all of his heart that it could have been so.

"I'm sorry. I shouldn't have asked. It's obviously very painful…"

175

"She fell and the case landed on top of her. Her neck was broken."

Tyler swallowed, then reached for her glass, which she held by the stem but did not pick up. She kept a grip on it, twisting it between her fingers, forming an agitated vortex in the wine.

"It was very quick. That's what the post-mortem said."

"That must be such a comfort for you."

"Comfort?" He wasn't sure whether he said the word aloud or not.

"And for your son..." Sensing she was on dangerous ground, but not how dangerous, she knocked back a mouthful of wine. She chased some chicken round her plate. She broke off the end of the bread.

"My son, yes. Yes, for him, too." He couldn't eat any more.

"You don't have to, you know – talk."

"No, I want to." He blinked in surprise at himself. "Most people don't ask."

"Well, I'm asking."

There were traces of herb mayonnaise on his plate, which he drew out into an abstract design using the tines of his fork. "Have you got kids?"

"No-ooh–" What began as a quirky smile never quite made the grade; it slipped and flickered, faultily. "No, I don't have."

He sat making tiny spider's webs out of mayonnaise, sticky constructs that allowed him to say nothing.

"Should have done, would have done, but it never – right person, wrong time / wrong person, right time – it never happened." Arriving at the far side of her explanation, she went a little slack. She leaned her elbow on the table, leaned her head in her hand. "Phew!" She fanned herself, although the air was growing cool.

"It's not too late," ventured Colin gallantly.

"It is way, way, way too late."

He rested the fork on the plate and folded his arms. For a few moments he made a careful study of the varnish on the saloon door, staring at the brittle glaze. He thought that when their trip was finished – at the very idea his skin prickled as if a cold breeze had blown across it – he would re-do all the varnish on the *Dragonfly*, make it his project for the autumn, seal himself up inside his shed and really set to work.

For the first time ever, he found himself dismayed at the prospect.

"It must have been very hard for your son."

Colin pressed his lips together. He lowered his head; he could have rested it in his arms and wept. "We're not on good terms, my son and I."

Across the river, the lights in the kitchen of the hotel boat went out.

"That sure is tough for you."

Colin nodded. "We were close when he was a boy." He was conscious of the strange octave his voice had found, "Very close."

She leaned on the table, her arm within touching distance, the hairs on it standing softly in the cool air. Without saying anything she stretched over and folded some hardened wax back into the candle flame, so that it melted all over again.

"I was closer to Michael than I was to my wife. Maybe that was the problem. She left me for another man…" Part of him was aghast to be sharing his private humiliations, but he was beyond being able to help himself. He shook his head. "She took him with her. When she left." He glanced in her direction. Her face was partially lit by the diminishing light of the candle flame, her eyes lost in shadow. "What brings you here? On your own"

For a moment her smile filled the little pool of light, before collapsing softly. "My ever-loving husband left me for someone fifteen years his junior when she told him she was pregnant. Not much of a body blow there. Hardly a setback at all." She drank some wine, regarding him over the rim of her glass. "We had our own business, importing kit houses from Sweden. We built our own first – that's what gave us the idea. God, I loved that little house–" she broke off and leant back out of the reach of the candle flame. All he could see was the shape of her, the darkness denser where she sat, with her arm still cast across the table. He watched the movements of her hand, fidgeting. "But I couldn't stay in it, not after – not when–" She drank more wine. "He – *they* – bought me out, bought my share of the business." With her thumb she scratched at a pearl of wax on the table, so that it flaked over her nail. "I've always been a bit of a pyromaniac," she observed disparagingly to herself.

He reached across, imagining for a single wild moment that he might net her hand within his own – the quick flutter of their fingers touching – but at the last second he finessed it; he pulled at his earlobe, he pushed his sunglasses up the bridge of his nose then remembered he wasn't wearing them.

"I wondered if I might buy a picture?" he asked, to cover his discomfort, clearing his throat. "That's partly why I came over."

She contemplated him for a moment and then shook her head, "They're not good enough. I do them for me, really. Kind of you to offer, though."

There was a long pause. "I'd better get back to my granddaughter, I suppose…"

"What you are doing with her is so wonderful," her words were soft with sentiment, "You're doing real good. And, you

know, however things work out between you and your son,
I'm sure this trip will mean something to him."

He concentrated on not clenching himself up into a
bitter knot.

"And I really appreciate you sharing your–"

"Chicken?" he suggested, hoping she might change tack.

"–your story–" the momentum of her laugh caught up with
her, "–*and* your chicken."

She jumped up, so he had no option but to stand up too
and he tried his best to crack open a smile, but inside he felt
a fraud because he hadn't shared the half of it; he had hardly
shared anything at all.

They walked together to the top of the gangplank and she
stood on tiptoe and brushed her cheek against his own, wings
of a dragonfly, the feel of a woman's skin after all this time.

"Good night," she said, the aftertaste of laughter still in
her voice.

"Thanks for a great evening," he began to reverse his way
down the gangplank. "And I'm sorry – about what happened."

"There's nothing to be sorry for."

"But I am – all the same."

"Good night…" she called again.

~~~

When he returned to the *Dragonfly*, Amandine was on weary
sentry duty at the cabin door. Tucked into the Velcro fastening
on her paw was a torn off piece of paper.

"Colin is very nice to Delphine and Delphine is very nice
to Colin."

He read it several times and then folded it up and put it in his
pocket. He took off his sandals and left them outside on the

deck, crawling his way backwards through the hatch. Twisting himself into origami folds, he slipped out of his clothes and into his sleeping bag. He lay on his back, staring into the darkness for a couple of minutes, then fished her message out of the pocket of his shorts. It was too dark to read it again, but he kept hold of it, admiring its even-handed statement of fact, then he put it safely on the shelf above his head.

~~~

He couldn't sleep. He lay on his side, his back, his other side. He studied the interior of his eyelids, trying to hypnotise himself with the different, veiny patterns that materialised.

When the cathedral – or was it the abbey? – clock struck two, Colin wriggled into his clothes once more, crept out of the cabin and set himself up on the bathroom locker with his feet propped up in the kitchen, the chiselled blocks of the quay at his back. The barbecue was relinquishing the last of its warmth and poking around among the coals he found some that were still serrated red and lit his one cigarette of the day, the one he should have had earlier in the evening.

Grimly, he smoked and smoked, only removing the butt from between his lips to flick the ash before he took another drag and after a while his thoughts returned to the photo album on the shelf above Delphine's bed. He didn't want to pry, but the prospect of what it might reveal exercised him: picture after picture reamed with unwritten stories; the archaeology of Michael's life. He reached into the cabin.

It felt as bad as reading someone else's letters and he sat for a moment with the album heavy on his knee before he opened it. The spine of the book cracked like a rifle shot as he turned the first page and Delphine stirred and the abbey clock – or was it the cathedral? – struck the half and he almost put it back where he had found it. He turned one page and then another, while the tobacco burned unsmoked until there was more ash than cigarette, ash which cooled and fell, covering a picture of the three of them, father, mother and daughter, in cindery dust.

In the end, although he studied Charlotte, he could find no signs of her complicity. He scrutinised a snap of her smoking – he tossed his own cigarette into the river – in another she was peering at the camera over some huge dark glasses, then drinking the last few drops from a bottle of mineral water. On the beach without her props, her red gash of a mouth gone, her pale skin freckled with sun and wind, she looked so ordinary: an ordinary mum, slightly self-conscious at having her picture taken. He couldn't see her as the siren to her own doom.

The album's transparent adhesive film had bubbled up from the picture in places. He ran one finger over it, pressing it down, but it wouldn't stick. Charlotte's face looked up at him, enigmatic and unchangeable, and he found he couldn't meet her gaze.

He ran through the story he had constructed: his son was an impressionable and inexperienced youth traduced and manipulated by a sophisticated older woman who used him for her own childbearing ends before she dumped him. He ran through it again. At the very worst, if Michael was guilty, *which he couldn't be*, it was a crime of passion, anything, rather than his boy standing vengefully at the top of the flight of stairs, with his arm raised to strike…

For the first time ever, he felt a twinge of doubt.

The river stilled, the night leaned in close and Colin shoved the album to one side and then straightaway retrieved it, leafing through it, studying picture after picture to try and understand:

Charlotte happy, Charlotte and Delphine mottled and shivering after a swim, Delphine and Michael on their bikes, Charlotte looking bored, Michael waving from a window, Charlotte paddling on a lilo, Delphine eating an ice cream, Charlotte combing her hair. They seemed like a perfectly happy family. Where did it all go wrong?

CHAPTER TWENTY-TWO

Laroche did sign up for a literacy course, sneakily, and Michael only found out about it when one of the kangas mentioned the unlikeliness of the fact as he came to collect him and escort him to the class. He raised his eyebrows at Michael as he went through the door and it only occurred to him afterwards how bulked up he looked. Remand prisoners could wear what they wanted and he was testing that one to the limit: sweatshirt, hoodie, scarf. More than you'd strictly need for the precarious season when summer threatens to spill over into autumn.

Two hours later and he was back, whistling.

They observed a silence while the kanga slammed the door and locked it and then removed the key.

"What did you learn, then? You kept that one very quiet."

"Ssshh," said Laroche, noisily. He unwound his scarf. "Fuck me, it's hot." He unzipped his hoodie and shrugged it off. "I learned," he said, "that money can buy you whatever it is you want." He elbowed his way out of his sweatshirt and there hanging from a strap around his neck was an inflated bag of the sort that comes in a wine box, a silver one with a plastic tap. "It's me birthday," he said, rubbing his hands together, "let's party!"

"What on earth—?"

"A little bit of finest lap. Want some?" he lifted the strap over his head and laid the bag reverently on the table.

"Where did you get that?"

"Got it in Education, wotch you got me started on."

"What's it made of? Is it wine?"

"Wine?" Laroche scoffed. "It's a hundred percent certified moonshine, made from carpet fluff, or whatever the lads can get their hands on: potato peelings, used tissues, it all goes in oink oink. Fetch us that glass." He nodded in the direction of a clear plastic tooth mug, clouded with spit and toothpaste. "On second thoughts…" he went bouncing onto his bed and lay back. "Chuck it over." He nodded at the bag, which Michael passed him. "Let's get the fade on!"

Laroche poured some alcohol directly into his mouth, shortening and lengthening the stream of it by lifting his arms until it overflowed, trickling along his cheeks and into his ears, down his neck, into the pools of his collar bones. His white face flushed and he started to splutter and sat up. "Man oh man thass the bomb diggedy! Wanna try?"

Michael eyed the dripping sack of hooch. He was primed to refuse, to sit at the table and do a crossword, to write a letter to – somebody, his lawyer, somebody. He bit his lip. "Well, just a taste, then."

"Have a day off from yourself," said Laroche, handing him the bag. "Just this once."

~~~

In the end, Michael had about a fortnight off from himself – at least that's what it felt like. He lay on his bed as the room gently repositioned itself around him, gathering speed.

"What's it made of again?"

"Fuck knows," said Laroche, dreamily. "What gets left down the plug for all I know – best not to ask. Works, though, doesnit?"

It worked so well that Michael thought he might already be going blind, until he realised that it was mid-evening and the light was fading. "I don't know when I was last this pissed."

There was what passed for silence in the remand wing of a prison: hollering, the occasional raw shout; outside in the neighbourhood a car alarm was sounding. Michael floated in and out amongst the noises.

"My W.I.F.E. – as in Wash. Iron. Fuck. Etc. – is going to call the kid Marianne. Whaddya make of that then? She's going to call the kid we both know isn't mine after my ol' girl. Woss the game?"

He surfaced briefly. "Maybe she *is* yours?"

"Tell us another," Laroche belched. "Not according to my sums, leastways."

"Maybe your sums are as ropey as your writing was. Maybe you're scared because the sums are right."

"Fuck off. I ain't scared."

"If you want to be the baby's dad, then saying so makes it so."

Laroche rolled his head to one side and looked at Michael. He closed one eye, trying to focus, then half-closed the other; open, close, round and round, chase, chase.

"If you say something often enough it gains currency. If your," Michael hesitated, "wife," he said delicately, "is offering you a line–"

"I wish she was. Bit of charlie now would go down nicely."

"–then take it."

"More red-eye?" Laroche squirted some alcohol into his own mouth, but he was having trouble with the tap; fumbling, misfiring; then he seemed to be having trouble with the bag as well, mastering its almost empty shapelessness. "Aw fuck it. Trousered anyway. Woss the point." He was sprawled across his bed, but he seemed to slump further. "Be a crap dad anyway, in 'ere. What kind of dad would I be?"

Michael tried to wrestle with the answer, but his tongue was like wire wool and his mouth was dry and the blood was turning to rust in his veins and he'd never missed Charlotte more than he missed her at this moment, never missed her more, and because saying something makes it so – "I loved her."

"…You're malcolmed…" mumbled Laroche "…yer sappy one…"

"I did though; I really, really loved her. She wasn't always easy to love, but I did."

"Wotch you love about her, my old drinkin' bud?"

"I loved the fact that she was different. She wasn't like anyone else I'd ever met. It took guts to set up house with me, when everyone was being so negative about her living with a younger guy. I do believe she loved me, for a bit, and I loved her because of that."

"Sorry, run that past me again…"

"It wasn't always easy, but it was worth it."

"Yer gets back wotch you put in – ha ha," Laroche gave a guttering laugh. "Didn't have you down for a toy boy, mind."

Michael lay looking up at the ceiling, following the cracks in the paint work, making continents out of them, the warmth from the liquor ebbing. He turned on to his side and the room slung itself after him. He felt sick and curled up on his bunk, trying to block out the world. He let his eyes fall shut. "Is it really your birthday?" he asked thickly.

"Nah."

CHAPTER TWENTY-THREE

Colin awoke the following morning, when Delphine prised his eyelids open with her finger and thumb.

"Breakfast in bed," she announced, passing him a mug of orange juice and a chunk of stale bread plastered in jam, which under her acute gaze, he felt obliged to try, at least.

"I'll save the rest for later," he said, brushing the crumbs from his sleeping bag. There was no escape from the orange juice, which was fizzing slightly from having been in a hot locker for too many days. She sat on the opposite bunk, monitoring his progress.

"What shall we do today?" she asked, when he had finished.

"What would you like to do?" He was about to add, mechanically, *after you've apologised to Tyler*, but he realised the real apology, the one that mattered most, was being made there and then.

"Swim," she said without hesitating. "Amandine is very good at swimming and it's going to be hot."

Colin tried to rally himself. He smoothed the back of his hand across his cheek, dimly recalling the touch of Tyler's skin as she kissed him good night. He wondered what it would be like to wake to an innocent day, saunter around the town, drink beer (and *Coke*) in different cafés, mooch round the market buying fruit, feed the swans, and then bump into her doing one of her paintings in a shady square…

With a sigh, he brushed the thought to one side, allowing his eyes to rest upon his granddaughter. She had her lavender tweed hat on backwards and jam at the corner of her mouth; the early-morning air was vibrant round her.

"Well?"

"There's a place that's supposed to be nice a few hours away along the Nivernais. It's called Saussois. It gets a good write-up in the book."

"Has it got a cathedral?" she asked suspiciously.

He shook his head. "It's got some rocks for climbing and there's supposed to be a nice spot for swimming in."

"What's the Nivernais?"

"It's a little squiggle of a canal." He unzipped his sleeping bag and swung his legs to the floor. "It goes through some very pretty countryside and there's lots to see and do."

She scrutinised him, then velcroed Amandine's feet around the monkey's neck, turning her into an intricate little ball. "And will it be just us?"

Colin glanced around the cabin. "There's not much room for anybody else."

~~~

He saw Tyler once before they set sail. Not to speak to, she was cleaning the deck with a hose and gave him a watery salute that sent spray everywhere. He waved at her and she waved back, her manner studiedly casual, a reminder that they were immune to each other's comings and goings, and there was a boat to scrub.

The scarlet prow of *Sabrina Fair* looked conceited and clean, shining in the sun, but there was no sign of her owner when

THE DRAGONFLY

Colin pulled the starter cord and the *Dragonfly* went charging off up the Yonne towards the start of the canal. They cruised along past hire boats which seemed to be knitting according to a very complex pattern rather than sailing in a straight line, stopping to wonder at the distant curves of the countryside clad in old gold, embroidered with stooks of wheat and laden vines and the darker thread of boughs and bark and rocks, until they reached Saussois where they idled for two days, just because they could. The Yonne intertwined itself with the Nivernais and Colin spent a whole afternoon fishing beneath the rocky outcrop which broke like a limestone wave high about their heads, while Delphine played with a Scottish girl who had escaped from one of the barges. In the evening he sipped sparkling wine beside the sparkling river.

He was lying in the reedy water the following afternoon, sculling with his hands so that he stayed afloat in the thin green seam which was warmed by the sun, when the cherry-coloured prow of *Sabrina Fair* came into view. *Holy God, she'll see me naked.* He stopped sculling so that his body drifted back to the perpendicular, the freezing sheath of the current closing in. *Not quite naked.* Mercifully he was wearing his oldest pair of pants, although that felt like cold, very cold comfort. He swam to the end of the pontoon in pursuit of some dignity and when he turned to swim back, Tyler had moored up and was leaning on the guard rail, looking down at him.

"Are there sharks in there?"

"Too cold for sharks. A pike or two, maybe."

"Mind if I join you?"

He swallowed some river water with a gulp, "Why not–?" He made an extravagant sweep with his arm, as if to suggest the whole of the waterway was hers, but it set him off balance and he had to pedal hard beneath the surface to keep himself afloat. Tyler vanished below decks and when she reappeared she was wearing a turquoise swimming costume which he was very careful not to look at, hoping that she would accord the same discretion to his underpants.

She dived in and struck out for the opposite end of the jetty, her lean limbs scattering droplets in all directions. Shivering, because he'd been in a long time, but couldn't contemplate getting out in the current circumstances, he executed a cautious kind of crawl up and back until she surfaced a few feet away, laughing and out of breath.

"I wondered if it was something I said?" she began, flicking the water from her eyes, "When you left like that?"

"What? Sorry?" Colin's neck was at full stretch, with his head tipped back so that the river came right up to his chin.

"When you went? I was a little – you know – I was wondering if I had said something or–? It was kinda sudden, that's all."

"Oh, that. No. No, no. No." He dunked himself under for some respite. "Not at all," he added, when he had sucked some air back into his lungs. "It's just that Delphine – well, she runs to a very tight schedule…"

By pulsing with her fist just below the surface, Tyler was sending jets of water up into the air, "That's fine, that's cool. I just thought I ought to… check. In case."

For a moment both of them watched the little fountains shooting upwards and falling back. He was conscious of the mortuary colour of his arms as they worked to keep him buoyant. "Did you finish your paintings?"

"I did a couple. One or two. The thing about cathedrals," she looked at him and then looked away, as bashful as a woman on nodding terms with middle age can be, "Is that when you've seen one, you've kinda seen them all. I didn't mean that," she said straightaway, contradicting herself. "But I'm a bit cathedralled out, just now…"

"Tell that to Delphine…" The second toe on his right foot locked itself under the first and without any warning his calf muscle started to tie itself into a variety of nautical knots – a bowline, a double hitch – then something very tight indeed.

"Where is she?"

"Ahhieee," he gasped, "I've got cramp!"

"Where?"

"She's out cycling – with a Scottish family."

"No – where's your cramp?"

He was thrashing about in the water, doing the swimming equivalent of standing on one leg while he tried to massage some life back into the other.

"Don't panic – it's really important not to panic," Tyler swam towards him.

"I'm not! I'm not panicking!" He couldn't keep hold of his foot and ducked down, trying to retrieve it and before he knew it she had him first by the neck and then by the chin, adjusting her sensible grip, and he found himself being towed from behind, the weave of her turquoise costume brushing against his back – *think about the cramp, just think about the cramp* – as she propelled the two of them towards the boats.

"It's because you've gotten so cold," she observed, handing him a towel as he sat in his smalls, dripping onto the deck of *Sabrina Fair*. He wondered how long it would take both of them to excise the memory of him scaling the ladder up the side of the peniche, with Tyler's slippery assistance, if indeed either of them ever could.

"I trained as a life guard. A long time ago. When I was a student – holiday job. It's like riding a bike – something you don't forget."

191

"Hmmm." He was busy kneading his calf with one hand, while clutching the towel around himself with the other.

"Would you like a cup of tea? To warm you up?"

Her question was tremulous; the tone of it made him turn his head. She had rubbed her hair dry and the towel was looped around her shoulders; she buried her face in it as he glanced at her, occupying herself with wiping her neck and then her shoulders. He could see that her turquoise swimming costume was paler in places where the water had dried. Her figure was made up of stringent curves, shaped by her outdoor life: it was unremarkably beautiful. He found himself wanting to place his hand on her slight, childless belly and let it lie there, just let it lie, with that listening attentiveness that touch can have.

With a sharp intake of breath, he gulped, "Tea? Tea! Yes, that would be lovely. Only I ought to put something on, get changed – dry clothes," he added as an explanation. "That would be lovely. Or something cold, if that would be easier?"

"Tea's easy enough," she answered and then apparently as an afterthought, just as she was heading for the cabin, she ventured, "I was thinking of walking up the Rochers later on, when it's cooler. I thought I might take my watercolours. I wondered if you…?

Colin wrapped the towel more tightly round him. "Rochers?"

She nodded towards the fold and swell of limestone high above their heads.

"Ah, the *Rochers* – yes, well; that would be – lovely – too. Yes." Then looking more closely at the rough escarpment, he asked uncertainly, "Walking?"

"There are footpaths, for oldies like us."

He was so beguiled by that *us*, so thrown, that he said in a rush, "You're not old," then stopped dead in his tracks. "Not like me…" He was saved from his floundering by the scorching

192

sound of rubber on gravel as his granddaughter skidded to a halt beside the *Dragonfly*, a lantern-jawed child with determined red hair following hard on her wheels.

"Delphine…!" He raised his arm to wave, revealing the unedifying spectre of his underpants as he did so.

Breathless with the details of her day, the child turned at the sound of his voice. She took in the peniche, Tyler's turquoise swimming costume and Colin's state of déshabillé.

"Oh."

"We've been swimming, and I got cramp and Tyler had to rescue me. Thank you, Tyler." He rose and made a flustered bow, edging towards the gang plank as he did so. "Have you said thank you to Sara's mum and dad?"

Delphine wasn't listening. She was staring at Tyler, uneasily. If Amandine had been there, she would have held her to her neck and stroked her paw across her cheek.

"Shall I come and call for you?" asked Tyler as Colin retreated. "Later?"

Delphine was motionless.

"To climb the rocks?"

"What rocks? What climbing?" she demanded as soon as he reached dry land.

"Oh," Colin sounded vague, "We thought we might, you know, when it's not so hot, have a go at climbing the… possibly…"

"Amandine is very good at climbing rocks."

"Maybe later…" He shouted back at Tyler, remembering not to wave.

"And mountains. Very good," said Delphine firmly.

"Excellent," he smiled down at her, half perceiving her possessiveness and feeling weirdly touched by it. "We must take her with us. But first you must go and thank Sara's mum and dad and give them back the bike." In a bid to reassure her, he looped his arm around her shoulders as they walked along.

"*Colin!*" the child averted her eyes, "It is not possible. You're in your–" she couldn't bring herself to say the word in English, "*Calecon!*"

~~~

Even in the cool of the evening, the going was tough. The baked earth of the footpath was crazed and cracked, wiry grasses sprung from crevices where you would think no seed could possibly take hold and close to, the limestone lost its sunlit sheen and looked more like cement, porous and grey.

Occasionally, Delphine lagged behind, "Is it far? I'm thirsty. I'm tired," but most of the time she remained on task, glued to her grandfather's side, a diminutive but tenacious chaperone. When Tyler turned to point out a sly red kite feigning indolence on the highest thermals, she was on the case straight away, "What?" standing between them with her hands on her hips, "Where? I can't see. Oh, that," but at moments when she straggled behind, scuffing her sandals through the dust, her body seemingly twice its normal weight, too heavy to transport any further, he glimpsed a lost expression on her face, a distance infinitely greater than the one which separated them on the rocky slope.

"Come on," he called encouragingly. Once, he went back down and grabbed her hand and towed her up behind him. On an easy stretch he walked up backwards with Delphine standing on his feet, while Tyler looked on, laughing. At last, she flopped down on some abrasive grass and hung her head.

"It is not possible. I can go no more," she stated, with the kind of melodrama to which he was becoming accustomed: Delphine's comedy always had sadness at its heart. He was about to head back down to fetch her, when Tyler went bounding past him,

"I'll give you a piggy back – no, seriously," she went on, to quell any protest, "Last one to the top is a custard!" and off they went, scrambling up to the summit, the child's shrieks pitched somewhere between anxiety and delight as she was jolted and nearly dropped, accidentally on purpose.

"What did I tell you? Isn't it worth it?" panted Tyler.

In the distance he could see the arm of the canal wall reaching into the Yonne; the sinuous arches of a bridge; one or two cottages with their whitewashed faces turned to catch the dying light; all of it mere detail in the great, green tangle of river and trees. The sun was swimming lazily – sculling – at the rim of the horizon, sending splashes of colour up into the gentian sky.

"Amandine is very good at painting," said Delphine stoutly as Tyler unpacked her box of paints and fixed a sheet of thick cream paper onto her clipboard.

"Is she, now?"

"Yes, very." For a moment, Delphine took her eye off the ball, as Colin produced a bottle of sparkling wine, two mugs and a can of *Coke* from his rucksack, but as soon she had secured her drink, she was back in post, standing at Tyler's shoulder, breathing heavily.

"What about you? Are you good at painting?"

Delphine didn't answer. With her face creased up in concentration, she read the writing on the side of the can, mouthing the words under her breath, "What's sodium, Colin?"

From the top of the rocks, the *Dragonfly* looked no bigger than his thumbnail; with the slightest inclination of his hand he could obliterate it entirely.

"Salt," he replied.

"Bleugh!"

"I'll bet you are," observed Tyler, marking out the line of the horizon with a watery brush. She glanced at Delphine who was only inches from her, "Good at painting."

The child rested her chin on her chest, defensively. She muttered something, took a swig of *Coke* and smacked her lips. On a whim, she marched to the edge of the slope and sat down as if the urge to go bottoming over the grass was too great to resist, then she froze, remembering her duties and hurried back, patrolling all the way around to Tyler's other shoulder, where she could keep an eye on Colin too.

"Shall I show you how to do the trees?"

Delphine shrugged.

Tyler mixed some green paint with water until it was as thin as rain, with only a ribbon of colour left in it, then soaked it up with a small sponge. "Look, you just blot it on the page like that, there, and like that – see?" She held out the sponge.

Delphine viewed it as if it were ticking and would shortly explode.

"Go on, have a go."

With a preposterous sigh, she took the sponge and splodged it into the middle of the paper.

"That's right, and again…"

Splodge, splodge, splodge. She peered at the effect and then with a little more care, dabbed another tree in, and then another.

"Why don't we mix a different shade of green? If you look down there, you can see trees that are almost black, some apple-coloured ones, some that look as if they are tipped with silver… what do you think?"

Delphine crouched down. She plastered the inside of the lid of the paint box with emerald and sloshed some water on.

Dab, dab, dab.

"I'm really liking that! Let's put some of the trunks in – we have sepia or sienna or what's this – Van Dyke brown. You choose."

Colin sensed that he had better keep his distance. Sitting with the bristly grass pricking through his shorts, he drank his wine, tuning in to the quiet exhalations of the day. He listened while they debated whether the river should be blue or not, a subject on which his granddaughter had violent opinions,

"But water is blue. The sea's blue, isn't it? It's a fact."

"Well, I was just wondering, if we had a little bit of grey, a little bit of green, it's lots of colours, isn't it?"

"It's blue."

"OK, I'll go with blue, but I'm going to put a little bit of green in it as well, just there, like that."

The first hint of darkness rose from the land like smoke. With a shiver, he hugged his knees. Delphine had no strong views about whether bridges should be buff coloured or cream; she was impatient to paint the *Dragonfly*.

"I sleep on the left side, so you won't be able to see my porthole, but I will paint Colin's, and the kitchen locker, and the bathroom locker, and the everything locker, and the flagpole, and the engine…"

"And shall I paint *Sabrina Fair* moored next to her?"

"If you want."

The moon glinted like an old coin. A moth went drifting by. Discreetly, Colin rubbed some citronella into his shins, for the air was sibilant with insects.

When it was too dark to tell rose madder from Venetian red and the wine was all but drunk, they packed up their things. Delphine went spinning round and round in circles trying to make the picture dry and as he followed her, his arm brushed

Tyler's bare shoulder. Their heads turned and for a moment they searched each other's faces in the twilight, until at length Colin, for whom such delight was unimaginable, looked away.

~~~

They formed an eccentric convoy, *Sabrina Fair* and the *Dragonfly*, locking their way up through filmy golden fields and hillsides coiled around with vines that were heavy with fruit. Helped for some of the time by two itinerant lock keepers, young students made indolent by the last days of summer, they bobbed up through locks selling honey, locks selling pottery and locks with unlabelled bottles of premier cru cellared in the boots of boiling cars.

Delphine seemed to like the mystery each one presented. It was impossible to tell from the bottom whether they would be rising up out of the shady slime to find a stall of produce, or a vegetable garden, or a donkey hungry for apples, or an ancient privy toppling over. She flicked their ropes over bollards and lassoed them off again; she helped the students wind the paddles to release the water and then open the lock gates; she cajoled him into buying gooseberry jam and when they couldn't fit anything else into the kitchen locker, she set to work on Tyler who, with a flighty smile, claimed to have more cupboard space than a woman travelling alone could ever need.

Although Tyler wasn't travelling alone, not any more. Nothing was said, but each time they tied up for lunch, it was somehow accepted that she would tie up too, just as it was somehow accepted that she would wander over to the *Dragonfly* with some oozing Époisses cheese…

"Hey guys, this stuff is really stinking me out, I can't possibly finish it on my own…"

…And that Colin and his granddaughter would stroll back along to *Sabrina Fair* with a bowl full of cherries, "Delphine bullied me into buying these."

"I did not!"

"She showed no mercy – help us eat them, please."

Nothing was said, though. There was no exchange of glances. Colin thought he must have misread her stilled expression of wonderment, which the dusk had half-revealed to him as they descended the Rochers du Sauccois, and he cursed himself for being a presumptuous old man whose imaginings had been inflamed by spending too long in the Burgundy sun.

CHAPTER TWENTY-FOUR

"What kind of a fucked idea was this?" Laroche swung round to face Michael. "Your kind of a fucked idea, that's what it was. Gimme some help, will yer? You said do literacy. Fuck! Nobody mentions tests when you sign up. Nobody mentions written tests. Fuck!"

"Well, if you want to work in the library…"

Three steps and turn. Three steps and turn. Laroche was pacing up and down the tiny space available to them. "I don't want to work in the library. Changed me mind. Don't want to do no tests neither. You have no idea what you've got me into. *Write something about yourself.* Sod that! I'm down the hobbit shop with you."

"It's only a paragraph."

"You write it for me then." He stopped his pacing. "Ackshly, that's not a bad idea."

"I can't come into the room with you. Exam conditions."

"You write it out an' I'll copy it on me arm. Job done. Sorted."

"It's life writing. It should be easy. It's writing about what you know."

"I don't have a life. Hadn't you noticed?" Laroche stopped his pacing as what he had said caught up with him. "I don't know nuffin', besides."

"Write about what happened to you before you came in here."

"What? And get sent down for longer oink oink?"

"Write about your childhood. Your best birthday. The first CD you bought. Keep it simple."

Laroche stood in the room with his hands hanging by his side. He looked like a cartoon sketch of a man: a few lines drawn and a bit of shading. "Thass wotch you think they're looking for, eh? Them examiners. My first record was a breaking and entering when I was eleven. Criminal, not vinyl. My best birthday? Ooh, let me see. It'd probably be me ninth, when me uncle had a fiddle with me as a change from me step dad. That was a cracker."

Michael felt a small collapse inside himself – the ebb of optimism, of anything positive.

"Will that do the job?"

"I – I had no idea. I'm sorry."

"Nobody has any idea. Nobody has a fucking clue." He sniffed and cuffed his bent arm over his face.

Michael hesitated, then took a step towards him.

"Don't you fucking dare."

"I was only going to–"

"Well, don't. Save yourself the bother." Laroche gave himself a quick shake. A shudder. "Oi Rosbif! Yer gotta man up!" He came sparring towards him, jabbing him in the ribs and the shoulder. "Thass wotch yer gotta do. Don't let the buggers grind you down."

He landed another blow, then another, until in a fit of crazy sadness the two of them started shadow boxing, swiping and ducking and dancing, until they heard the turning of a key and one of the kangas slammed the cell door open wide.

"Which of you is going to Education?"

~~~

Laroche came back from his exam whistling.

"Took yer advice, Rosbif. For me life writing question I wrote about the first CD I ever nicked." He whistled a few more notes, executing a sideways shuffle, with a bit of beat boxing to finish off. "The first CD wot I ever nicked was *Now That's What I Call Music 53*. I wrote about the standout track *The Ketchup Song*. What it meant to me oink oink." He flung himself down in his chair, "Reading and comprehension tomorrow," he said lugubriously.

"Why didn't you write about – what you told me?"

"Yesterday's news."

"But if the authorities knew, it might make a difference – mitigating circumstances. When it comes to your trial."

Laroche gave him a scornful look. "You're such a noob, Rosbif."

"It might help."

"You and your wossname circumstances. Half the crims in France would be out on the street instead of inside if that counted. We've all got our – you know, wotch you said. Ask anyone in 'ere if their ol' man, or their neighbour, or whoever, didn't try their luck. When they stop doing it, you know you're one of the big boys. Moving quickly onwards..." he said, "Woss the first CD you ever... bought?"

CHAPTER TWENTY-FIVE

The day that Amandine fell into the lock began in speckled sunshine under clouds so perfectly formed that they looked as if they had been cut out and pinned onto the sky. It started with Tyler knocking on the *Dragonfly's* cabin door, bearing three plates of scrambled egg and lardons.

"Hangover food. Go on, try some. The French really know how to do bacon – not that watery stuff we get at home – this is the real deal." She licked her fingers. They had moored the night before near the village of Coulanges, "So much red wine, so little time," she'd carolled as they'd set about putting to the test more Burgundy appellations than perhaps they should have done.

Colin emerged blinking a little, already on nodding acquaintance with his headache, "Ouch. Maybe some coffee first…"

"Nope, it's got to be a fry up. Research has shown that a cooked breakfast is the best cure. Coffee will make it much, much worse: all those stimulants…"

Still in her sleeping bag, Delphine pushed the food around her plate. "Amandine doesn't like these *oeufs*…"

"Well, has she tried them?" demanded Tyler briskly, poking her head into the cabin.

Delphine regarded her with uncertainty. "Ah mais non," she shrugged.

"Then she must," she swooped down and removed the monkey before her owner could protest, settling her in a corner of the deck with a saucer of scrambled egg on her lap. "If she likes it, you might find that you like it too…"

Delphine would not allow herself to be convinced. "She prefers pain aux raisins and at the weekends sometimes she has brioche with jam."

"Lucky old Amandine."

Defiantly, the child picked out all the bacon bits and ate them one by one, ignoring the egg, just to emphasise her point. Colin, who in his time had learned hard lessons about choosing which battles to fight, leaned over.

"I'll have that if you don't want it," he said scooping her egg onto his own plate. "Breakfast in the fresh air – there's nothing to beat it."

They set off in convoy, the David and Goliath of the waterways, the agile *Dragonfly* nipping ahead then making showy turns, flashy figures of eight, killing time while *Sabrina Fair* made more sedate progress behind them. Delphine squealed as they went hurtling past the barrage at Basseville, where the canal crossed the Yonne, tangling the currents, slewing their light boat close to the weir's edge. One lock later and they were back on the river, not much more than a stream now, haemorrhaging water over a spillway, the banks unkempt and tousled, also spilling green: easy going for the *Dragonfly*, but a navigational nightmare for the peniche. Tyler made her way through inch by ponderous inch.

"Why do we have to wait?" grumbled Delphine.

"Because it's friendly," he answered, frowning. "Because she might need a hand. Pick some flowers, why don't you? I can get you right in close to the bank."

She turned and regarded him witheringly.

"You could dry them in the sun and then send them on a card to Papa..." He tailed off. She occupied less space when she was sad, he'd noticed that. Now she drooped, staring at some tiny insects as they strafed the bows of the boat, then looking beyond them to where the bank curved round, the river ahead empty as absence. He watched her rouse herself; she stretched out over the verge, wobbling slightly as she reached to pick a buttercup and then a poppy and then something blue that he didn't know the name of, private and apart from him.

By the time *Sabrina Fair* came prowling up behind them, the cabin roof was strewn with crucifers and mignonettes and doubtless several different kinds of wort, none of which Colin recognised, their wafery leaves contracting in the heat. They made their way in uncompanionable silence through the outskirts of Clamecy, until he gave in to the compulsion to tell her something about the town, although he knew she wasn't interested, that it annoyed her to hear.

"You see that funny chapel over there? The book says that it is the first example of the use of reinforced concrete in the whole of France." Sometimes he appalled himself, but even so, on he went, and on, and on, and on.

"Have you got some card?" she asked him suddenly. They were just entering Les Jeux lock and he was doing his usual trick with the boathook, looping their line over a bollard set high above them on the quay while the *Dragonfly* skittered over the water that the peniche was churning up behind them.

"Hold on a sec—"

As the lock keeper closed the gates and started to wind the paddles to let the water in, Colin was busy dismembering a box of rice that he found in the kitchen locker.

"This should do just the job," the cardboard was off-white, flecked with grey. He handed it to her. It was one of their rules that they never had the cabin door table up when they were doing manoeuvres, so she squashed herself onto the bathroom locker beside Amandine, who was still staring pitifully at the saucer of scrambled egg in her lap.

The *Dragonfly* bridled and started jibbing at her line, becoming frisky as the water swelled beneath her. Delphine selected a pencil from her pencil case and stared hard at the cardboard, the expression on her face sombre, then she swept her hand once across the card as if readying herself to begin, sending Amandine flying over the side.

Looking back, Colin might have expected some filmic, slow motion effect to kick in the way it is supposed to in moments of crisis, but everything happened so fast: the little monkey was splayed over the surface for a matter of seconds as the saucer of scrambled egg hit her in the neck, forcing her under with dizzying speed.

"Amandine!" shrieked Delphine. "Amandine!"

Before he could stop her, before he even knew what was occurring, the child flung herself off the boat into the lock, just as the sluice gates opened to release more water into the chamber. All he saw was her arms scissoring the air as she disappeared.

Oh my God. Oh my God. Oh my God.

She surfaced a few feet from the *Dragonfly* with a saturated scream. He had the boat hook hooked over the lock ladder and hanging from the end of it he leaned as far as he could, reaching and stretching for her, his feet skidding on the deck, his fingers grasping and grasping at nothing.

"Colin!" He would never forget her gargled cry, as if the river was already rising in her throat.

"Grab my hand – come on Delphine, grab my hand. You can do it. Come on!" A convolution of the water swept her towards him and for a moment he thought he had her, his grip slippery on her wrist, but the turbine effect spun her away so that she slipped from his hands like a piece of soap. Briefly he glimpsed the twist of her skirt like rag in the current.

"Delphine!" he shouted, "Delphine!"

From above his head flew the life buoy, slung by the lock keeper, who was now racing back to close the sluices on the front gate. The water was roaring in Colin's head like grief. Another revolution brought his granddaughter close to the surface, her skin already the colour of reeds. One of her feet breached for a second and he heard a splash as Tyler, wearing a life jacket, plunged over the side of *Sabrina Fair* and struck out for the drowning girl.

He couldn't bear to watch and he couldn't look away. He saw Tyler searching intently, calculating the water's torque, swimming around to where she figured Delphine might next appear. As the sluices closed again, the current turned back on itself, sucking inwards. The lock was unnaturally calm and still, sated, the only movement an apostrophe to the main event, an afterthought: a small eddy close to the rear gate, around which the child's body swirled listlessly one last time.

"It's OK, it's OK, I've got her," the damp acoustic of the chamber circulated Tyler's words, passing them from wall to wall, so that he couldn't be sure that he had heard them right, but the next moment she was swimming backwards in his direction, her hands cupped under Delphine's green grey chin and muffled up inside him he remembered her insisting *but water is blue. The sea's blue, isn't it? It's a fact* and he knelt down, leaning out to receive her from the river and somehow Tyler delivered her, as glistening and limp as a newborn, into his arms.

She lay on the deck as bedraggled as litter, her limbs tumbled carelessly and he turned her onto her back. He crouched over her, trying to make out if she was breathing, and then began pumping both hands on her chest, because he must do something, anything, and he had a fleeting recollection that this was the kind of thing you did do, to drowning girls. He couldn't bring himself to look into her face, with its terrible oxidised colour, and was transfixed instead by a cigarette butt caught in her hair. There was lipstick on it and he was appalled by its casual redness and wanted to untangle it and throw it away, but he knew that he must keep pumping and he looked instead at a leaf that was snagged there too, and a twig, and drops of moisture that still clung like cobwebs, and he kept on pumping.

Then, without warning, Delphine burped like an old man and her head cracked against the deck in a spasm of surprise. She started to choke; half sat up and was very, very sick.

Tyler, who had streaked round the boat to the ladder in the lock wall and was climbing up it, shouted down, "Put her in the recovery position, lay her on her side…" but Colin couldn't let go of her and thought that he never, ever would. He held her in his arms, rubbing her back as if she were a baby and she retched again and again and then she started to cry.

~~~

THE DRAGONFLY

He made it through the lock, barely conscious of what he was doing. Delphine was lying in her wet clothes on her bunk and he held the tiller at arm's length so that he could sit as close to the cabin door as possible and he checked up on her so frequently that the *Dragonfly* tacked treble the distance to the port de plaisance and was, for the first and last time, overtaken by *Sabrina Fair*.

Tyler was standing on the bank to receive their ropes. "You need to get the kid to a doctor. I'm sure she's fine, but you need to get her looked at."

He nodded. He discovered that he was shaking and to conceal the fact busied himself retrieving Delphine from the cabin. She was stiff with shock and he found it extraordinarily difficult to lift her through the narrow hatchway because his hands were fumbling and it seemed to him that the *Dragonfly* wouldn't keep still beneath his feet.

"She'll be fine," said Tyler with anxious encouragement.

He nodded.

"Would you like me to come with you?" She was still in her life jacket, the scent of the Yonne rising from her damp T-shirt and shorts in a bracing, just got *back from a dip* way. Delphine, sodden and waterlogged, lay heavily against his chest. He shook his head.

"No, I'll – I ought to–" he swallowed, gathering the child closer to him. "Thank you."

Tyler shrugged.

"For what you did."

"It's nothing," she smiled her fugitive smile, which was too sad to sustain itself for long. She glanced in the direction of the town. The air was turbulent with things unsaid: "I wouldn't hang about…" she said gently.

Another strange town, another taxi ride, another hospital. He made it his mission to keep talking to Delphine. "There's a wonderful museum here," he began, "The Romain Rolland Museum, it's got all sorts of…" and then, mortified, he stopped himself. She was shivering and her teeth were chattering. He wrapped her close. It could have been Michael he was holding. "I remember taking your dad to hospital. He was a bit younger than you are now and he cut himself on a glass at his birthday party. On his actual birthday! Can you imagine that?"

She shook her head, almost the first response that he had had.

"And another time I had to take him when he stood on a weaver fish in Cornwall. You'll be keen to know what a weaver fish is, I expect," he went on, gazing down at her, throwing her a line so she could keep up. "They hide in the sand right by the sea shore and if you step on them they sting you hard."

She half listened, but it was as if she were still beneath the water, floating beyond his reach, so he kept talking, to save himself as much as her. He told her how they bought Michael a cassette player and one day found him threading his willy through the sprocket of a cassette of *Old MacDonald Had a Farm* (*Old Madonna Had a Farm* he called it) in the hope that talking about his boy, though it touched on old wounds, on raised red scars, would draw the heat from the emotion of the moment, that the past might be an antidote to the present, an anaesthetic.

~~~

"Are you able to be exact about how long your granddaughter was unconscious?" the doctor asked. He wanted to keep her in overnight for observation and some function tests.

Delphine levered herself upright on the trolley. She looked around the examination cubicle as if she had only just realised where she was, then lay back forlornly against the pillow. "I don't want to stay–"

Colin squeezed her hand. "It's just for tonight. Just to keep an eye on you. A real bed with proper sheets, you lucky girl. They might even let you have a bath if you ask them nicely."

She shrugged, making the foil in which they had wrapped her lisp and whisper.

"You look like a chicken all ready to go in the oven. I could eat you for my supper..." he said to her, foil bright himself, trying to make light as the doctor passed him a clipboard full of forms to sign.

"Will you stay?"

"I'll stay as long as they let me."

"But will you *stay*?" she urged.

The doctor ducked out through the curtains, carrying the paper work with him.

"Actually," fastened round her wrist she had an identification bracelet made of shiny, laminated card and he started to fiddle with it, turning it round and round, "Actually, I thought I might go back to the lock, while it's still daylight, just to see if Amandine..."

He watched the penny drop, painfully.

"Isn't she – didn't you–?" The child spoke from that place of sorrow where anger blurs with disbelief, "But Colin–!"

"All we could think of was rescuing you. Tyler saved you." He spoke judiciously, weighing out the reprimand. "You should never have jumped into the lock, you know. It was a very courageous, very silly thing to do."

She turned away from him on the trolley with a flounce that was recognisably hers and he almost smiled to see the old Delphine returning, even though her gaze, staring off to one side, was sullen and the quarter crescent of her face that was visible to him was closed up, her mouth a brutal line. Colin bowed his head. He recognised the roaring ugliness of bereavement: he knew it well.

"There wasn't time to look for Amandine."

She hunched herself further away, straining to emphasise the distance between them.

"I'll stay if you want. But if I go now, maybe there's a chance that I might find her; that she might still be there…"

She didn't answer.

"If you think it's worth a look, I'll…"

This time she roused herself and glanced over her shoulder. She said something in furious French which he couldn't understand but gathered meant *Do what the fuck you like, I don't care*. She was only nine. She had seen and heard too much.

He sat waiting by her trolley until a hospital porter appeared. She kept her back to him throughout. "I promise I won't be long," he said, as she was wheeled away.

~~~

He walked back from the hospital, from the new fringes of the town to its old heart, the shock of what had happened still registering. The noise of the traffic, the pulse of the passing cars, was soothing. It felt good to be out in the ordinary sunshine and he stopped for a moment and tilted his head so that he could feel its commonplace warmth on his face. It was going home time. People were retracing their steps, laden with shopping, or busy on their mobiles, still carrying the day's events with them, halfway to exchanging them for a quiet night in, and he tried to imagine falling into step beside somebody and strolling back with them all the way to their home life. It was the one thing he didn't really have.

He set off down the hill, the roads narrowing, the houses ageing from baroque to mediaeval within a couple of streets. He liked the frescoes of faded adverts on ancient plaster, the stooped doorways, the peeling shop fronts, the stressed angles of the half timbering – Clamecy was a timber town – the old brass lanterns strung from building to building, the water pumps on pavement corners, and set in high niches, the religious statues trying to horse trade with fate.

The lock keeper had gone home. The gates were closed and the chamber was empty. As he peered down into the water, he remembered the flicker of her arms and her skirt twisting like rag as she disappeared. He wiped his hands across his eyes.

There was some weed and a couple of sticks, but no Amandine.

He searched the length of the lock on both sides, checking behind the ladders and in the corners by the gates. A fish teased the surface with its tail, but there was no little monkey, the side of its head worn with too much loving.

He made his way along the quay and looked over his shoulder. At the end of the lock arm that stretched out into the Yonne was the bust of some local dignitary – the book would surely know which one – who contemplated Colin, giving nothing away. Colin, in his turn, stared back at him, until his eye was caught by some movement close to the far bank: a coot was threading her way through the overhanging grasses, trailing her tiny black babies like beads behind her, darting out into the current to avoid obstructions: branches, boulders, something felty.

Something felty!

He broke into a trot, down the quay, over the bridge, past the reinforced concrete chapel (the first of its kind etc) through a small park until he reached the spot, more or less, where he had seen it. No gently shelving shore to make life easy, but a sheer drop of about five feet. He leaned out as far as he could, craning his neck this way and that, but he couldn't see anything. There was only one thing for it. He lay down on the path and hung himself over the bank, reaching down with both hands hoping there was nothing there which might bite, and began to feel his way between the rocks and pebbles and the muddy clefts, making his stomach muscles sing whole arias of pain, probing and groping until at last his fingers closed over something which could only be material. He yanked hard, sending water bucketing over himself as he prized his trophy from the river's grip.

It was Michael's lavender grey tweed hat.

He struggled into a sitting position and wrung it out, watching the drips fall with a keen sense of the futility of life. He sat there with it wetly in his lap, picking some grit from the weave and then with a suddenness which startled him, his phone rang.

"Bonjour Monsieur Aylesford…" It was Michael's solicitor.

Colin hunched his shoulders, as if he were protecting his softer parts. "Yes?"

"I visited your son last week."

He drew up his knees and gripped them with his free hand. "How is he?" He could hear a reedy note of need in his voice.

"He's doing OK," she spoke English with an American accent, bestowing on him that sense of total focus which comes with a five hundred pounds an hour price tag. "We have a date for the trial. Things can be more quickly expedited because of his guilty plea."

"There's no chance that he will change that, is there?"

"To not guilty?" she queried. "Do you have some new information?"

I have only doubts, only doubts, he wanted to say. *No certainties, no belief, no hope. I am thinking things which to me should be unthinkable: Michael, standing vengefully at the top of the stairs...* "No," he said.

"We could look at mitigating circumstances. Your son has made it clear that he does not wish to put forward a defence, but if you have grounds to believe..."

"Mitigating circumstances," he echoed, thinking, *the guilt is mine. I let him down. It's my plea.*

"You are caring for his daughter, no?"

"Yes. I'm caring for Delphine..."

"Then is it possible that she has said something?"

"She hasn't said. I'll ask. I will ask. She hasn't said."

"The trial is in October."

"October, yes."

"We'll talk next week, perhaps? When you have spoken with Delphine." There was an emollient and respectful silence. "Au revoir, Monsieur."

"Au revoir..." he clicked the phone off and slid it back into his pocket. The lavender grey tweed hat had fallen onto the path and he stooped to pick it up, his knees cracking. It was almost dry. He smelt the inside of it: the metal scent of the river; then held it to his face the way that Delphine sometimes did. *We're all bloody guilty,* he thought, *all of us, one way or another.*

~~~

When he arrived at the hospital, Delphine was fast asleep and he stood in encroaching stillness beside her bed absorbing her peaceful abandon: her round-cheeked rosiness and the rhythmic catching of her breath at the back of her throat were a kind of benison, so different from the wan, grey-skinned child – Colin blinked. To banish the image of her straggled body lying on the deck of the *Dragonfly*, he leaned forward and smoothed a trickle of hair from her forehead, hesitating in the hope that she might stir and wake up. He found himself wanting her back. He found himself longing to hear her caustic little voice upbraiding him, holding him to account. She made a slight questing motion, as if a cool current from the open window had disturbed the air around her. With the exaggerated movements of a mime, he laid Michael's hat on the locker beside her bed and turned for one last look before he tiptoed from the room.

He couldn't find the doctor – any doctor – but managed to corner a nurse on the main ward, whose reassuring words were limited by her elementary English and he set off back to the port full of renewed anxiety about antibiotics and maladies from the urine of rodents. "Precaution," the woman kept saying, "Precaution," but he wasn't entirely comforted.

Colin wanted to buy something for Tyler, some inadequate gift incapable of expressing the extent of his debt, but Clamecy had shut up shop. The florist was closed, the boulangerie was closed and even the supermarket was locked up for the night. He wandered into a tobacconist thinking he might be able to find some chocolates and saw, on a wire rack of esoteric publications (books on crochet, books on road safety) a book of photographs of rural France. He headed for the port with it tucked beneath his arm.

Sabrina Fair was at the far end of the mooring reserved for larger craft and as Colin hurried over to it he felt a prickle of anticipation almost in spite of himself. He rehearsed the giving of his present: *This is nothing really, but I wanted to thank you…/ I don't know how to thank you for what you've done but I hope that this…/ This is a small token, I can't begin to…* His mouth was dry when he reached the foot of the gangplank. He licked his lips.

She wasn't there. The peniche was empty, its door was locked and the curtains were closed. He stood for a moment staring at a picture of what he took to be a culvert – something watery at any rate – that was hanging in the window in front of him. On closer inspection maybe it wasn't a culvert, maybe it was a bowl of something – fruit, possibly…

Disappointed, he turned away.

Planning his supper for one – he ought to be hungry, if he put his back into it and made a bit of an effort he could be hungry – he trudged home to the *Dragonfly*, reflecting on the merits of tinned salmon versus chips from the chip shop if there was any damn chip shop open, when he caught sight of her.

She was wearing a dress, a sleeveless shift dress in a vaguely retro print. He'd never seen her in a dress before. She was sitting on the quay next to his duck egg blue boat, her feet dangling over the side, writing postcards.

His heart did something crazy: it *leapt*, and he started to run, calling out her name.

"How is she?" Tyler jumped up, "How's Delphine?"

"She's fine," he panted. "At least I think she is." He had difficulty catching his breath. "They've kept her in overnight. For antibiotics. They've put her on observations." Still breathing hard, he shoved the book into her hands, "This is for you."

"Why, Colin this is such a – what a wonderful – you didn't have to…"

"To thank you for what you did."

"What I did was nothing – it was just…" Tyler began leafing through the book and as the moments passed and he recovered himself, he took a step closer on the pretext of looking at the photographs too, and as she turned the pages one by one the atmosphere between them was so charged it was as if they were already touching. She closed the book with enormous care and turned to look up at him and it would have been the easiest thing in the world to put his arms around her.

"Those are the most beautiful photos," her smile hovered at the corner of her mouth and then faded.

He could have leaned down and kissed her then.

She swallowed, "You can learn so much from photographs," she hesitated, "If you want to be a painter…"

He nodded, feeling her breath go glancing past him, her soft breath, her warm scent. He kept nodding, very slowly, as if there was much in what she said for him to understand. "I… er…"

She waited. "Yes?" she whispered.

His courage failed him. He ran his fingers through his hair. "I… er… wondered if you'd like to stay for supper?"

"Colin!" she exclaimed, "Don't you want to – you know, like – kiss me? What does a girl have to do–?"

His head felt as if it was spinning, so that his hand moving shyly towards hers turned from a single action into a flickering sequence. Their fingertips touched. "I wasn't sure… I didn't want to presume…"

"Presume what?"

"I'm not exactly a young man any more…" he said as she stood on tiptoe and kissed him on the mouth. It was a tentative kiss, a kiss which gathered up and let go in the same breath. "A kiss as long as my exile…" he whispered, losing himself in Tyler's gaze.

THE DRAGONFLY

"I bet that's from Shakespeare," she grinned, and then to his amazement she looped her arms around his neck and drew him down to her again.

CHAPTER TWENTY-SIX

"*Amarillo Brillo* – Frank Zappa"

"*Brooklyn Dreams* – Neil Diamond."

"You can't have Neil Diamond," Laroche objected. They were playing cities in song titles, alphabetically, in the terminal stages of boredom. "On taste grounds. You can have *Barcelona* by Freddie Mercury, if you like. I had it up my sleeve ready but I'm giving it to you."

"I don't like. I'm going with... *Billericay Dickie* – Ian Dury."

"*Century City* – Tom Petty and the Heartbreakers, which is a double. Woop, woop."

"OK. *Buried in Detroit* – Mike Posner."

"*El Paso* – can't think the fuck who... it's coming, it's coming..."

"I'm going to have to hurry you."

"Marty Robbins!"

And so they went on, ploughing from *Kashmir* by Led Zeppelin, through *Meet Me in St Louis* by Judy Garland which was a bit of a low point, to *Viva las Vegas* by Elvis Presley, all the way to *Youngstown* by Bruce Springstein. They couldn't think of a Z, so Laroche suggested song titles where you replace the words *love* or *heart* with *knob*. "*Can't Stop Knobbing You*," was his opener.

THE DRAGONFLY

Michael was still trying to think of a song title with a city in it beginning with Z on his way to the hobbit shop. He tried not to let his spirits sink as he filed into the shed with its queasy lighting and its damp walls. He was working on a child's bike so heavy it was difficult to lift and he glanced around the room as he heaved it into position, checking what was what and more importantly, who was where. Chapot was in which was unusual, looking sleek, but he didn't think anything of it.

There was a clot of earth with a few wisps of grass jammed into one end of the handlebars and it made him wonder briefly, about the child who had thrown it down on some lawn... *Rosbif... Rosbif...* or some verge, before hurrying in for tea. He started digging the dried mud out and it went crumbling onto his shoes... *Rosbif... Rosbif...* and he tried to picture the discarded bike with its pedals still turning and the tick tick tick of its wheels slowing: that sense of adventure, put on hold.

He felt the hairs rising on the back of his neck, the pricking sensation of somebody walking a little too close to him. He glanced up to see a guy he hadn't come across before... *Rosbif... Rosbif...* A heavy-set bloke with a dented nose in a face that had seen too many fights, arcing past him en route to the supplies cupboard, curling the long way round the room with a speculative swagger, before sauntering back to the privileged corner near the stove, where the men parted as he approached, Michael took note.

He wasn't concentrating; he was watching the bruiser. That was his first mistake. During the instant in which he ceased anticipating trouble, trouble struck. Somebody knocked his wrench off the workbench – Belfiore, who never looked as if he could move quickly enough? As he stooped to pick it up... *Rosbif... Rosbif...* it was kicked beyond his grasp and he was diverted again as it was passed and passed back in a scuffle of feet. There were taunts in the air, although nothing was said. Incitements. The wrench was further up the line now, beyond the reach of easy retrieval.

Same old, same old, he thought; which was his second mistake. He gave the wrench up for lost and turned his attention back to the bike, gripping the front wheels between his knees so he could straighten the handlebars. Out of the corner of his eye, on the far side of the room, he saw the new guy remove a sock from his pocket and unroll it and although that seemed odd and he was curious to know what the sock was for when rags were supplied for polishing off, he went on with his adjustment of the handlebars – a little bit this way, a little bit that way – squinting through a half-closed eye to see if they were level. He'd learned how to absorb himself into the task in hand, blotting out the murmurings; a transcendental concentration that gave him space and peace in which to be. He didn't hear the whispers ebb, the flow of silence into stealth. Even the diversionary fracas on the far side of the room failed to divert him, although the kangas went racing across to deal with it – there was always some kind of a dust up going on. He was thinking of song titles with cities beginning with Z, that it'd be good to get one over on Laroche. He didn't notice the footfall or the sweat stink, though he thought for a second that he heard the words *wife killer* wreathe around him, although he couldn't be sure and he swung round to see, glimpsing the sock but not the wrench inside it and as the blow caught him on the side of the head he thought – *Zanzibar – Billy Joel!* – before he went sprawling face down onto the floor.

~~~

"I'm sure there must be a song about Zamboanga City somewhere," said a voice.

Michael was trying to work out where he was, piecing himself together until a blurry sequence of memories gathered momentum and he remembered everything – the prison, Charlotte, all of it.

"But I'm buggered if I can come up with it."

He opened and closed his eyes. The subdued light of the room he was in – not his cell – stung.

"Rosbif! You're back! At bleedin' last." Someone leaned over him. He took in the shaven head, the bony face, the close-set, pale-lashed eyes. "See you've met Joubert," the man said. "Chapot closed the book; he was calling in the money. Yer number was up."

"Laroche?" said Michael. He was feeling slightly sick. His skull burned as if his brain had swollen inside it.

"You're in the ding wing. How many fingers am I holding up? Who's the president? What day of the week is it?" said Laroche. "You'll live."

"What are you doing here?"

"I used up some credit, let's say, without going into the small print. Somebody owed me. Can't stay long though. Five minutes, maybe."

Michael put a hand to his head, which felt like broken eggshell. There was a bandage, some tape. "I saw a doctor, I think. I think I can remember that. And having some stitches." He lay carefully on the bed, cautious with himself. "What about Joubert? It was Joubert, wasn't it? I saw Chapot, too."

"Somebody else'll take the rap – you won't catch Joubert on the block. 'S all trade. Chapot was there to see fair play."

"Fair play?" said Michael derisively.

"Following the rules."

He let it go.

"I did warn you. I did tell you it was going to happen. Tried to toughen you up, woss more. Education ain't juss ritin.'"

A key turned in the lock and they fell silent. The kanga looked round the door and jerked his head at Laroche. "Time's up." Laroche strolled out with the kind of insolence that follows the rules, but only just, with a little oink oink to punctuate his leaving.

"You're wanted," the kanga said to Michael. "You have permission to receive a telephone call."

~~~

"Hello?"

"Michael?"

It was his father's voice. He felt unsteady on his feet. Like the bicycle handlebars, the ground was not quite level and even if he half-closed an eye he couldn't adjust it. He couldn't straighten anything out.

"Hello Dad," he said warily.

"I'm ringing you because – well, it's Delphine. She's had an–"

"Delphine? What's happened? Tell me what's happened? Is she–?"

"She's had a little accident. It's nothing – she fine, she's OK. I don't want you to worry, but I thought I ought–"

"An accident? What kind of accident?"

"She fell into a lock."

"Into a lock? For Christ's sake! Is she alright?"

"She's alright. She's alright."

Michael felt out of breath, as if he'd been running and running.

"She's alright," his Dad said again – the salient news, the phrase to hold on to. He rested his forehead on the wall of the phone booth, forgetting the bandage and the stitches and the sock with the wrench, forgetting everything except his daughter.

"It was a fright, as much as anything, for all of us. But I took her to the hospital, just to be on the safe side, so that the doctors could have a look at her and they've kept her in overnight."

"You took her to hospital?" he said.

"Just to be on the safe side. I'm on my way to collect her now."

"And she's alright?"

"She's fine."

"She fell into a lock?"

"Yes."

"I can't see how–" he began. An incoming tide of tiredness washed over him: his head was throbbing. There were moments, which he tried to fight, when the burden of remorse was simply too heavy for him. "Never mind," he sighed.

"Michael–?"

"Will you give her my love? Tell her–"

"The solicitor thinks you should change your plea. She telephoned me to say," his father blurted out.

Michael took a moment to reply. "Just tell her that."

"Please will you consider it? Please. Think what it would mean to your daughter–"

The bandage felt tight as a tourniquet round his temples. "I think about that all the time," he said curtly.

"If you go for not guilty, at least you have a chance."

"I don't want to talk about it."

"Think of the damage–"

"You have no idea what you are asking me." His heart felt as if it were beating in his head; he was all pulse.

"Parents sometimes have to make difficult decisions. As a father–"

"I've got to go," Michael said abruptly. "Sorry. Send her my love." He hung up, then stood with his hands pressing against either side of the booth, holding himself steady.

"You had three more minutes," the kanga said sardonically, checking his watch.

"I'll save them for another time," said Michael.

CHAPTER TWENTY-SEVEN

Delphine was sitting on her bed waiting for him, when Colin arrived at the hospital. She was wearing Michael's lavender grey tweed hat sideways on her head and the sight of it made him wince. She took one look at him and the expectancy went out of her. She didn't ask about Amandine and he didn't say anything. Disconsolately, she accompanied him through the corridors.

"We have to follow the green line on the floor and when that stops we follow the yellow dots," he explained, "All the way to the exit. How are you feeling?" He saw the beginnings of a Gallic shrug. "You're looking much better."

"I'm OK..." she said in a small voice, her bottom lip protruding. She tucked her hand into his.

The yellow dots took them all the way to the car park where she stopped, squinting up at the sky, which was infused with a sulky colour that promised a change of weather: grey clouds lanced with the last shafts of light. She looked up, a critical frown on her face.

"Papa told me that the rays of the sun are the souls of the dead climbing up to heaven," she said. No names were mentioned; no mums, no worn monkeys were referred to. "Is it true?" she asked, turning to him.

Colin bit one side of his lip and then, for good measure, the other. "Well," he said prudently, "I don't think we should rule anything out."

"I think it is not possible," she stammered, her voice choking as she turned on her heel and walked off.

"Wait a moment! He had to hurry to catch up with her. "Wait – I've got something for you – a treat – when we get back to the boat."

She glanced at him as if he'd been stringing her a line all this time, making promises he couldn't keep; as if he'd let her down.

"Just you wait and see!" He sort of understood; he thought he did: this new unhappiness lighting the blue touch paper of her other sadnesses. As they neared the port de plaisance he overtook her and sped on ahead, so that he was able to greet her at the *Dragonfly* with a flourish.

"There!" he trumpeted. He'd put the cabin door table up and sitting on a plate in the middle of it, plush with cream, was a magnificent cake in the shape of a swan. "I'll bet you a euro you can't finish it!"

Holy God, there were tears in her eyes.

"Amandine doesn't like–" she responded automatically and then broke off.

"Three euros?" he offered, as a single tear fell. "Five?"

~~~

Had he been able to sleep at all the previous night, Colin would have woken with a woman in his arms for the first time in Lord knows how many years, but as it was he kept himself awake, entranced by the feeling of Tyler's head nestled under his chin, scared that if he took his eyes off her for a moment she might disappear. There was also the question of limited space. Some strange scrupulousness and a need to hold and be held prevented either of them from rolling over on to Delphine's empty bed. Gallantly, he insisted that she sleep on the inside of his tiny bunk, which left him a narrow strip on the edge and on the couple of occasions when he was close to nodding off, a sense of his precariousness swiftly woke him.

They made love, and they made love again, and he thought that he could easily die from happiness. When he came, he found that he was weeping, and he couldn't let her see.

Around dawn, she stirred too. "Colin?"

"Hmmm."

"Just checking…" she whispered, and kissed his chin, and went to sleep again. He feasted on the rainwater scent of her hair fretted with silver, drawing out one dark curl to its full extent and coiling it round his finger.

"Colin?"

"Hmmm."

"Are you looking at me?"

"Would I do that?"

"What time is it?"

"Do you really want to know?"

"Well, I do, quite…"

"Because if you do, both of us will have to get up and one of us – probably you – will have to go naked onto the deck to give me enough space to look for my watch."

"Forget I asked."

"Though actually, I mustn't be late for the hospital…" With elaborate leaning and stretching (and kissing; with elaborate kissing) he managed to locate his watch on the floor under some clothes. "Seven thirty. Loads of time…"

"Colin?" She tilted her head back to bring him into focus. It was a while before she spoke. "What's happened, this – thing, between us, well it is just… a thing, isn't it? Only–" She smoothed her hand along his jaw and up to his temple and he had to struggle to keep at bay the plummeting feeling in his stomach. "Only… I'm not really a people person, you see."

With tremendous concentration, straining to keep the tremor from his voice, he said, "Yes, I see."

"And you are such a great guy…"

He stared up at the bottom of the shelf above his bed, not answering.

"And it's really important that we are clear and honest with each other…"

"Why? Why aren't you a people person? That's if you don't mind me asking…"

She fanned herself with the corner of the sleeping bag. "Is it hot in here, or is it me?" she said nervously. "Because I've been hurt in the past."

"God, Tyler! We've all been hurt. Nobody gets off scot-free."

"–and I don't want to be hurt again."

"Well, fair enough." He wondered how brusque he sounded; probably not as brusque as he felt, rattled by this giving with one hand, with one strong, beautiful hand and this taking away with the other all at the same time. "I don't want to be hurt, either. But I wouldn't imagine either of us is lying here planning how much pain we can inflict, and how…"

"No-o."

"I know I'm not," he leaned up on one elbow, the better to see her. "I want to make you happy. I want you to make me happy."

"It sounds like a pretty neat equation, when you put it that way," her doubtful laugh tailed off. "Have you had other... like, *relationships*, since... you know...?"

"One serious but failed attempt," he scratched his cheek, "And a couple of false starts."

"What went wrong?"

"I was still in love with my wife. I loved her for an awfully long time."

"Being a victim is such a great role to play – you get all the good lines, the big scenes," agreed Tyler dryly. "But if things didn't work out before, for either of us, who's to say that this time...?"

He thought hard before he replied, "Because we're different people now." He paused, testing out the credibility of what he had said. "I'm different."

"Different, how?"

"And my guess is that you are different too." He touched the tip of her nose. "I'm less certain about things and more grateful," he kissed her nose where he had touched it, "Maybe that's a promising combination."

Distractedly, she kissed him back. "Why?" she demanded. "Why've you changed?"

His arm was getting tired; his hand was crackling with pins and needles. He laid his head upon her breast bone. "Are you interviewing me for the post?" he asked.

She twisted so she could look down at him. "Kind of," came her blunt reply. "Is that OK?"

He was listening to the flooding of her heart, the breathy flow of blood. "I've stopped blaming Sally, that's the main thing. I've loosened up a bit – spending time with Delphine would thaw the hardest heart." He reached up and touched one corner of Tyler's mouth and then the other, teasing out her smile. "And yes," he said, "Being interviewed is fine, as long as I get the job," and he kissed her smile before it could disappear.

"Don't get me wrong," she sighed a moment later, "This – what we're doing here, now – it's lovely…"

"It *is* lovely. It's very, very lovely."

"It is…" she nested closer to him.

"Well, in that case, we could just go on doing it, a little bit at a time and if it keeps being lovely…"

"Even though you do have Delphine to look after…"

"I do, but sadly, she's not mine to keep. I'm going to have to give her back at the end of the summer."

"And we come from different countries…"

"But we both like being in France."

She nodded. He watched her lips part, trying to anticipate what she might say next, then in watching, completely lost the thread and kissed her again.

"Don't get me wrong," she said weakly, "I'm not against doing this," so he kissed her one more time, "In principle…" and then again, "But I just think it's important," and again, "That we are honest with each other right from the start."

Colin flinched, but he was in too deep to turn back now, ready to drown; he told himself he hadn't lied to her – *her mouth, his mouth, their mouths* – he had been honest in what he'd said – *her throat, the thrill of her pulse, beating* – he just hadn't told her the whole story – *her brown arms, her slender legs ensnaring his, all the mysteries of her skin* – but he would. Of course he would. He'd tell her everything, when the time was right.

~~~

They set off along the canal in the middle of the morning, with the Yonne dithering beside them, heading off in one direction and then doubling back, neurotically indecisive. The weather couldn't make up its mind either, oscillating between drizzle and a thin scarf of mist, and Colin and Delphine sat side by side under the fishing umbrella, speaking only a little, lost in their own damp abstractions. Now that his lack of sleep was catching up with him, what had happened the previous night seemed like a sweet hallucination, brought on by an excess of emotion in the aftermath of Delphine's accident and he found himself closing his eyes to picture it all again, to make it real.

"Colin!" Delphine said crossly, snatching the tiller from his grip. "Regardez–"

"What? Sorry?"

"You cannot sleep and drive. It is not possible, practiquement. We nearly hit the bridge."

He glanced back over his shoulder. *Sabrina Fair* was gliding beneath the central arch, a narrow fit, and he could see Tyler in silhouette in the wheelhouse; he stared at her outline just to make sure of her. "I'm sorry," he said to his granddaughter, but his eyes lingered, following the ripple of their wash back to the peniche, always back to the peniche, like a refrain his gaze returning.

Marshalling himself, he took the tiller from her. "Right!" he declared, making a statement of intent which Delphine didn't acknowledge. She was lost in some inner landscape too and although her limbs were folded close, there was a lopsided look about her, as if, without Amandine, her centre of gravity had shifted.

"Are you hungry?" he tried not to think about the swan-shaped cake, which she had picked at but he had ended up feeding to the ducks. "Because if you are, I thought we could stop at the next village – Tyler says it's market day there."

She didn't answer and as they put-put-puttered along he couldn't help reflecting that the various hazards between Paris and the butter-melting south were as nothing, navigationally speaking, compared to the perils of conversation: what can be spoken about, what can be alluded to and what must never be mentioned. *Why can't I just ask her?* he thought, hating his own ineptitude, the way he fiddled about in the shallows for fear of floundering right over the barrage. *Straight out? Why can't I just ask her what happened?* He cleared his throat. "The book says–" he began, kicking himself.

Her shoulders sagged.

"The book says there's an excellent brocante in a village called Asnois – a real Aladdin's cave – and I'd like to take you there so that you can choose something that you like." He took a deep breath, "Because I'm very sorry that I couldn't find Amandine."

She turned to him and for a moment her face was undefended, so that he glimpsed the extent of her anguish.

"It doesn't matter about Amandine," she answered briefly, retreating from him.

"Well, I was very fond of her and I didn't know her half as well as you did," he ventured, conscious of the complicated currents now in flood, "Are you missing your Mum, too?" he said, steering the small craft of their chat close to the weir's edge.

She looked at him as if he didn't get it, as if he didn't get it at all.

"And Papa?" he went on recklessly. "I miss Papa, all the time."

"Yes," she said dully. "All the time."

Colin swallowed. "Did they argue – ever?" His voice seemed to go up an entire register and he couldn't bring it down again. "Did they used to…?"

Delphine held out her hand so that the drips falling from one of the spokes of the umbrella formed a little pool in it. She watched each raindrop as it broke the surface tension.

"Did you ever hear them… talking, saying things… shouting – perhaps; or even fighting?"

She tipped the rainwater onto the deck and wiped her hands together until they were dry, a gesture that was more theatrical than practical, and then she bent her wide-eyed gaze upon him, as if she were trying to discern if he really wanted to hear what she had to say. "I heard Maman panting, once," there was something ruthless in her tone. "In their bedroom. She was panting as if she was running somewhere very fast. And then she cried out. I did wonder if something was hurting her. Then Papa cried out too, although I don't think he'd been running."

"Oh," he remarked, feeling himself flush.

"I didn't go in to see."

"No."

They measured out the silence, negotiating terms.

"How far is it to Asnois?" she asked, politely.

Colin found himself back in the shallows, "Not far." He was uncertain of what he had achieved, except perhaps to have been reprimanded by a nine-year-old. "Do you think you'd like to visit that junk shop?"

Delphine regarded him, her innocence undiluted. "If I will be honest I would prefer to have a pet…"

~~~

The three of them walked to the village in the loose embrace of the rain, which was fine yet persistent.

"Is it far?" asked Delphine.

"Not far," he said.

"A couple of miles," said Tyler, who had never had children and was ignorant of the essential etiquette of half-truths and evasions, "but there's a bridge where we can play Pooh sticks and maybe when we get to the market they'll have a crêpe stall and we can eat crêpes with honey *and* chocolate," she added, because she meant well.

"And... *guimauve*?" asked Delphine. "I don't know the name for it in English." Amandine's preferences, a feature of so many of these exchanges, resonated quietly between them.

"Guimauve? Sure you can have guimauve. You can have double guimauve if you want. Whatever it turns out to be..."

The market was all but closed when they arrived at the little town. A lad was whistling as he piled crates of unsold vegetables onto the back of a truck, scattering torn pieces of lettuce and the outer leaves of cauliflowers; the butcher was cleaning the pavement round his stall, sloshing water over it then brushing hard until filmy blue membranes were aggregated into fat and gristle, clogging the gutter. Someone was loading cheap trainers back into their cardboard boxes.

"I probably need some trainers," said Delphine in a speculative aside. "I cannot wear flip-flops in winter. It is not possible."

"Well it's not winter yet," replied Colin, robustly ignoring the rain spurting down on them. The smell of fried onions began to mingle with the wet weather whiff of the inside of his cagoule.

"I love French cuisine, but *andouillettes*? I don't get them, do you?" said Tyler, hurrying past the catering van.

Delphine was holding out for her crêpe.

They watched the raindrops plop into the empty buckets from the flower stall, disturbing the discarded petals of Sweet William. All around them they could hear the drag and snap of trestles being dismantled and the churn of engines as vans reversed. Leaving the market behind, they headed down the main street. The boulangerie shut up shop as they approached and the three of them stood under the overhanging roof of a haberdasher's, dolefully eyeing some embroidery kits.

"We could go and look at a lavoir," suggested Colin, "The book says there are two of them…"

"What's a lavoir?" asked Tyler.

"… and at least they can't be closed."

"It is like a launderette," answered Delphine in unreconciled tones of despair.

"A mediaeval wash house," explained Colin who, given that their options were currently limited, took it upon himself to lead the way.

The lavoir offered little consolation. Its dark timbers, their grain an ancient and inaccessible text, supported a tiled roof that seemed to be entirely held together by moss. Loose spools of spider's web trailed from the rafters and abandoned birds' nests frayed in high corners. The pool itself, fed from an invisible spring by a dented leaden pipe, was a perfect oval, its limestone rim worn away by ancient knees. He contemplated the water, twists of green algae dispersing through it like washed blood. Tyler stooped to fish out a beer bottle. The air of neglect was as penetrating as damp.

Sensing that if he didn't do something radical the afternoon would become irretrievably steeped in melancholy, Colin seized Delphine by the hand, "Come on – we can't get any wetter!" and he jumped in, pulling her after him, and started to run up and down. The water was shin deep and he kicked a sparkling arc up into the shadows and as it scattered and fell Delphine's expression changed from disbelief to astonished delight and she started to scoop water into the air, whole armfuls bursting over her head, chasing him round and round.

"Come on in, the water's lovely!" he yelled as he went sloshing past Tyler.

"Have you ever *had* campylobacter?" she answered doubtfully, "The germs in here probably go back five hundred years."

"At least," he shouted, making flakes of plaster and grit and hardened mediaeval bird shit pepper down on them from the eaves. He held her gaze for a moment, asking her and then to make his point, reminding her…

"What the heck!" she leapt in and started batting fat handfuls of water at him.

Under cover of the grown-ups having gone stark raving mad, Colin grabbed her by the wrist and started to whirl her round. The two of them spun in drenching circles, creating spray as bright as sparks, a liquid Catherine wheel.

"Stop, stop!" laughed Tyler and panting, he released her, unbalancing their small constellation, sending them off at unpredictable angles. They flopped down on the limestone rim with its patient erosions, catching their breath, a subversive glow keeping them warm. Staring at his saturated shorts, he gave a little snort of amusement and Tyler looked at him and giggled and then stopped herself. Without warning, a gale of laughter came soaring out of her and then he began to laugh as well.

"What are you laughing at?" asked Delphine in a quiet voice. Deliciously helpless, Colin couldn't answer her and though he wanted to get a grip on himself – needed to – he couldn't for the life of him sober up.

"Stop, stop!" gasped Tyler, clutching at her side, "Oh, stop!"

But Colin didn't want to stop, he wanted to go on laughing, laughing like this at nothing and everything, laughing until he was spent, he wanted to go on laughing till he cried.

Like musketeers, the two of them swaggered wetly through the town, with Delphine trailing behind. By some fluke or oversight the boulangerie had opened up, but when he saw the state of them the baker came hurrying to the door, barring their way. Puddles formed around them as they chose cakes from the window.

"I bring them to you," he wiped his hands fastidiously on his apron. "Attendez."

They made their way back to the Nivernais, all the colours of the countryside running together. Colin started to sing snatches of a hymn – *the golden evening brightens in the west* – but neither of the others joined in.

"You can't sit under your umbrella in this…" said Tyler when they reached the canal, looking at the strumming rain, "You folks will catch your death and besides, I have *radiators*," she played her ace with a gleam in her eye.

"Radiators, eh?" With a twinge of guilt he looked at Delphine, whose level stare seemed like a small test. Then, contemplating the stern horizon, he told himself defiantly that Tyler was right, they'd catch their death in this downpour. "Well, maybe just for a little – while it's so heavy – what do you think?"

Delphine glowered at him long enough for him to understand that if this was a test then he had scored forty percent maybe, barely a pass, that he was in the *could do better* category of the grandparental league table. Yet to be in the league at all was rather mystifying, when he considered that a few weeks ago he had been living in the kind of sustained solitary confinement that solidifies the heart, makes mutton of it, and now here he was, a man who had a social circle – almost – and competing demands on his attention. He scratched his chin and water ran down his wrist inside the sleeve of his anorak. "I'll just get some dry clothes for us to change into…" he said, as if the decision had been made on purely pragmatic grounds.

Snug in the cabin of *Sabrina Fair* they filled the first few moments' silence by discussing radiators, "I have a diesel boiler," Tyler explained, "and they run off that. It saves draining the domestic battery – God, I'm boring *myself* – am I being too much of a techie?"

Colin was watching her making the tea with a sidelong sense of wonder: heating the water, filling the mug, putting the tea bag sachet on the side, but never mind that. *I love it when you're techie*, he thought to himself, *be as techie as you want, I can take it.*

Steam lipped at the windows; there was the scent of wet hair in the air and little by little he became aware that Delphine's pout had settled in for the duration. "Do you want to play cards?" he asked, suddenly remembering his obligations, and he tweaked the brim of her hat. "We could teach Tyler Damn It."

She scowled at him. "Damn It's boring…"

"Or Spit?"

"Spit's–"

"I know–" Tyler interrupted inspirationally. She picked up the beer bottle she had fished out of the lavoir, which she had brought home with her because she couldn't find a bin to put it in. "Let's send a message in a bottle. I'm going to draw a picture of the three of us in the rain and perhaps you could write the message," she said to Delphine, "And there's sure to be an old cork in the trash, so we can plug it up and throw it over the side when we've finished…" She produced paper and pencils from a drawer. "Here we go!"

Stiffly, Delphine reached for a pencil. She stared at its sharp point.

"What will you do, Colin?" demanded Tyler, now that her organisational blood was up.

"I thought maybe I could watch the two of you – be on hand to answer any questions, that kind of thing…"

"Or maybe you could be cork deputy…?"

"Maybe I could…" But he did watch them – her – he watched her. He watched her sitting next to his granddaughter; he watched the swift movement of her hands as she sketched something, then rubbed it out and sketched again, chattering all the time to Delphine, relieving her of the awkward freight of conversation,

"D'you know what? I find people really difficult to draw. I really do. I guess I'm not really a people person. I like landscapes. You look like a people person to me – I'll bet you are. I'll bet you draw really neat people. How's that message of yours coming along? Have you thought what you're gonna say…?"

Her voice faded out as he focused all his energies on willing her to glance his way and when she did look up and smile, he jumped. She didn't speak. Her smile widened, not flickering this time, and his mouth moved a fraction as if in answer, although he had no idea what he might say. Phrase by phrase, in stealth, a silent dialogue began. They talked of kissing, of the slow stroke of tongue on skin, of clothes sliding, of the delicate violence of touch.

They never drew breath.

"I've finished!" Delphine slammed the pencil on the table.

Colin blinked as if coming into the light. He took in the child's downcast face and the clench of her jaw. She appeared poised for action and yet withheld and as he clocked the danger signs, he wasn't sure if it was rage or misery that was building in her.

"I'd better find you a cork…" he said circumspectly and then, while they sealed up the bottle with the message and the picture inside it, "Will you tell me what you said?"

She shook her head.

"Is it to Papa?" he asked with a kind of lazy intuition that he recognised too late was a substitute for proper interest. He swallowed and found the imagined taste of Tyler was still in his mouth.

Delphine didn't answer.

Quite right, he chided himself. *She's no fool. She knows when she's been short changed.* "You don't have to," he said awkwardly, "Even though I'd really like to know. Look–" he wiped some steam from the window with reluctant fingers, as if the cleared glass provided a view into his own shortcomings. He didn't want to leave and yet he knew it wouldn't be quite right for him to stay. "The rain's easing up. It's time for you and me to go."

He disciplined himself to keep his gaze neutral, to say goodbye to Tyler and take his granddaughter by the hand. Together, they wandered mournfully along the riverbank to the next bridge and he was conscious of the slight sounds of the countryside drying out: a single drop falling, a leaf shifting as it lost its weight of water. Along the wooded bank a silver birch was caught in the flare of evening light, its white trunk illuminated fleetingly, before being extinguished for the night.

He had to lift her up onto the parapet of the bridge so that she could throw the bottle in.

THE DRAGONFLY

"Do you like being with me?" he asked her, all of a sudden. He could feel the small case of her ribs, her thinness. Her answer mattered to him.

Delphine thought for a moment, weighing his question, making her choice. She cocked her head to one side. "What day is it today?"

"Let me see, it must be… Saturday – yes, it's Saturday."

She twisted round to look at him and then, with a generosity that made him feel ashamed, she said carefully, "Well, if it's Saturday, then I like being with you very much."

"I'm sorry–" he blurted out. "I'm very – sorry."

She was watching the bottle, already collared with a strand of weed. "De rien," she whispered, innocent of the extent of his transgressions.

CHAPTER TWENTY-EIGHT

Michael was back in his cell. A medical orderly had removed his bandage, checked the stitches and discharged him. He'd had a migraine for two days, with bright razorings in front of his eyes. There was a provisional feeling to everything.

Laroche, returned from his first stint in the library, was all for playing another list game. He started making a list of all the list games they could play. The A to Z of sexual positions, the A to Z of criminal offences...

"How about countries or birds, or characters from Shakespeare?" Michael asked wearily. He sat on the edge of his bed, gripping the mattress, his knuckles gleaming. He was conscious of the unkind light. The conversation with his father still bothered him. *Parents sometimes have to make difficult decisions.* Asking Charlotte to have an abortion? Not wanting to see Delphine when she was born? There were two, for starters. For difficult, read wrong. He took a breath, and then another, to give himself ease. He released his hold on the mattress and flexed his fingers.

"Birds?" said Laroche. "Ones you've pulled? I could go several times through the alphabet with that, though you," he eyed Michael quizzically, "would probably be stuck at C. Am I right or am I right?"

THE DRAGONFLY

"Let's not do birds," said Michael with a sigh. As an afterthought he covered his mouth with his hand, but there were thoughts he couldn't stifle: how much he loved his father; the bewildered ache for him when he was gone. The disbelief – that was it – that such a thing could happen: that his Dad could let him go. No fight. No court case. No righting of wrongs. No bitter custody battle. A nod and a wave and a *see you in the holidays*. Brave faces all round, but Michael never felt brave, he felt bereft. He glanced up, conscious of Laroche's eyes upon him. "What about films set in prison? – *The Shawshank Redemption, Midnight Express* – that's two for starters."

Laroche pulled a face. "Busman's holiday – no thanks." He thought for a moment. "We could do escape films, I s'pose…"

"*Chicken Run?*" Michael said doubtfully. The divorce had robbed him of the certainty that he was loved. In their different ways his parents tried to make things up to him, *have an ice cream, I've got tickets for the footie, I'll take you to the cinema, let's go fishing*, compensations that only left him feeling wary. "…I'm sorry?"

"I was saying," said Laroche, as if he were fed up with talking to a halfwit, "that we didn't really watch films when I was a kid. Or if we did, they were ones bought down the market with more crackle than picture. Which might give you the edge."

"Right," said Michael, who was struggling to listen.

"Which we wouldn't want, obvs. We could do *ways* of escaping…"

"If you like…"

"Except I'm stuck on A. I don't suppose you'd let me have arse licking, although I guess that might sometimes do the trick."

"What?"

"Farkin fark, Rosbif. I'm workin' really hard at this. Ways of escaping beginning with A. Or we could try something else. You could ask me if I'd had a nice day at the office."

"Oh! I'm sorry. The library. It was your first day."

"And I could say, thank you, dear Rosbif, for asking, except I'm bored of this already. This is definitely not a good game for passing the time. You could help me out here."

"I'm sorry. My head still hurts and I'm worried because my daughter's been in hospital–"

"Yer gotta man up–" said Laroche irritably, going over old ground.

"And I know I've not been very good company. OK then, I'm on the case: ways of escaping beginning with B – boring, as in tunnels.

"Boring, as in boring." Laroche did that thing with his spine, that quick collapse of vertebrae. "Alright then, here's some news: I've got a conjugal coming up – not that kind of conjugal, a family one. My missis is bringing in the kid. Little ickle Marianne. Though talking of conjugals – have you ever played that game where you wank onto a biscuit?"

"No... Let's do the A – Z of birds."

CHAPTER TWENTY-NINE

Colin awoke in the morning with a sense of discomfort that wouldn't go away: he was feeling guilty about Delphine, guilty about Tyler and he lay there worrying until he was filled with the inescapable certainty that he must tell her everything.

When she popped round first thing, "Isn't it just the most beautiful morning? I was going to walk into the village.. I wondered if you'd like some croissants…" hooking her arm behind her head in a way that he had come to know meant that she was feeling ill at ease, he understood the subtext of her offer.

Schooling himself, he looked beyond her to where the canal curved round. In places, the banks were obscured by the branches of trees, the burden of a long summer weighing them down as far as the water. His eyes rested on a crooked fishing platform bearing faded notices, discoloured threats and blandishments. "Actually," he stood there, thinking that when it came to it, he couldn't bear to tell her; thinking, obscurely, that he needed a shave; that he needed… that he couldn't… "Actually, we were planning on making an early start–"

"Oh," her arm fell to her side. "Oh. Right."

"Just to – you know – get a bit ahead… Time to be moving on, and all that–"

"Sure, sure." She started inspecting a callus on her palm.

"I mean, we'll probably see you at the next lock – you know how these things are…"

"Yeah…"

"… What with delays – lock keepers' lunch hours, that kind of thing. And hire boats getting in the way…"

"Hire boats… Yeah. They do, don't they?"

"Yes."

"Get in the way…"

"Yes."

Several ducks went clattering past, laughing raucously at their own jokes, and Tyler shoved her hands into the pockets of her shorts. "OK…" she squinted up at him, although the sun was not directly in her eyes. He could see that she was disconcerted, that she didn't understand. "Catch you later, maybe…" she said abruptly, after a beat or two.

"Yes," he said, on the threshold of regret, "Yes, maybe catch you later…"

~~~

"Look, if you don't fancy the brocante, there's a little museum that has an exhibition of tools used by forestry workers in the Morvan, according to the book…"

"OK, OK, let's go to the brocante."

Colin was balancing the guide on his knees, reading and steering at the same time. Delphine was watching him through the binoculars. "Colin, you have hairs growing out of your ears."

"Yes, alright, alright."

"It is dégôutant."

"It happens. When you're my age. Lots of men…"

THE DRAGONFLY

"Yuck."

They moored close to the bridge leading up to the village of Asnois. The road was dusty and there were strange crops in the fields: piles of roof tiles, rusting iron work, tractor tyres and several burnt out dormobiles. The telegraph wires were strung with silent birds. The first house they saw had a rotting mattress bulging from an upstairs window. They exchanged glances and she reached for his hand.

"Or we could just go back to the boat..." in a squeaky voice Delphine resumed a conversation which they had never started.

"We could, but now we've come this far, we might as well..." Rounding a corner, they found themselves right in the centre of the village – in fact, almost out the other side. Ahead, there was a dilapidated chapel and nailed to what must once have been the parish notice board was the skull of a goat.

"Hmmm," said Colin, trying to sound noncommittal as his head filled with thoughts of devil worship and he was about to second her suggestion about going back to the boat, when she slipped her hand out of his and ran through the gate and up the path before he could cry out, "I wouldn't go in there if I were you."

He hurried after her. It wasn't some kind of rural coven where they sacrificed passing river folk, but the brocante. The straggled space around the entrance was crammed with old prams, zinc baths, enamel coffeepots, an umbrella stand stuffed with *swords* – yes, swords, cracked panes of stained glass, a bicycle with wooden wheels, an ancient twin tub, several stone bottles, piles of saucepans, broken ceramics...

"Look at this!" she had found a porcelain lavatory glazed with blue hydrangeas, with a picture of a splendidly moustachioed man on the bowl at the front.

Together they went inside the chapel, Delphine speeding on ahead. "Did you mean it?" she called over her shoulder, "Can I have something? Because of…"

Happy to indulge her, he smiled and nodded, distracted by high tors of china crockery, their irregular strata consisting of side plates stacked on dinner plates stacked on saucers which even a sigh, let alone an over-excited nine-year-old, might dislodge. There were leather suitcases, their travels bragged about on peeling labels; boxes of door knobs; hundreds upon hundreds of odd glasses, some of them sticky, all of them dusty. He was just reaching for a small silver mug, its vine leaf engraving tarnished yellow, when she came bounding across, "Can I have this?"

He was stretching up to a high shelf and turned incrementally, with his breath held, fearful of sending a pile of butter dishes crashing to the floor. "Absolutely not," he said, missing a stained crystal decanter by a hair's breadth.

"Please–"

"Certainly not," in a complicated but compressed contortion he brought his arm back to his side. "Put it back where you found it. Now."

"But look–"

"I'm trying not to," he retorted, feeling himself blush. From some dark recess of the junk shop she had found what appeared to be a lamp made from coloured glass. It showed a jolly friar in the later stages of arousal, with a naked woman slung over his shoulder. She had a frayed electric cord with a Bakelite switch on it coming out of her bottom and he dreaded to think what might be illuminated when it was turned on. "Now," he barked, as a woman appeared from behind a hedge of ashtrays and said something in French. He could feel the hot roots of his hair.

"She says it's from the 1930s," translated Delphine, unabashed.

"I don't care when it's from, put it back."

"But you promised…"

"I might possibly have said… but I'm not going to… certainly not that."

"OK." She put the lamp down and for one brief, naive moment he marvelled that he had got off so lightly. "Then you will let me have a pet instead…" she said with a subtle smile. "Non?"

~~~

Colin bought Delphine the little silver mug with its vine leaf engraving even though she said she didn't want it. He breathed over its tarnished surface and then buffed it on his T-shirt. "It'll polish up quite nicely," he said, holding it out for her to see.

Round-eyed, she regarded him and shrugged.

It looked like the kind of thing you might give as a christening present and on the way back to the *Dragonfly* he fell to wondering if she'd been christened and whether she was a catholic and what promises had been made on her behalf.

"I'd like you to have it anyway."

She received it with casual indifference, though she did pause to inspect her reflection in it, opening her mouth wide and scrutinising her teeth, then closing her jaws with a snap.

"I thought it might be rather good for drinking *Coke* out of…"

"Have you got any *Coke*?"

Once they were underway, he poured her some and as his beautiful duck egg blue boat fizzed along the canal; she played at rinsing her drink round and round until it went foaming up her nose. A good deal of spluttering ensued.

After he had patted her on the back and done some light mopping up, he said, without considering the failure of their previous conversation, "What do you miss most about your mum?"

Her mouth was full of *Coke*, which she took her time in swallowing.

"You don't have to talk about it if you don't want. Her. You don't have to talk about her…"

The effervescence was all gone. She hunched over the little silver mug staring at the trailing vine leaves.

"I'm only asking, because I didn't really know her, not properly – I only met her a few times and I wondered if you could tell me what she was like…?"

Delphine was breathing heavily.

"I'm just interested, that's all," he went on, as kindly as he could. "It can be a way of keeping someone with you, talking about them, you know…"

She looked away.

"I thought she was very pretty," he said. "Very striking. She used to wear lots of lipstick, didn't she? I remember that," he tailed off, casting around. "And I remember…"

"Her smell. She put on nice *parfum* when she went to see her friend."

She spoke so quietly that he could hardly hear her above the noise of the engine. Little by little he lowered the revs, letting the *Dragonfly* drift, and as he did so Delphine started to hum. It wasn't a soft and melodious sound; it had an abrasive edge, a hard, industrial tenor. She was humming through gritted teeth. It wasn't a tune that he recognised; it probably wasn't a tune at all.

"What friend was that, then?" he asked, as casually as he could.

Her strange, riven music grew louder and he thought that sometimes he could read her like a book, a tender, slender volume; at others, everything about her, her moods, her wants, her history, was written in a language that he couldn't fathom. "What did she smell of?" he asked, when she didn't answer.

"Powder," she replied carefully.

"My mum smelt of rather old Chanel No 5. She had the same bottle for years and years and years," he tried to be conversational, the thought of Charlotte's "friend" lodging itself like a thorn beneath his skin.

"And cigarettes."

"Did she smoke a lot?"

"Quite a lot."

"My mum gave up smoking and sucked on a cigarette holder instead, a little ivory one."

"Is your mum related to me?" she asked curiously, pouring the last drips of *Coke* into her mouth.

"Bound to be," he said, "I'm not good at that stuff. Some kind of grandmother, I should think. Great-grandmother?"

She nodded.

"Were they happy together, do you think? Your mum and Papa?"

Delphine looked minutely at him and then looked away. She looked at him again, as though she wasn't sure that she had heard the question correctly, and then she looked away. She looked at him as if to say, *how can you ask me that*, and then looked down into her lap.

"I suppose I'm trying to make sense of what has happened, you see," he faltered.

"Maman was very nice to Papa and Papa was very nice to Maman," it was more of a delivery than an answer and her voice had a welling sound, as if she might start humming her strange, raw song.

He recalled the note that she had written him, the night of the mashed potato. It was safely tucked away inside his wallet. *Colin is very nice to Delphine…* It had been a hopeful whitewash of recent history: not a statement of how things were, but how she had wanted them to be.

"Very nice…" she said uncertainly.

"What do you miss most about your dad?"

"Everything," she whispered and Colin had to lean in close to hear her matchwood answer, syllables which might split and snap.

"What, though…? he repeated gently, filled with his own yearnings – for Michael's confidences, for those shared moments that weren't shared anymore, for the hobbies, the question and answer sessions – *What? Why? How? Why? Where? Why?*

"I miss the stories he used to tell me."

"The thing is," he hesitated. He could feel the great weight of his heart in his chest. "I love Papa very much and I can't understand why – I just can't understand." His head was once more full of that terrible apparition of Michael standing at the top of the stairs with his hand raised to strike, an image which he struggled to extinguish. "I thought that maybe you could help me…"

"I miss riding on his shoulders. I haven't done it for a long time because he said I was too heavy…" Delphine appeared to be in a state of suspension, as though any kind of action were possible, if only she could find a way to move. "I miss his mousse au chocolat. He used to write my name on the top in cream and once he wrote *Papa* with a big Chantilly heart around it." She broke off.

"Tell me what happened," he said, drawing out the question that he hardly dared to ask.

She flinched as if some scary tale were being recounted to her, full of details that she didn't want to hear. He half-expected her to put her hands over her ears. He watched the tiny hyperventilations at the base of her throat as she took anxious sips of air; he could see the workings of her frantic pulse. "Maman was leaving…" her mouth opened, "and…" her breath stuttered, "and…"

"And?"

Silence.

"I want Amandine…" the words came out in a jumble, "I am missing her so much."

He watched the spillage of tears down her cheeks. "Maman was leaving," he prompted, the words inching their way out of him, "and…"

"And Papa was cross," she cried as if that were the whole story, as if it were the end of everything.

"And then what happened?"

She shook her head. She shook it brutally from side to side.

"Did Maman fall… or…?"

Her breath came in little scissorings that cut and cut. She was rocking to and fro. "I can't–"

"Or did Papa–?"

"I can't – I can't – I can't – I can't – I can't – I can't–"

Colin sat with his head bowed, listening to her until he couldn't take the carnage any more. "It's alright, ssh, ssh."

"I can't–"

"Stop now, stop. You don't have to... I don't want you to... Ssh."

"Oh Colin! Oh Colin!" She pressed both hands over her mouth as if she might have said too much and went tunnelling into his embrace, into the darkness of his arms. He kept on holding her, wiping her eyes with the hem of his T-shirt, stroking her hair, rocking them both back and forth, back and forth, comforting her in the hope of finding some oblique comfort for himself.

~~~

"The navigation is about to get extremely interesting," he announced the following morning, as much to strengthen his own resolve as his granddaughter's. *Twenty-four hours and no Tyler.* Scores of tiny insects had drowned in the dew on the cabin roof and Delphine was arranging them into patterns, her face sombre. It would be hard to persuade her that the words *navigation* and *interesting* could belong together in the same sentence. "We've got seven lifting bridges coming up – I'm going to need your help with those – and then, wait for it–" he totted up the numbers, "Twenty-seven locks in eleven kilometres!"

She was unmoved. She was busy writing her name with dead bugs – D – E – L – P – H...

"Twenty-seven locks! What about that then?" He could see the beginnings of a shrug and went on, "And after that we've got three tunnels. That should keep us busy, eh?"

Raised up, the lifting bridges looked like emaciated wading birds bent over the canal, their angular necks dipped low so they could feed. They worked with a system of pulleys and counterweights and the first one that Colin heaved into the air

– the pont levis de l'Arc – left flakes of rust and ancient paint all over his hands.

They were approaching the village of Cuzy when he spotted some red flowers floating in the water, the waterlogged petals losing their colour. He stared at them as they eddied downstream, disintegrating, until the memory of Tyler's fingers nervously deadheading petunias sprang at him, and then he knew without turning to look that *Sabrina Fair* would be somewhere up ahead.

At the thought of her, every part of his body felt hot and he had to fight the urge to go throttling forwards, waving and calling out her name. He craned his neck as they went past the cherry-prowed peniche, twisting right round in his seat. He couldn't see her onboard, although the engine was idling in neutral, so she couldn't be far. As he straightened up he caught the expression of resignation on Delphine's face; a look of bitter deflation.

"It's alright, we're not going to stop, I promise," he said, trying to master his resolve. She rewarded him with a torn little smile, as if it were against her better judgement to believe him. With an extortionate amount of self-discipline, he pointed his boat's duck egg blue prow in the direction of the next lifting bridge, and then he saw her.

Tyler had hauled the bridge halfway up when she spied the *Dragonfly*. In the moment it took the two of them to exchange a diffident glance she relaxed the tension on the chain a fraction, but it was enough to allow the bridge to sink back gracefully to the horizontal, hoisting her four metres up into the air.

"Hold on," he cried, "Whatever you do, hold on." He rammed the *Dragonfly's* nose into the bank. "Turn the engine off, will you? And tie her up to something – a tree – it doesn't matter what–" he shouted over his shoulder at Delphine as he leapt onto dry land and started running, "Don't let go! I'm coming! I'm coming!"

Strange yelping sounds were issuing from Tyler as she tried to get some purchase on the chain using her feet, causing the end of it to whip and swirl like the tail of an enraged animal. "Oh my God," she wailed. "I don't do heights…"

"Don't look down – youch!" The chain struck him on the shin, "Ow, ow, ow. It's alright. It'll be alright. Hold on tight," he said, hopping about rubbing his leg.

"Oh my God."

"It'll be alright. It'll be alright. Try and keep calm. If you can keep still, just so that I can grab–" The chain went scything past him again.

"I can't hold on any more. Oh my God."

"Hold on for a moment, just for a moment. Don't look dow–"

Her fingers unfurled; her body seemed to fall more rapidly than her limbs, so that she hurtled downwards in a crescent shape and he could almost hear the rush of air as she came tumbling into his arms. He staggered sideways, his legs buckling atrociously, so that he ended up flinging her on to the grass verge, before collapsing next to her.

"Bloody hellfire," he said, when he had caught his breath. They lay side by side. High above them, the white sails of clouds filled with wind and went scudding past. He stared up at them until that shifting moment when they stood still and the earth began to move instead.

Tyler was pressing her fingers against various bones, testing them out. "My," she drawled, "You sure know how to sweep a girl off her feet."

"Are you alright?" He let his face tip sideways so that he could look at her. A sprig of clover partially obscured her profile and there were moments when he could smell its sweetness and moments when it eluded him, when it was diluted by the fleeting fragrance of standing water and earth.

"For someone who's just been dumped – in every sense – I'm doing real good." She had concluded her examination, "No bones broken – I guess that's something."

He levered himself up and hunched forwards, hugging his knees. He could hear dark shades in her voice as she began to speak.

"I'd kind of assumed that I was the one who wasn't a people person, but you seem to be in a different league altogether. Was it something I said?"

Beside the canal was an old farm with a circular tower at one end. Broadleaved trees leaned close, framing a picture of that could have come straight from a child's storybook. The only thing missing was a beautiful girl at the highest window, letting down her hair. Colin gazed at it and sighed.

"I'm sorry. I must have seemed rather – abrupt."

"Abrupt? More like *incomprehensible…*"

"I wanted to talk to you, to try to explain, but it's not very easy when Delphine is…" his eyes strayed to his granddaughter, who was wandering down the tow path with her head bowed, kicking at stones. "I have – responsibilities…"

Tyler sat up. She studied her watch, gazing at the second hand sliding round, though she didn't seem to be curious about the time. She tilted her wrist so that the glass face caught the light, casting tiny flashes into the air, signals which he couldn't read. "I understand that."

"I don't think you do–"

"Well, pardon me, I'm sure."

"I don't think you can – understand." He ran his fingers through his hair. "You couldn't."

"Try me," she responded crisply.

"Anyway, I thought it was you who said that what happened between us was just a *thing*," he observed, attempting to head off his own explanation at the pass.

She peered back over her shoulder at *Sabrina Fair* and he had an intimation of how little it would take for her to stand up and brush the grass from her shorts and then walk away.

"I'm sorry," he said. "I haven't been quite–" he had to search for the word, "Quite – *straight* – with you. I'm sorry."

She turned to face him; there was a terrible fatigue in her action. "You don't say."

"No," he swallowed.

Although her head was tilted at a sorrowful angle, as she spoke her words hardened as if, exposed to the air, they had bonded into something tough and translucent, something resinous. "I have this kind of vague recall that I also said how important it was for us to be *clear* and *honest* with each other. Am I dreaming, or did I say that?"

He hung his head. He was loathe to speak. He sat there as the silence turned caustic, until he could feel all of its corrosive properties at work. He bit his lip and looked away, his eyes seeking out Delphine. She seemed to be lost in some tracking game, crouching low at the base of the round tower, her movements elaborately stealthy.

"If you're going to tell me that you already have a girlfriend, or you're going back to your wife, I'd rather hear it straight, so shoot–"

On the brink, beyond beating about the bush any longer, Colin said, "My son is on remand for murder." There, it was done. He felt vertiginously, dangerously light.

"Jesus!" Tyler's eyes flicked wide. She stared at him for a moment, her mouth opening "But–" she looked as though he must somehow be mistaken.

"The trial is in a few weeks. He's pleading guilty, so it will only be a formality."

"*Oh my God,*" she breathed. "Who? Who did he–?" She broke off and as her gaze swept over Delphine, who was still on safari along the old farm wall, he could see her answering her own question.

"Her mum didn't fall," he said.

They could have been sitting on different continents, so far apart they seemed.

"It'll be all over the papers soon," he went on reluctantly. "I'm hoping his legal team will get the charge reduced to manslaughter: a crime of passion." He felt sadness like a sharp blade drawn along the length of him.

"Why?"

He covered his face with his hands as if he were bathing it in water, as if all of this could be washed away.

"Why did he do it?"

"I don't know," he sighed. "I've asked myself a hundred times, over and over, and I just don't know. Charlotte was leaving him–" He shook his head, trying to blot out a mental image of his son with arm raised, a static picture in which the blow never fell. "But the boy I knew, my son, couldn't – Michael wouldn't…"

A silence like lead encased them both.

"It makes you question everything you thought you knew," he said, in grief.

"Yes…" Tyler was motionless and yet alert, as if listening to some distant and indecipherable sound. "I guess…"

"I should have told you. I know I should have told you. I should never have allowed myself to–"

"To what?" she asked tensely, "To fuck me?"

"To get involved…" he said, flinching, "But you were so lovely…"

"Jesus!" she exclaimed and he braced himself for the tirade to come, but it was her tenor of regret which floored him, of lost opportunity and disappointment. "I'm not lovely. I wish I was. I'm just me, an ordinary person who deserved to be treated with some respect and told the truth."

"I was frightened that you might walk away."

She didn't answer. She was a study in quietness.

"And there was Delphine to consider. In a sense the story wasn't mine to tell…" She darted him a sceptical glance and he went on, more truthfully, "I didn't want you to think badly of me…"

A small, wry sound escaped from her. "I might have walked away," she said, thinking the matter through, "but when I'd had a chance to, I don't know, sleep on it – whatever – I might have turned round and tiptoed back…"

"But you won't do that now?"

She pressed her fingertips to her temples, "I'm not getting this. I'm just not getting this. Yesterday morning, in that oh so polite, oh so evasive way you Brits have made your own, I had the distinct impression that you were giving me my marching orders, and now–" she turned to him, her palms raised in incomprehension, "What's the story, Colin? What's the plot? Because I can't figure it out. Can you shed some light here for me?"

"The plot's a little bit complicated. I'm struggling myself. It involves a middle-aged man and a needy little girl and a boat not much bigger than a matchbox. I didn't know my granddaughter until we came on this trip. Sometimes I think I hardly know her now, but what I do know is that she depends upon me, even if she doesn't always like me very much."

"I think she likes you," she said, pulling at a frond of grass, the high note as she slid it from its sheath catching the sadness in her voice.

"And then you came along. You're just about everything I've ever wanted. But your timing is rubbish, because of what has happened to Michael. Because of Delphine." He allowed himself to look at Tyler's face, her eyes that were green or grey, according to the light. "I thought for a few heady moments that I could have it all." He looked away. "Life isn't like that though, is it?"

She shrugged. "I don't know. It can be. It's up to you."

"I wasn't a very good dad. I tried to be, but–" He could remember the feeling of Michael's slight hand in his as if he were holding it now: that trusting, confidential grip. He closed his fingers over nothing, over thin air. "And I haven't got off to a great start as a grandpa, but that is something which I can put right."

"I'm not sure where that leaves us…"

He didn't answer.

"Isn't it weird how we protect ourselves from what we most want?" she whispered. "In some ways I'd have liked nothing better than to be… well…" she couldn't finish. "There we go…" Awkwardly, she rose to her feet. "I hope it goes well for your son. I really do. And I hope that you and Delphine…"

Colin stood up. All he wanted was to press rewind – *actually, this isn't what I meant, this isn't how I wanted it to be. I want to have my cake and eat it, too.* He studied his T-shirt, examining the weave of the cotton. "I do like you. It isn't that I don't–"

"Best not go there," she rebuked him softly.

For a moment they stood there, looking out over the canal, neither of them knowing how to leave. From the corner of his eye he saw Delphine, her trek over, sprinting towards the *Dragonfly*. She leapt onboard and started rummaging in the kitchen locker. When she realised he was watching her, she slammed the lid down and sat on it, beaming insouciantly.

"You ought to go–" said Tyler, following his gaze.

He bit his lip. There was something he wanted, more than anything: to kiss her, just once, to say goodbye.

As if she could read his thoughts, she lowered her head.

"At least let me lift the bridge for you…" was all he said.

She hesitated and her mouth moved fleetingly – the mirage of a smile, nothing more than a shimmer in the heat.

"Tyler–?"

But she hooked her arm behind her head and then turned and walked away.

CHAPTER THIRTY

Laroche said, out of the blue, that when he was six he saw his stepdad hang his mother over the banisters by her ankles till her teeth rattled, and without thinking Michael said that he once saw his dad hit his mum around the face.

That shut them both up for a bit – the sum total of an afternoon's conversation.

Looking back, Michael could remember his mother from when he was young – her brisk hands swooping down from on high and wiping his mouth, the wrap of a hot towel around him after bath time, her standing in the kitchen doorway and bursting into tears at the end of a wet afternoon, the birthday cakes she whisked up: the football pitch, the circus, the guitar, the skateboard: elaborate creations that reflected his every passing interest. She made him a star chart for his reading – he might try that on Laroche who was making heavy weather of *The Monstrumologist*. She lay on the floor and they played with his garage by the hour: wheeling the blue car up three stories and down again, up three stories and down, filling it with petrol, taking it to the car wash. He always had the red car, but the routine was the same.

He could remember her dried up and dying, but he didn't remember much in between. It was his dad he was trying to get to, elbowing her out of the way. When people talk about what hurts them most, they smile; they don't look sad. He'd noticed that. He remembered his mum smiling, the contraction of her gaze as he hurried to go fishing, or off to football. He could remember the breathless radiance in her face when he first saw her with Étienne, and the complete understanding he had of what was coming.

She gave him a choice when she went to France: *you can come with me or stay with Dad, it's up to you*, and he was so overwhelmed with guilt at the wringing relief he felt because she'd said he could stay with his dad, that he stammered in a rush he wanted to go and live with her.

He remembered one dirty morning lying late in bed with Charlotte in her flat, when they had only just got together and were thirsting for every kind of knowledge of each other. He was trying to explain the situation to her: how he'd ended up in France, the awkward wreckage which his parents had created.

She lit a cigarette and for a while the two of them watched the slow dissipation of smoke into the room, the pale convolutions catching the sliver of light through the curtains, drawn against the midday sun.

"I'm not sure that I'll ever be able to forgive them," he was tentative, wanting her to know about him, nervous about telling her.

She leaned on one arm, sweeping her last exhalation up and away. "Mon petit Chéri." He felt her beautiful French words rather than heard them, on his skin, in his hair; her voice like smoke tangible in the air. She trailed her fingers over his chest as if she might write something there, things which could not otherwise be said.

"Charlotte–" her name twisted out of him. He was convulsed with wanting her, wanting everything about her, all five senses of her: touch, smell, taste, sight, sound.

"If you don't forgive you can't forget," she said, "and you'll have to carry the past with you always and the weight of it will become très lourd."

Uncertainly, he moved to kiss her and she caught his face in her hand and he could feel the grip of her fingers, the urgent grip, "and you will never be free."

He ducked his head. He was way out of his depth, deliciously, terrifyingly. She leaned across to stub out her cigarette and he felt the graze of her against him as if she had burnt his skin. He was consumed by her. The last thing he wanted was to be free.

Michael looked up at the barred window, at the drain pipe on the hospital wing with its slick of green algae. He should have listened to her. He felt the glint of a migraine in the corner of his vision, like the half-seen slap to his Mum's face, the sight of Charlotte crashing down the stairs.

There was silence in the cell, brief and rare.

"About this kid," said Laroche. "If I agree it's mine – wot then?"

CHAPTER THIRTY-ONE

They ascended the Sardy lock staircase in the glazing heat, sixteen locks in three kilometres and nowhere to stop, with the sun coming at them from that end-of-summer angle which inveigles its way under fishing umbrellas put up for shade, and the brims of hats. The two itinerant lock keepers who accompanied them looked like extras from the film *Deliverance* (too much leather and too many chains for Colin's liking) but the lock keepers' cottages had exhibitions of sculpture and pottery and – *oh Tyler* – watercolours to keep them diverted as they climbed up and up and up.

He was starving by the time they reached the top. "I'm famished!" he panted, hammering in a stake for them to moor to.

"What is famished?"

"Hungry."

With that, Delphine bolted from her place on the bathroom locker to the kitchen locker in the twinkling of an eye. She sat down and crossed her arms and then as an afterthought she crossed her legs as well. She became absorbed in looking at the view.

"Aren't you?" Colin chucked the mallet onto the grass. "I could eat a horse."

She half-turned her head. She didn't look at him.

"What about it then? Bread and cheese? Fried egg – I wouldn't mind a fry up? What do you think?"

"It's too hot."

"Bread and cheese, then."

"I'm not hungry."

"Well, I'm ravenous – shift over."

She darted him a glance. "Perhaps we could have an ice cream, at the next village?" She spoke airily, although there was a little seam of anxiety stitched into her voice.

"This is the next village."

"I won't bother then…"

"Or maybe a cheese omelette. That would be just the ticket." He climbed back on board, "Now, if you wouldn't mind parking yourself over there…"

Delphine took a deep breath. "Did you say tunnels? The other day? Did you say we'd be going through some tunnels?"

"Yes. Move over a sec, will you? You're sitting where I need to be."

"I'm really interested in tunnels–"

Colin regarded her with the first twinge of misgiving. He wiped his sleeve across his forehead and blew upwards so his exhalation cooled his face and wondered if the heat was getting to her, too.

"Does it say anything about them in the book?" she asked avidly.

Taking some grandfatherly license, he scooped her up under the arms and sat her down on the bathroom locker. "Excuse me," he managed not to call her *young lady*, as he suspected that might irritate her, but she sounded irritated in any case.

"Colin!" she bounced back up, but he already had the kitchen locker open and was lifting out the Primus stove.

"Keep your hair on," he said, *that's what he said* as he noticed that the lid of the Tupperware box they kept the cheese in wasn't properly shut, but as he wanted to get the remains of the Gruyère in any case, he took the whole thing off and there, laced round and round in neat coils, was a small, snub-nosed brown snake.

"OH MY HOLY GOD!!" An extraordinary yodelling sound escaped from him and he almost let go of the box, as if it had become too hot to hold, making the snake rear up in alarm, but Colin reared higher and far more swiftly: he retrieved the box with the snake half out of it and threw it as far away as he could up the bank.

"Hector!" wailed Delphine, scrambling off the boat, stumbling over the mooring line so that she floundered into the shallows. She recovered herself, her arms windmilling, slipping in her wet flip-flops, and went skating up the slope. "Petit Hector–"

Colin was gasping for breath. Convulsively, he kept brushing at his shoulders and neck, swiping here and there as if serpents were seething all over him. He could feel the cool ooze of them winding down his arms and under his T-shirt and kept picking up his feet, capering painfully as if the deck were writhing with them. He shuddered. He tried to marshal his breathing: he made himself inhale and exhale with deliberation, but he couldn't help himself, his head whipped round to look behind him, his flesh crawling. *Inhale and exhale.* He gripped his knees, bending like an athlete, overwhelmed.

"Colin–"

His head snapped up, "Don't come near me with that–" he couldn't say the word – he didn't even like the shape of it written down.

Delphine had the Tupperware box in one hand and the lid in the other and she gestured with them, using them as evidence. "See what you have done! No Hector. See–? I cannot find him anywhere."

Colin was merely trembling by now. "Well, thank God for small mercies."

As she advanced towards him, brandishing the box, he took a step back and then another. When he felt the bathroom locker against his calf he jumped. "DON'T come any closer – let me see first."

She shook the box upside down, "It is empty! He is gone!"

He leaned forward a fraction, peering at the box, then leaned forward a fraction more so that he could inspect the foot or so of water between the boat and dry land. *Do they swim? Do they slither up mooring lines and slide round fenders?* He surveyed the bank, blade of grass by blade of grass. He checked behind him one last time. "Alright," his shoulders slumped down from round his ears, "You can come back on board."

"But we must look for him – he is only a little baby."

"*What?*"

"We must find him–"

"If you think–"

"He is very small, he is very young, he is in great danger–"

He could see the tell-tale welling of sorrow in her face and was conscious of her facility for expressing emotion – heartfelt emotion – while at the same time gauging its effect. For once, his instinct to pacify and compensate deserted him.

"I am not going to look for…" avoiding the specifics, he went on in a quiet voice, "…whatever. We are going to have lunch," though he had never felt less like a cheese omelette in his entire life, "…the two of us. You can help me cook it if you like, but I have no intention–"

"He was my pet!"

"I don't care if he was the Queen of Sheba."

"You said I could have a pet–"

"I said nothing of the kind. You said you wanted a pet, which is a very different thing."

"–because of Amandine…!"

"Oh for Pete's sake–"

She burst into tears.

"I'm sorry," he collected himself. "I'm sorry. I'm sorry about Amandine and I'm sorry about – everything else. But I can't have Hector or any other kind of – you know – on the boat. I just can' t."

"I *hate* you."

It took a moment for both of them to digest what she had said. Fearing that she had gone too far, Delphine grew reckless and went further, "I wish I'd never been born," she sobbed.

Nervously scanning the bank, he stepped ashore.

"I'm sure you don't mean that," he began, thinking that she probably did and in the circumstances he wouldn't blame her one little bit. To rub salt into his own wounds, he thought of Tyler and the price he had paid to have this troubled scrap of a girl all to himself. He stifled a sigh and after a moment he went and stood a little closer to her. He could see her tears rolling into the corner of the Tupperware box. "Here–" he held out his handkerchief, "I'm afraid it's got a bit of grass stain on it and some engine oil…"

Delphine looked at his handkerchief and fell to weeping harder. Gingerly, he mopped one side of her face and then the other. "You have no idea, Delphine, how very, very glad I am that you were born. Blow–!" He wiped her nose. "Very glad." He cleared his throat. "I know you are going through a really hard time at the moment, really hard, but it won't always be like this," he tucked a strand of hair behind her ear. "You're going to have to trust me on this one."

A long, stuttering sob escaped from her; it sounded as if it were taking her soul away with it.

Silence.

"Are we friends?"

She lowered her head. He liked to think it was a nod.

"Look – I'm very sorry about…er…Hector. He gave me a terrible fright."

She wiped her face on the inside of her arm and for a moment, streaked and grimy, she looked beautiful, in the way that ancient faces can look beautiful. She looked scarred and worn and sweet. He held his hand out, palm side up. "Put it there, pardner," he said.

Hesitantly, staring down at the ground, she slipped her hand into his and the small weight of it made him feel humble and blessed all at once. He just kept holding it, until at length Delphine wound herself round and into his arms, and she leant against his chest, giving him the gift of all her sorrows, the great gift, and the two of them leaned against each other and he stooped down to kiss the top of her head, thinking that in the grand scale of things, if he had paid a price at all in saying goodbye to Tyler, then it was the right price and a fair price and it must surely be worth it.

"If you're going to have a pet," he said, disengaging himself slightly and leading her back down towards the *Dragonfly*, "Then it's probably best to have one that doesn't need to live in a Tupperware box…"

After an improvised lunch (chunks of bread with lumps of chocolate) they played Spit and Damn It, and Delphine managed to be reasonably patient while he tried to teach her Backgammon, but when she'd had enough she plugged herself into her phone, though he couldn't be sure that she was listening to anything, just that she wanted to seal herself away.

"How long had Hector been on board?" asked Colin, an anxious thought occurring to him as they prepared for bed.

"For not long enough," she said pointedly. "Since Tyler went up with the bridge. I found him in the long grass, while you were talking."

He nodded, "He didn't have any little friends, did he? Or relations?"

"I think he was an *orphelin* – I do not know the word. All alone, without parents," she added, to be sure that he understood the extent of their association.

He checked the bottom of his sleeping bag, all the same.

~~~

They passed from leafy light to darkness as they went through the Tunnel de Breuilles, then the Tunnel de Mouas, then all seven hundred and fifty-eight metres of the Tunnel de la Collancelle. Outside, the netted sunlight caught in the branches overhead and spilled down creepers which hung low like viper's tails. The air felt used; it couldn't circulate and filled the cuttings bronchially, damp with other people's breath.

"Our first down lock," Colin rubbed his hands together, "Easy as pie – no messing about with boat hooks, looping ropes over bollards that are far too high. You just pop the centre line on like that–" he demonstrated, "–and Bob's your uncle you can put the kettle on and have a cup of tea."

There was none of the turmoil of the up locks, where the water tumbled and churned into the chamber, sending the boats skittering to the end of their lines. The *Dragonfly* became indolent, so that each descent was little more than a recline, a stretch and lean that allowed her joints to settle.

As they bowled down past Bazolles and Mont-et-Marre they established a routine: Delphine jumped onto the lock side as the little boat swooped close, looped her rope, then hopped back onto the cabin roof and lay down in the sun. She had her headphones on, creating distance, but from time to time if she caught his eye, she waved at him with a happy/sad, brave/sad, sad/sad expression and Colin waved back, revving the engine, accelerating after coots to try and make her smile, or pulling faces at the pale Charolais cattle which haunted the banks like wraiths, quenching their ghostly thirst.

Faithlessly, the Nivernais had given up on the River Yonne and was pursuing other options. Approaching the little town of Chatillon en Bazois, it hitched up with the River Aron and the two of them idled side-by-side, leaning into each other's curves, placid in the warm afternoon. The *Dragonfly* dawdled through the town, dodging a hire boat which had come firing out of the open lock like a bullet from a gun. Colin listened to the furious recriminations of the crew as they went hurtling past: *I couldn't reach! It's not my fault. We need to get the rear line on first…*

Perhaps the sun was too soporific; perhaps the fields were too warm and golden; perhaps the trees whispered too beguilingly, perhaps the walls of the chateau by the lock were too achingly ochre, so beautiful he had to look back, like Orpheus, to crane his neck and stare.

Perhaps it had just become *too* easy.

Lazily, possibly (in retrospect) smugly, they nipped into the lock and pulled up alongside so that Delphine could do her thing with the rope. Colin did his thing and reduced the revs, twisting round to contemplate the knuckled branches of a row of trees which had been pollarded in the spring and were wrestling their way back into growth. Beyond them lay the ornamental gardens of the chateau, the hedges clipped and controlled. Sunshine glanced off round towers and chimneys, while reptilian black tiles glittered on the ancient roof. The late afternoon light was hazy with pollen and heat, dust and tiny seeds floated down through the thermals and Colin sat there, absorbing everything with the keenness of someone who has learned to live in deficit. He was so spellbound he barely acknowledged the lock keeper, who had closed the gates behind them and sauntered past to open the paddles at the front. He listened to the winding sighs of the machinery and the lethargic creak of their rope, his little boat imperceptibly floating down as the water began to drain away, and he was so intent on straining to see the last bright weathervane of the chateau disappear from view that he barely noticed the fact that the rope was no longer creaking, but griping insistently. He was roused by a squawk from Delphine, who had flipped round onto her hands and knees, *"Colin–?"* There was a note of query in her voice, rather than alarm, so he was slow to surface from his slumberous trance and he didn't come blinking back to life until he saw the navigation book slide down the everything locker. His Swiss Army knife was sitting on top of it to weigh down the pages and it was only when it bounced over the side and into the water that he realised something was amiss.

"Colin!" There was pure fear in her voice now. She scrambled up the roof of the cabin, which was tilting at thirty degrees and flung herself onto the lock side. She managed to get the trunk of her body on first and twisted round. "It's the rope," she cried, "The rope's jammed." Until then, Colin had been preoccupied with the loss of his knife, his head full of idiotic thoughts about how long he had had it, whether there was time to fish it out, how quickly it would sink, but as the deck began to shelve beneath his feet – forty degrees, fifty degrees – sending him lurching towards the water himself, he became ferociously alert, the hot flare of adrenaline spurting through him. He spun round and balancing on the kitchen locker, no longer a flat surface but an escarpment, with one hand he reached port side of the boat, now disorientatingly above his head. He hauled himself upwards and inched his way along the duck egg blue flank of the *Dragonfly* towards the snagged line. The loose end, instead of spooling freely, lowering the boat, was caught, and the more the water drained away, the more trapped it became.

"Stop the lock," he bellowed. "Tell the keeper to stop the lock."

He was conscious of so many sounds fading in and fading out: a child whimpering, the clatter of the propeller slowing in the air, a man's voice shouting in French, the tangled noise of cutlery and crockery falling, the soft acoustic of clothes and bedding tumbling through the cabin, the pious squeak of his shoes on the paintwork, his heart beat, the faint reproach of birdsong, a man's voice shouting in French…

"Allez, allez monsieur!" The lock keeper was standing above him gesturing, stooping to reach down to him. In the man's shadow, he glimpsed Delphine, crouching low with her eyes closed and her hands covering her ears. Colin tried to lever himself upwards, grit embedding itself in his palms like glass. He could feel the suck and slime of the lock wall against his thighs; his feet went shooting off in all directions; he lost a sandal. The man had him by the T-shirt, by the shoulder; he was shouting at him. Everything happened so slowly, until everything happened so fast: the pale, mild chateau, the pollarded trees, the terrified little girl, the meaty arms of the lock keeper, the chlorophyll green of the lock wall and then the wide, forgiving sky all chased each other helter-skelter round and round until before he knew it, he was sprawling breathless on the stone quay.

He stumbled to his feet. The man was still shouting at him. "Non comprend," Colin turned away from him. "I've lost my sandal. And my knife." He made his way to the edge of the lock. *Don't look down*, he told himself, *once you look down...*

The *Dragonfly* was dangling sideways from the centre line about a foot above the water. He stood with his head bowed. Some of the junk – the torch and the mallet – had spilled out of the everything locker and was caught in the corner of the deck; Delphine's turquoise pinafore was in the water, dragging down.

Delphine.

The man was in his face, talking coercively right up close. "Yes, yes" said Colin, pushing past him. "My granddaughter–"

She was curled up, as small as small can be, her face pressed into her knees and her arms covering her head. When he reached out his hand to touch her, she was rigid with fear.

"It's OK," he said, his voice blurting and shaky. "Everything's going to be OK. I just need–" He had no idea what he needed: to feel steady on the uncertain ground, perhaps. He looked at the chateau. He looked back at the town. Three or four people were clustering round. "I just need to–" The lock keeper had him by the sleeve. "I just need to sit down, as a matter of fact," he said, his legs folding up beneath him.

He managed to lift Delphine into his lap. That seemed to be the most important thing. The longer he held her, the smaller she felt.

"You alright, mate?" asked an English voice.

"What?"

"Are you alright?"

"I don't know. I'm fine. I'll be alright in a minute." He peered up at the inevitable group of helpful boaters, trying to locate the speaker. "I'm fine," he repeated, apprehensively.

A man stepped forward, scratching his cheek. He had a huge belly slung above a disproportionately long pair of shorts. He rolled his lower lip against his teeth, chewing at a tuft of beard.

"About your boat, mate. I've had a word with the lock keeper – GCSE French and all that – and the thing is, I think you need to check your insurance, because as far as I could make it out, I think he's planning on hiring a crane…"

Delphine was so still in Colin's embrace that he wondered if she'd gone to sleep; or perhaps she'd died of fright – he bloody nearly had. He clambered to his feet, hefting her weight. Her legs clashed against his and he could feel the drape of her arms around his neck. Cautiously, he returned to the side of the lock and stared down. The *Dragonfly* looked like a discarded toy. He hadn't realised it was quite so small.

The lock keeper came hurrying up, still hammering out suggestions, but now that Colin had come to and could take him in properly, he could see that he was a young man, not much more than a student, with his hair tied back in a ponytail.

"Can't he just fill the chamber up and refloat her?"

The helpful boater shook his head. "Not when she's lying at that angle. She'd just fill up with water," but he translated Colin's query all the same. The lock keeper spread his hands flat, signalling finality, and went to make a phone call. The helpful boaters started to drift away. Colin rested his chin on Delphine's hair. Upstream, a queue of hire boats was forming. One or two of them had tied up already, the others were noodling around, wondering what on earth was going on. A crane? The lock could be closed for days. They could be stuck in Chatillon, with its treacherously beautiful chateau, until the end of the week, or longer still. "Look," he said to Delphine, "You're too heavy for me to carry. I'm going to have to put you down now." He loosened his hold and she slid to the ground. He caught her before she crumpled up. It was as if she had vacated her body, as if there was something about her that wasn't working any more.

"Delphine?"

Apart from a tiny tightening of the muscle around her eyes, there was nothing.

"Are you OK?" He glanced round to see if there was somewhere they could sit and started to head for the stairs up to the street, limping because he only had one sandal. He sat down on the bottom step, so that his face was on a level with hers. "You and I need to have a chat," he began, putting his hands on her shoulders because she was visibly shaking. "We need to clear something up," he leaned in closer, tilting his head one way and then the other, trying to engage with her. She stared at the ground. "What's happened is completely and utterly my responsibility. I should have checked the line. I should have checked it every time, and the fact that you were so fantastically good at coping with it doesn't let me off the hook. Is that understood?"

She gave a sigh so small it was inaudible.

"It turns out that I'm a bit of a crap sailor." He studied his hands; the hands that had built the *Dragonfly*. "I'm rubbish, in fact. I've got a lot to learn," he added shortly. "I can't apologise enough. It was my mistake; my mistake entirely. Is that understood?"

She might have said, "It was my fault," perhaps she mouthed the words, it was almost impossible for him to make out. She might have done. He couldn't be sure. At that moment there was a shearing sound that cracked wide open, fissures of noise splintering crazily, then the slap of wood on water as the rope which was holding his beautiful, duck egg blue boat snapped and the *Dragonfly* went crashing face down into the lock.

CHAPTER THIRTY-TWO

On the morning of the conjugal, Laroche was restive. He kneaded the muscle in his forearm as if he wanted to separate it from the bone. The lines around his eyes were pulled tight.

Michael shot a look at him. "What's up?"

"It's me bleedin' wossname conjugal, that's what."

"Ah."

"Don't want to see 'em. Changed me mind." He shifted his weight in the chair, got up, walked to the door, kicked it, then came and sat back down. "Besides, got a daughter already. My little Zazie. Don't need another one." He sniffed then wiped his nose on his shoulder. "Nobody likes to be made a fool of, Rosbif – do they?"

"Who's making a fool of you?"

"Her bloody mother, that's who. It's not the kid. I like kids – couldn't eat a whole one yada yada oink oink. But she's having a laugh. Well, fuck her."

"You've got nothing to lose…"

At that, Laroche leaned his forehead into his hands. He slumped against them. "Thanks for pointing that out, Rosbif," he said in a low voice. "I feel shitloads better now. Lilian Laroche – the man with nothing to lose. Merci bleedin' beaucoup."

Michael couldn't help himself. "Lilian?"

"Yeah?"

"*Lilian?*"

"*Yeah?*"

"It's just that – it's a girl's name, isn't it?"

Laroche eyed him coldly. "Let's do a list of things that frost me muffin: number one, Rosbif ponces."

"Isn't it?"

"It's both." His leg started jiggling. A vein surfaced beneath the skin of his temple. He cracked the knuckles in one hand.

"Alright, alright."

He cracked the knuckles in his other hand.

"About your daughter – Marianne," Michael said quickly. "Her mum will have got her up and washed and changed and fed and changed again and probably caught three buses in order to bring her here to meet you. It wouldn't do you any harm to go along."

Laroche looked askance at him. He laced his fingers together and cracked all the bones at once.

"You've got to man up," said Michael apprehensively. "It's what you keep telling me I must do – *Lilian.*"

~~~

There were days when time didn't pass, it congealed, and the afternoon of Laroche's conjugal seemed to last a week. Being alone in the cell felt a bit too close to solitary confinement. *I've got half a lifetime of this ahead of me.* He tried reading a book, but it failed to grip him. *How am I ever going to bear it?* He attempted to do a pencil sketch of Delphine from a dog-eared photo he used to keep in his wallet, but it came out full of all the fear he had for her. *How will she manage? Where will she live when Lisette is too old to look after her? Would his father step into the breach on a long-term basis? Would he even want him to?* He was drawing a picture of Charlotte's mouth from memory, when he heard the particular articulation of the key turning in the lock. *The law of unintended consequences is harsher than the one that sends you down for twenty years.* He observed a kind of silence within himself, a stilling of his thoughts.

Laroche burst in through the door as if he were fleeing from the paparazzi, his hands, palm outwards, screening his face. "Leave me be, leave me be." The air crackled around him as he sat on his bed, tilting himself away from Michael. Instead of jiggling, he rocked back and forth, a movement so slight it was no more than the beating of a pulse. "Can't get me head round this," he muttered. "Can't get me head – oi, Rosbif."

Michael was extending his drawing of Charlotte, shading the line of her jaw, pencilling in the lobe of her ear. He couldn't bring himself to draw the intimate sweep of her neck. "How did it go?"

"Like that." He threw a photograph onto the table.

Michael studied the picture. A bald baby with close-set, white-lashed eyes.

"I'm basically fucked."

"She is very like you."

"Poor little rug rat." He sniffed. "Let's do a list of ten ways to shaft your kid: kill its mother – that's a good one, that should come top in all fairness. Next one: get yerself sent down for armed robbery–" he wiped his nose on his sleeve, then glanced at the photo again and looked away. "Your turn," he said. His gaze was drawn back to the photo. "She's quite like me, isn't she? You know. Just a bit."

"Don't they say babies always look like their fathers? Makes the dad invest."

"Think she's got me mouth – whaddya reckon? And me hair, obvs." He bit his lip.

"I think she's got your eyes."

"Did you say *invest*? Fat chance. Five years, that's what my lawyer said I'd get. She'll be half way to leaving home by then."

"You can still be some kind of a dad – while you're in here."

Laroche grunted. "Don't have much to do with the other one – Zazie. Her mum's not so keen. Got a court order against me, as it happens. We could do a list of all the court orders that've got my name on them if you've the time."

"Marianne's mum seems quite keen."

"Yeah, well."

"You could write her letters, when she's older."

"I could record her bedtime stories an' all. I've got the leaflets. I know the drill. But."

"It's better than nothing." A heaviness descended on Michael. He stared at the picture he had drawn and with a few swift strokes of the pencil sketched in Charlotte's neck, her broken neck, at a pitiful and incongruous angle. "We're in the same boat, you and I. Fathers of daughters we won't get to see."

A laugh cracked out of Laroche, "Result!" he said mirthlessly. "You made it in the end. You took yer time about it but *yeehaw!* – here you are."

"I'm sorry?"

"You blew in here all *I'm not like the rest of you*. Look at you now, me old Rosbif. I'm not the only one who's been doin' Education."

CHAPTER THIRTY-THREE

Did Delphine disappear in that agonising moment when the rope snapped, or did she vanish later? Talking to the police, Colin couldn't be sure. He recalled sprinting to the side of the lock and seeing with horror his boat splayed upside down in the water, its revealed hull looking unbearably vulnerable. He remembered staring at the gauzy green stains on the paintwork, the river's fingerprints, thinking, *what do I do? What do I do? What have I done, and what do I do?*

He swung into action then. With blinding velocity he climbed down the ladder into the lock and reached for the *Dragonfly's* broken line. The cabin was already filling with water, sitting heavily, forcing the stern up and he was desperate to stop it sinking further. He tried tying the short length of rope to the ladder he was standing on. The propeller was snapshot still. Some of their possessions were floating on the surface: a couple of plastic plates, the navigation guide open at the correct page, a few of Delphine's felt tip pens. They looked shamefully personal and he couldn't bear to see their big adventure reduced to so much flotsam.

The lock keeper, who was talking into his phone, raised his arm peremptorily to indicate that he had words to say to Colin too. Behind him, Colin could see that another hire boat had joined the queue to pass through the lock, and another, and then he noticed that beyond them a cherry red prow was stealing round the bend in the canal and more than a sense of humiliation at his own foolishness, he felt relief and a kind of ludicrous delight. Tyler was coming. *Tyler was coming.* Merely the sight of *Sabrina Fair* seemed to have a calming effect on him and as he watched the small peniche ease through the sloping curve of the canal walls he marshalled himself enough to make a short to-do list in his head: find a bed and breakfast where he and Delphine could stay the night (he groped in his back pocket and his fingers closed over his wallet and his phone: another relief); buy sandals in order to be able to walk round Chatillon and accomplish the former; possibly buy a case of wine and take a bottle to every boat waiting in the queue and apologise profusely; make peace with the lock keeper (another case of wine?); ring the insurance company. As he stood watching the progress of the cherry red prow, he fell to wondering where and how Tyler featured on his list. He contemplated compiling a second list, of all the things that he might do to try and make things right between them. He wasn't sure if this was a list that he should write. There wasn't a manual, a handy book with diagrams, to show him how to square the circle of being a lover and a grandpa.

He did think of Delphine at that point – he thought that he would take her to the shops as she'd need clothes to replace the ones that were currently drifting down to the bottom of the lock; he was thinking that perhaps he could buy her an ice cream, when the lock keeper snapped his phone shut and addressed himself to Colin.

He got the gist of it: *grue… demain… après midi*, with the mention of an eye-watering sum of euros. The crane would be arriving tomorrow afternoon and would cost a month's wages.

The lock keeper was keen to emphasise the disruption – *de Clamecy jusqu'à Decize*, before striding off.

"Yes," Colin kept nodding, "Comprend," he said, "Désolé, désolé."

Desolate was about the size of it.

Throughout all of this, he was pretty sure that Delphine was sitting at the bottom of the steps – no, *huddling*; huddling at the bottom of the steps in an abandoned little ball; he couldn't be certain, but he was reasonably sure, because part of him wanted to be huddled there as well pretending that none of this was happening.

The reason that Colin didn't turn round then and go back to the steps and flop down next to Delphine and loop his arm around her shoulders or pat her on the knee and say, "It's not the end of the world, you know. I shall have a great time this winter getting the *Dragonfly* shipshape again. Perhaps you can come and visit me in the holidays and I can show you my shed and take you to Sally Lunn's for a bun…" The reason that he didn't say any of these things, for which he castigated himself, was that from the corner of his eye he saw Tyler strolling down the tow path, shading her eyes from the sun, and at the sight of her his heart, which had been fidgeting and fretting ever since disaster struck, settled quietly in his chest. He was inexplicably moved by how familiar she seemed: there were things he knew about her, as well as so much that he didn't know. He knew her late night fragrance and her early morning scent; he knew the sound of her footsteps and the length of her stride; he knew the colour of her eyes, but he didn't know her birthday. He didn't know how long she'd been married, where she had lived, if she'd been to college, if she had brothers or sisters, what films she liked. He didn't know if she would want to speak to him.

THE DRAGONFLY

He could tell the exact moment that she saw him. She glanced back over her shoulder, hesitating, then with her head bowed, she began to retrace her steps. She was so graceful and athletic, her supple outline moving sadly down the tow path.

But then she stopped and raised her arm and he thought that she would hook it round behind her neck, but instead she ran her fingers through her hair and shook her head as if she had come up from the depths and was scattering a halo of bright spray. She spun round and started hurrying towards him. She reached the lock a little out of breath.

"I just wanted to say," she began and then she stopped and peered more closely at him. "You've only got one sandal on–"

He stared at his feet. "That's the least of my problems."

"You wouldn't by any chance be involved somehow in this delay? A guy back there said the lock will be shut for two days at least."

"Somehow," he glanced sideways at her and then nodded in the direction of the lock.

"Oh. My. God."

"The rope jammed…"

"Oh my God–"

"…and we just managed to get off in time before it broke."

"Colin, I am *so* sorry. I'm so *sorry*." She covered her mouth with her hands.

He shrugged.

"You built it yourself, didn't you? Your beautiful boat…"

"Well… the insurance will cover it, I suppose."

"Yeah, but…" She looked around. "Where's Delphine?"

Shoving his hands into his pocket and starting to turn with comfortable, presumptive certainty, he replied, "She's over th–" and then he froze.

The step was empty.

~~~

They searched around the lock and the street above it, Colin speeding along as best he could at a lolloping hop.

"We're not going to get very far with you like this," Tyler said presently. "You go and check with the hire boats and I'll scoot into town and get you some shoes. What size?"

"Eight."

"What's that in real money?"

Colin was already hobbling off down the tow path, "Forty-two," he called back.

"What was she wearing? Just in case I…"

"That pink sundress we got in Auxerre," he answered, "With some kind of cardigan thing tied in the front. Orange. And Michael's hat. You couldn't miss her…"

There followed a terrible sequence: *Have you seen a little girl – she speaks English with a French accent / I'm looking for a little girl in a bright pink dress / I've lost my granddaughter, she's about this tall* again and again and again. Some people didn't understand; others shook their heads; one man began, "Is it your boat that's–?" but he didn't stop to answer. The helpful boater who had translated for him said, "That little girl? Yeah, yeah, I saw her–" and Colin wanted to seize him and hug him, "She was sitting at the foot of the stairs going up to the street…"

"Did you see her after that?"

The man rolled his bottom lip, capturing his little tuft of beard between his teeth, "No mate," he shook his head, "Not after that. Do you want us to help you look?"

"Would you? Would you?"

Tyler came running up, brandishing a pair of espadrilles, "Best I could do." She shook her head as well, in answer to his unspoken question.

Colin took a deep breath, "Perhaps you two could start with the town and I'll check the canal in both directions. I'll radio the lock keepers," he broke off. His VHF was at the bottom of the Nivernais.

"*I'll* radio the lock keepers," Tyler offered, "while–?" She looked questioningly at the helpful boater,

"Peter–"

"While Peter makes a start – is that OK, Peter?" She turned back to Colin, "Have you any idea where she might…?"

As Tyler spoke, Colin remembered how Delphine had slipped off to find the otters, and his panic at seeing her empty bed when he woke up. He felt the same bitter fear now. He remembered the sound of her laughter leading him to her, how it coloured the air.

~~~

At five o'clock, already frantic, Colin went to the Gendarmerie and reported his granddaughter missing. He sat in an office with windows too high to look out of, staring at a poster with a cartoon of a pickpocket that was blu-tacked on the wall and as he tried to give an accurate description of her, he felt as if the whole ghastly process had set in train a self-fulfilling prophecy which could only end with a blank-looking, out-of-date photograph of Delphine splashed across the evening news. The policeman told him in almost accent-less English that her description would be forwarded to all the patrol cars in the department and that in nine out of ten cases the missing person turned up unharmed and oblivious to the furore.

But what about the one in ten?

Colin stumbled out of the police station. He glanced at his watch. It was six thirty: there were about two more hours of daylight left. He was distraught at the thought of her alone in the darkness. He yearned for the sight of her curled up in her bunk with Amandine tucked under her chin and her lavender tweed hat tipped back on her head. Where would she sleep? How would she keep warm? Would somebody take her in? Would they care for her? Would they *hurt* her? Holy God! For the first time the possibility that she hadn't gone, that she'd been taken, began to gnaw at his innards; anxiety, like bared incisors, ripping into him.

Tyler came hurrying over the town bridge. He went rushing to meet her, but she quelled him with a single shake of her head. "No luck so far," she sighed. "I ran into Peter just now – he is such a great guy, so kind – he's going over to the chateau to see if she might have wandered into the grounds. It's possible. And the shops haven't shut yet. She may appear from somewhere at closing time – you know what she's like, she is *such* a girl for new clothes…"

They stood side by side without speaking, wretchedly computing other possibilities, until Colin said, "We'd better go back to the lock. Perhaps we could walk along the canal and look there." He told himself that it was something to do; it was better than having stiff drink after stiff drink; it was better than throwing himself in the Nivernais; it was better than doing nothing.

Walking felt like therapy; it felt purposeful, until Colin remembered how as a child he'd had a macabre fascination with the discovery of an old shoe or a draggled scarf or a discarded pair of tights – he'd always pictured them being the prelude to the uncovering of some terrible dismemberment. He shivered, forcing himself to look into the ditch beside the tow path, fearful of glimpsing a torn length of something fuchsia-coloured or a crumpled orange cardie and he wished he could trade these well-founded adult terrors for his morbid childhood imaginings.

"Are you OK?"

He grimaced. "I'm OK." Casting his mind back to the ordinary innocence with which the day began made him feel a little unhinged. "I'm feeling bloody awful, to tell you the truth. Bloody terrible."

They walked on, dusk dispersing through the countryside like ink dissolving. Colin cupped his hands around his mouth and shouted her name. "Del-phine! Del-phine," using the singsong intonation of the searcher, "Del-phine!" They left the path and walked through the verges, kicking up leaves, delving into undergrowth until the only light left seemed to come from the pale bark of the trees. Colin's phone rang and he almost dropped it, his hands were shaking so.

"No news," said the policeman. "I wanted to let you know that we are scaling up our search. I have asked for more men and for divers, so we can examine the lock."

"Perhaps we should go back," said Colin, when he had hung up. Coming to any decision seemed beyond him, he was finding it increasingly hard to believe that anything which anyone could do would make a difference. "If they're going to drag the lock…"

"Colin," said Tyler, "Would it be OK if I – without any kind of, you know, obligation – or anything like that – if I held your hand…?" Tentatively, she intertwined her fingers with his. "I hope you don't mind me asking."

He shook his head in the forestry dark.

"For comfort…" she whispered.

They looped the long way back to the centre of the town. They asked in the auberge, they asked at the petrol station, but no little nine-year-old, overtired and abashed, came scuffing out from the shadows, unwilling to meet their gaze, unsure how to say sorry. *It is not possible*, Colin kept rehearsing her saying inside his head, *it is not possible.*

As they approached the centre of Chatillon, still holding hands in a loose and non-committal grip he turned round and looked back the way they had come. "This afternoon," he began, "At the lock, you were going to say something..."

She nudged him forwards, "Was I?" she asked casually. "Oh, yes. It seems such a long time ago already."

The town was subdued; the houses had their shutters up. As they walked from hushed street to hushed street, still hunting high and low, every movement seemed magnified by disappointment.

"Maybe now is not the moment," she faltered, as they crossed through the main square and passed down by the church. They stood facing one another, the street lights casting conflicting shadows. Tyler was squinting off into the middle-distance, automatically searching still. "I've never had a... you know, a kid of my own, and what I was going to say before all of this—" she gestured round the square, at the empty benches and the trestles piled up ready for the market. She swallowed, "—you know, before Delphine... what I was going to say, what I want to say... is that I know she has lost her... mom... I don't want to presume, or, you know, go where I'm not wanted, but if there's a way of spending some time with you and maybe helping her—" her words slowed to a trickle. "Oh my God, this is turning into a whole long speech. Wrong place, wrong time, as usual. Sorry, sorry – let's go."

The canal side throbbed with light, arc lamps illuminating the lock. Several police cars were drawn up nearby and there were officers conferring in groups. The policeman Colin had spoken to earlier came over as soon as he spotted them.

"No news," he reported; he looked tired but extremely focused. "We are still within a positive time frame. We are using all resources. We have a family liaison officer – I will introduce you," he broke off to speak into his radio and then was hailed by one of his men. "One moment, a moment please."

Like a moth in the glare of the arc lamps, Colin stood on the lock side, the realisation of what had happened as searing as if he had come to it new and unprotected. He shaded his eyes from the horrible limelight, which seemed to illuminate his loss for everyone to see. He watched the dark shapes of the divers in the water, thinking that his own heaviness would drag him under, wishing that it might be so.

Tyler touched his sleeve, "Why don't I make you a cup of tea? You need to keep your strength up and we'll be close by if they need us."

He couldn't speak, he couldn't answer, he could hardly think. He was intent on making promises: *let her be alright, please let her be alright, let her come back safe and sound, I'll do whatever it takes, I'll do anything at all.*

As they walked along the towpath in the darkness Tyler clasped his hand in both of hers and held it to her cheek. "Don't be too hard on yourself," her eyes sought out his, holding his gaze by degrees. "It'll come out right in the end, I know it will."

~~~

The only sound in the cabin of *Sabrina Fair* was made by the clock, each tick tearing up what was left of his hope. Colin sat hunched at the table staring at the grain of the wood, those journeying lines which never meet, while Tyler was curled sideways at the far end of the sofa, her tea growing cold.

At last, when they were ashen with tiredness, with the strain of waiting recorded in every muscle, the phone rang.

"Oh Jesus," he breathed before he answered it. He held the handset in his hand.

"Do you want me to take it?" asked Tyler in a low voice.

"No. No, no." In his head, they were lifting Delphine from the reedy water; he had seen the grey green colour in her face before, "Hello? Yes... Oh God, oh my God... yes... yes... straight away." He laid the handset on the table, matching it exactly with the grain. He rubbed the heels of his palms into his eyes and tears ran down his wrists, making salt pools over his blue veins. "They've got her," he stuttered, with a wrenching laugh that was born of grief. "They've found her; they've got her; she's safe."

It took him a minute to pull himself together; he leapt to his feet, hurrying, turning back, stopping, starting. "She's in somewhere called Eguilly. By the canal," he cried, halfway up the stairs. "She just walked off, heading south–" *Until the butter melts*. He was brought up short at the thought. "My phone," he rifled through all of his pockets. He ran back down again.

"Do you want me to come?"

"Yes. More than anything. But it's better if I do it on my own. Thank you," he made as if to kiss her mouth, "Thank you – for what you said. For everything you've done today." He wanted to wrap her in his arms. Instead, he cupped her face in his hands, regarding her searchingly. "When there's time to stop and think... can we talk? Can we? But not now – I really have to go."

Sitting in the police car driving sleekly through the darkness, the golden gleam from the instrument panel cast a glow over everything. He watched the outline of the Morvan hills roll past the window, their shapes only visible through inflected shades of black, his own reflection superimposed upon the view. The police radio provided a commentary on other people's heartbreak: burglaries, accidents, and God forbid, lost children, in a language that he didn't understand.

The gendarme explained that a young woman, putting out the rubbish, had found her. She had been curled up in a little ball, leaning against the wall of the lock keeper's cottage at Eguilly. When they arrived there, Colin flung open the door of the car before the vehicle had come to a halt. His head was spinning, but he walked as calmly as he could up the path, as if he'd come to collect her from a friend's house after school. The door opened before he had a chance to knock.

"Monsieur?"

"Yes, yes," he said, as if he were admitting everything.

He hardly took in the young woman or the interior of the house. He had a vague impression of terracotta tiles and dark furniture and lots of crocheted lace. Delphine was sitting docilely at the kitchen table with a glass of milk in front of her. For a moment she looked dazed, as though the arc lamps had turned their light on her.

"Grand-père–" she exclaimed, as pleasantly as if it was a coincidence which had brought him to this heathland cottage in the middle of the night. When she saw the policeman, her eyes widened and her mouth moved the way it did when she was reading to herself. Colin held back while she made her small and silent reckoning, although he was longing to offer her some sort of reassurance, to give her a hug and ruffle her hair. She slipped from her chair and he bent down and held out his arms.

She didn't move. She made the kind of little gesture that she used when she reached to find Amandine, but Amandine wasn't there.

"Delphine?" he began in an undertone, lowering his arms to his sides. "Am I glad to see you!" She looked like a creature at bay and all he wanted was to make things easy for her. "We ought to be making tracks," he suggested, speaking carefully and gently.

She pressed her lips together. She rubbed her sleeve across her eyes as if she was very tired. "It was my fault–"

"Darling girl," he knelt beside her. "It wasn't your fault. It was an accident. It wasn't your fault at all."

She turned from him to the policeman, her face disconnected and bemused. "It was my fault," she repeated. "When Maman fell. It was my fault. It was me."

CHAPTER THIRTY-FOUR

Laroche was given four years and nine months and seemed unmoved by the sentence. "This is me home, 'ere," he gestured around him, taking in the bed, the cell, the view of the hospital wing. "'S where I live. 'S where me mates are; got me little ickle job in the library. Board and lodging, no rent to pay. Who needs the outside? All that trouble? All them rellies? Nah." He resumed filling a carrier bag with his belongings. "Right," he said. "Got the kanga to give me five. Sit down."

Michael sat abruptly on the chair that was thrust at him.

"Don't move and this won't hurt," said Laroche from behind him.

"What–?"

There was a rustle of plastic bag then a click and a buzzing sound that Michael realized too late was an electric razor.

"Don't move."

"What the–?" The first featherings of hair sifted down onto the floor. "Get off me, you maniac!"

"I'm doin' it for yer own good."

"You're a madman. What are you doing?"

Hair, like feathers from a pillow fight, drifted downwards.

"Who's going to watch your back, now I'm crossing to the other side?"

KATE DUNN

Michael twisted his head round to look at him. "What?"

"I've only got five minutes. Don't move." The razor skimmed the contours of Michael's skull. "You're gonna have to watch your own back, because I won't be there."

"Have you been watching my back?"

"What do you think, ya murdering Rosbif ponce? You're bloody lucky Joubert only caught you a glancing blow with a wrench. Could've been much worse. Now turn round and look at me." Laroche surveyed him critically then zipped a strip of hair from above his ear. "That'll do. 'S toughened you up a bit."

Gingerly, Michael felt the scalp around his scar. "Were you really? Looking out for me?"

"Yer about to find out."

"Why would you do that?"

"Why would you teach me to read?"

He opened his mouth to say something about owing him one – two – for the phone calls, but then stopped.

"There's your answer, mate."

As they heard the key turn in the lock and the kanga stuck his head round the door and beckoned him into the corridor, Laroche slung the razor into the carrier bag, then picked up his copy of *The Monstrumologist*. "S'long, dude." He punched Michael on the knuckles. "Will you look at us now – me the bookworm, you the crim."

Michael ran his hand across his scalp, seeking out the soft abrasions. "S'long… *Lilian*, and – thanks!" he said, torpedoed by a feeling of aloneness as the door slammed shut. He listened to the sound of receding footsteps, that desolate childhood sound, and a faint *oink oink* filtered back to him on the stale prison air.

CHAPTER THIRTY-FIVE

The police car drove through the dizzyingly dark night, Delphine huddled in one corner of the back seat, Colin a stiff consignment in the other. After they had radioed their Paris colleagues, the officers in the front had given up trying to make conversation with them, or with each other. The wildness of the Morvan was only guessable through the blackness: a bleak incline lit by moonlight, the charcoal bone yard of a forest. He glanced across at his granddaughter; her face retained its white, strained aspect, although her eyes were closed and he assumed she was asleep. He leaned back against the headrest, too tired to sleep himself, caught in the headlights of what was happening and unable to think or move, waiting for the moment of impact.

Be careful what you wish for, that's what they say. *Be careful...* With the barest, most bitter of movements, little more than a contraction of muscle, he shook his head. Michael was innocent. He should have been delirious with relief, rhapsodic. Instead, he felt as if he were hardly inhabiting his body, barely breathing.

"I pushed her, and she fell," the child said, and while Colin tried to explain to the policeman about Charlotte's death and Michael's confession, she sat and drank her milk, detached from everything that was going on around her. The policeman squatted down on his haunches and asked her what had happened. "I pushed her, and she fell," she repeated, as if speaking from some far country, a distant hemisphere. There was a small moustache of milk on her upper lip and Colin handed her his handkerchief, without thinking.

"Wipe," he said abstractedly, and she said his name, whispered it – *Colin* – and the music of it seemed terrible to hear.

The policeman went outside to make a phone call. The woman who owned the house put a plate of biscuits on the table and fled from the room.

He ran his fingers through his hair. He went to the limits of the pool of light and then turned back to face the child. "I'm sorry," she said in a tiny, fractured voice and he could see that for her the word had lost the magical, healing properties of childhood, the kiss and make better facility that puts everything right. Her mouth was trembling. "Will I go to prison, like Papa?"

"No, darling. No, of course not. Of course you won't." He knelt down and reached to take her in his arms and she winced as if he had hit her, as if that were her punishment. She was standing at an awkward, bunched up, twisted angle, straining away from him, but he took her hand in any case and held it in his big paw. "Nothing bad will happen to you. I promise you. Cross my heart." He tried to draw her close, but she gave a jittery shake of her head, her body crooked with fright and he understood entirely what Michael had been trying to save her from. "I'm here," he said, "I'm here for as long as you need me. And everything will be alright."

~~~

THE DRAGONFLY

They arrived back at Chatillon en Bazois in the smallest hours of the morning. The arc lamps were still in place around the lock although the lights were out and the night was closed around the town like a vice. The car came to a halt above the tow path. The crack and crunch of the gravel died away as the policeman turned around in his seat.

"The family liaison officer will be on hand tomorrow. You have her number, yes?"

Colin touched the phone in his pocket.

"It is best that you have the day to recover yourselves."

"Then what?"

"Then you go with the officer to Paris. There will be some assessments. My colleagues will wish to interview Delphine."

"What assessments?"

"Everything will be handled carefully. We have special protocols…"

"Yes, but what assessments?"

"She is young. They will want to determine if she knows the difference between telling the truth and lying. They will want to look at her recall, her memory. Everything is very careful…"

Colin closed his eyes to the terrible seepage of tiredness. "What will become of her?"

"She will be looked after."

Heavy-limbed, he roused himself and opened the car door. He twisted to look back at the policeman. "Yes, but what does that mean?" He went round to the other side of the car and lifted out his granddaughter.

"They will take care of her. Therapy, counselling. She is young. There are experts to help."

Cold comfort to carry into the darkness with the sleeping child.

Tyler was propped up at the table in the cabin of *Sabrina Fair*, fast asleep. When Colin tapped on the window, she sat bolt upright, blinking, her hands clattering around her head in surprise. She scrambled up the stairs and on to the deck.

"Are you guys OK?" she gasped, catapulted from slumber into over-wakefulness. "Is Delphine–?"

"She's here." The inside of his head felt as if it were silted with ash. "Did you get my text?"

"Yeah – here, let me–" Tyler reached out her arms to take Delphine from him, but although the incline of the gangplank seemed impossibly steep, he lumbered up it holding the child to him, her head in the crook of his neck, her body limp against his chest.

"Is it alright for us to stay? We've got nowhere else..." he was too tired to explain, too tired even to finish the sentence.

"Of course it is," she was in lifeguard mode. "I've made the spare beds up. It's this way." She led him to a compact little cabin with two small bunks cunningly wedged in at one end. They were made up with fresh sheets – the benison of clean white linen – and he laid the child down in the nearest one still in her clothes, then fumbled helplessly with the buckles of her sandals.

"I'll do it..." Tyler removed Delphine's shoes and paired them neatly on the floor beside the bed. "Come with me–"

She sat him at the table in the saloon, then unobtrusively she made him tea and brought him slices of brioche spread with lock keeper's honey. She settled herself beside him, ready to accompany him through the wreckage and seemed not to mind that he didn't eat and didn't talk.

"It was Delphine–"

"I know. I know. You said…" she touched his wrist with her hand.

"Did I?" he searched her face.

"You did. In your text."

"Not Michael."

"No."

His head bowed of its own accord. "No."

"You need to get some sleep," she traced her finger down the side of his face. "Tired one."

He looked sideways at her. "In the little cabin…"

Tyler nodded. "Sure, I know. You need to be with Delphine and she needs to be with you. I understand."

"Thank you," he said, which seemed too brief a phrase, and with too brief a kiss on her rainwater hair he stumbled off to find his bed.

Dawn was spilling the new day carelessly through the porthole in splashy pools of light as he lay down on the bunk opposite his granddaughter. When he awoke in the shallows of the afternoon, she had crept across the little gap and was lying in the harbour of his arms.

~~~

They took things gently, the three of them, with the remains of the day. They ate a hybrid meal of breakfast and tea on the shady deck. There was ham and stinky cheese, and French bread which still felt warm, and cherries in a china bowl, and croissants and fresh juice and tarry black coffee and banana milk shake. To begin with, the child sat close to her grandfather and watched him, following his movements as if she had forgotten what one did at meal times; as though there were customs that she didn't understand. He hung cherry earrings from his ears and buttered her a croissant. She picked uncertainly at the crispy flakes of pastry and ate three cherries: *tinker, tailor, soldier…*

"Ah-ha!" said Tyler, remembering something. She disappeared into the galley and returned bearing a great big bag of marshmallows, "Look what I tracked down – guimauves, I believe!"

"Go on," Colin nodded, beginning to comprehend that this new, chastened Delphine needed permission for everything. "Tuck in." He ate an earring to encourage her.

Two or three marshmallows disappeared, swiftly followed by two or three more, as Delphine discovered that she did have an appetite after all. She made short work of the croissant and the milk shake, swinging her legs as she did so, something he observed with disproportionate relief.

"What do you want to do? Today? What would you like?"

The swinging stopped. "I don't mind," she hung her head and sat, taking up as little space as possible on her chair. "Are we going to Paris?" she asked, her voice sounding as if it had been ironed out, every wrinkle of emotion pressed away.

He put his arm around her and she leaned against him. "We will be. We'll go tomorrow, the two of us."

"Are you coming with me?" she quizzed him, needing to be sure.

"I'm coming with you."

She nodded. "Will I see Papa?"

"Yes, very soon," he promised, heedless of the legal niceties, wanting only what was best for her.

"You are coming with me, aren't you?" She had a searching expression on her face.

He nudged a marshmallow in her direction. "Yes, I'm coming with you."

THE DRAGONFLY

~~~

As it turned out, none of them wanted to do very much. They wandered into town with that strange, wading sensation of walking through water, patient and slow. Tyler took Delphine to buy a few clothes while Colin, on the pretext of making some phone calls (although Holy God he did have phone calls to make – Michael's solicitor, who confirmed that they were seeking bail for him pending the conclusion of inquiries, the family liaison officer, the insurance company, Madame Duvoisin) scoured the whole of Chatillon to find a pet shop. He wasn't strictly speaking a cat person: they made his nose run and his eyes itch and they crapped in his garden at home, but a cat, a small one, was better than one of Hector's little friends, and in the circumstances…

Colin spotted Tyler and his granddaughter on the tow path heading for home. The kitten, in a ventilated cardboard box, appeared to be going through the spin cycle, throwing itself round and round and round and he was keen to hand it over to Delphine as soon as possible, but as he hurried to catch up with them, following the bend in the canal, he stopped dead in his tracks. Ahead of him, the great claw of the crane flexed and reared and dangling from its pincers was the *Dragonfly*.

He set the box down, the better to shade his eyes. His beautiful, duck egg blue boat was showering half the contents of the lock onto the quayside, hopelessly incontinent. He followed its lurching progress through the air, the poor, sodden *Dragonfly's* last flight. No final gleam, no flash of blue, no whip and flick of its tail. He watched the crane deposit it on the strip of land at the side of the lock keeper's hut, heard the wail and scrape of the chains being removed. *A write off*, the loss adjuster had said. *A write off.*

In another time, he would have loaded the remains back onto his trailer and carted them home with him, setting the boat up on the trestles in his shed, to spend the winter – many winters – loving it back to life. He gazed up at the empty sky. *If you fall asleep by a stream the dragonfly will sew your eyelids shut.* Stiffly, he stooped down and retrieved the box. The kitten let loose a stream of invective as he broke into a run, hurrying to catch up with the others.

~~~

As romantic partings go, Colin's leave-taking from Tyler had a few obstacles to overcome: the presence of Frederique the family liaison officer for one; and Delphine, who with some of her old spirit said it was cruel and unkind to keep the kitten in her box and kept opening the lid to comfort her because she was frightened, while Colin, although he understood that it wasn't just the kitten who was frightened, kept trying to close it.

"I'm going to call her Libellule," she announced on their way into the station.

"What does that mean?" he inquired, pocketing their tickets while scanning the departure board and watching Tyler from the corner of his eye.

"It means *Dragonfly*," she replied, as if that were obvious. "I'll call her Lulu for short."

He tweaked her hat. "It's platform two," he said, "and we've got about a minute and a half…"

With a gentle discretion that he was coming to admire, Frederique ushered Delphine and her frazzled charge up into the nearest carriage, while Colin and Tyler stood at ground level on the station holding hands, and then, fleetingly, holding each other.

He breathed in her outdoor scent of cut grass, then closed his eyes and rested his cheek against her hair. He was acutely conscious of every point at which their bodies touched, as if he were learning her longitude and latitude, mapping her in his memory.

"Can we...?" he began. "Will you...?" He rested his forehead against hers. He could feel the downdraught from her eyelashes when she blinked. In close-up, her face had the strange, distorted beauty of a Picasso portrait, all intersecting planes and shadows.

She brushed her lips against his with the lightest touch. "We can," she murmured, "And what's more, I will."

He could hear the blunted percussion of train doors closing. He held her closer. "Thank you, for everything – really, *everything*," he said, kissing her. He flung himself up the steps and into the carriage. "Tyler–" he called back through the open window, the flare of her outlined in sunlight, a bright frame she broke through to reach up to him one last time.

"This is for you..." She tucked a small package into his hand and he could see the private face he cared for becoming public once again as she squared her shoulders and raised her arm in a waving salute, then with the strength and grace he thought he could easily come to love, or loved already, she turned and walked back down the platform, her figure fading into the dusty light.

~~~

Colin, his granddaughter, Lulu in her cardboard box, Frederique the family liaison officer and a workman with a bag of tools and what looked like lengths of skirting board, all piled into the lift at Madame Duvoisin's apartment block, squashing in together, pretending that their bodies weren't pressed uncomfortably close. Delphine was staring hard at the illuminated numbers which showed the floors flashing past, mouthing *un, deux, trois...* more of a child than she had seemed on their adventures; the summer bubble burst, the iridescence gone. As they walked along the corridor to the flat, Lulu complaining as the box knocked against her owner's knees, she glanced uncertainly at him.

"So is the butter melted, maintenant?" she asked with a wistful glance, starting to slip back into her French life, starting to slip away.

He looped his arm around her. "Oh, it melted a long time ago. I wasn't going to mention it, though."

She gave a sigh. "I thought so."

Madame Duvoisin was waiting at the open door, her fingers telling the pearls around her neck like rosary beads. She reached out her free hand, beckoning the child towards her with something you might mistake for impatience, if you didn't know. Colin looked away as she pressed Delphine's head against her diaphragm. Frederique the family liaison officer stared discreetly at the floor.

"Alors," said Madame Duvoisin, a note of trepidation in her voice, "There is something in the box, non?"

"Lulu!" cried Delphine, liberating the frantic kitten who disappeared into the apartment in a tortoiseshell streak of terror. As the child sped after her, she gave a rapid explanation to her grandmother over her shoulder in French: *Lulu is very fond of olives and fruit cake, but she doesn't like lettuce*, or words to that effect, and Colin was comforted to think that the cat, if it could ever be enticed from under the sofa or wherever it had taken refuge (an operation he didn't particularly want to be a part of) would be there to mediate the world for Delphine, and that when it had grown and she had grown up too, she would be mended enough to speak up for herself. He rattled the change in his pocket, turning over coin after coin.

"Delphine's father will be freed on bail within a couple of days," Frederique the family liaison officer was explaining in English, for his benefit. "Arrangements will be made for her to stay with him while she undergoes assessments. It will be good for the two of them to be together."

"And after that–?" Between her fingers, Madame Duvoisin's pearls grated against each other like teeth, grinding.

"The accent will be on treatment and support, not punishment. She will have psychological help," Frederique went on, "And help from her family, of course…" she finished with an upward inflection, a professional suggestion of positive outcomes.

Madame Duvoisin nodded; she glanced at Colin, her gaze saying nothing, volubly. "Will you be staying in Paris?"

"For a little while," he answered. "Until…" Michael's name hung in the air between them. "I'm not sure if…" He turned a coin over in his pocket, running his thumb along its milled edge. "For a little while," he said.

~~~

Colin found a hotel in the northern suburbs of Paris, not far from where he had parked his car, what seemed like months ago now. When he stood in the middle of his single room and stretched his arms wide he could touch both walls. The wallpaper was covered in beige bamboo; he ran his fingertips over the raised design. There was a beaker on the glass shelf above the basin and he filled it with water, then he perched on the bed. The counterpane was made of quilted nylon which had bobbled in places and as he sat there, he found himself sliding inexorably towards the floor. Bracing his knees, he sipped some water. The Paris street was hazy beyond the grey net curtains. He pressed his fingers against his palm, recalling the feel of Delphine's hand. It was a reflex of missing her. He felt as lopsided without her as she had been without Amandine.

Alert to the danger of depressing himself, he set about unpacking his belongings, up-ending a rucksack full of underpants and socks and toiletries onto the bed. Straggled on the counterpane, they looked more like flotsam that anything he had left behind in the lock at Chatillon en Bazois. He needed new clothes, badly. He'd lost count of how many days he'd worn the same T-shirt, there was green slime and goodness knows what else on his shorts, and espadrilles were definitely not the footwear du jour in the capital.

He checked his phone. Thanks to Frederique, everybody had everyone else's phone numbers, but nobody was ringing anyone.

He'd get cleaned up, that's what he'd do and then he'd go and find something to eat. Perhaps he could make his way back to Gautier's. He poked his head into the shower cubicle, which was not much bigger than the bathroom locker on the *Dragonfly*. The limp white curtain had hard water stains on it and the grouting was mottled in places. He started to empty out his pockets. Amongst the cargo, buried at the bottom, was Tyler's little package.

He sat back on the bed and ripped open the wrapping. Inside was a clear glass bottle containing a small scroll. He pulled out the tiny cork stopper and after several minutes of shaking it upside down, he teased the scroll through the narrow neck.

The paper was tied with a length of duck egg blue ribbon. He undid the bow, unrolled the page and spread it out.

The composition was slightly out of perspective, but a vast improvement on some earlier studies he had seen. It showed a small peniche with a cherry red prow and a valiant little day boat for fishing, sailing side-by-side through some rather crooked landscape, heading towards the sunset. The title of the picture was *Wintering in Dijon*.

Colin blinked. He put the watercolour on the rattan table under the window, anchoring it with a bottle of mouthwash and his shampoo to flatten it out. He stood looking at it for several moments, until the sore strings of his heart, frayed and tangled up for so long now, somehow seemed less taut. He sent her a text: *Book says Dijon excellent for wintering. Ducal palace worth a sketch or two. Good high-speed links to Bath...?* Then straightaway he sent her another one, which just had kisses in it.

CHAPTER THIRTY-SIX

Colin phoned his son without realising he was going to, as if the days and days since Delphine said *I pushed her, and she fell* hadn't been a vertiginous trial of longing and reluctance, of *not right now, but maybe later,* as if the thought of doing it didn't bring him out in a sweat.

He dialled the number, those quick, slippery digits that Frederique had given him.

"Hello?"

The sound of his boy's voice shot through him, the shock of it reaching right to his fingertips.

"Michael…?"

He was walking along the tow path of the Canal St Martin: walking as escape, walking as expiation. He stared at the green water lapping against the waterway's green walls, the green railings at street level, the green branches arching under the ribbed blue sky: the long, urban nave of the canal.

"Hello, Dad."

"Hello, my boy." He didn't want to sound too eager; he didn't want to sound too cool. "How are you?"

"I'm fine. I'm at home. They released me yesterday…"

"That's great news." In front of him, the tow path widened. A knot of people was listening to a busker playing the cello.

He took a deep breath. "You don't have to speak to me and you don't have to see me if you don't want to–"

"I do want to."

"–I'd quite understand."

"I do want to see you."

"Oh." Two cyclists went past in a blur, whirring, leaving behind them a slipstream of silver and blue. "Well, that's good," he said, his heart thudding in his chest. "I want to see you too."

There was silence on the line as the two of them acclimatised to the notion that they could fix a meeting place and just turn up, that bridging nine years of separation could be that simple.

"So where shall we–?" / "Do you want to–?"

"You go first," said Colin.

Michael cleared his throat. "A psychologist is coming here to see Delphine later on this morning. Perhaps I could meet you somewhere? I've got a parcel I need to post."

"Anywhere–" said Colin, his heart still ticking like a clock; a slow continuum of all the time spent waiting, the chronology of loss, of stupid, stupid waste.

"What about the Buttes de Chaumont? It's a park near where we live. I'll meet you at the metro."

"I'll be there in half an hour," he said, finding his voice, his mouth dry. "I'm on my way."

~~~

He messed up the Metro – he followed the line towards Nation instead of Porte Dauphine, taking the interchange at a swerve in his hurry, but he'd been running towards this for years and years and he couldn't stop now. He sat on the train listening to the slow pneumatic hiss of the wheels on the track, urging them onwards. He walked the length of all the carriages to the one in the front to be closest to the exit, but when he arrived at Michael's station, it said *Sortie* at the far end of the platform and he began to run again: up the stairs, through the barrier, up and up.

He raced panting into the daylight, shouldering past some bloke who was on his way down, and there, leaning against the railings, was his son. Colin stopped dead in his tracks. The proportions of his face had changed: his eyes were more striking, his head was shaved. He was so thin. It is easy to assume that suffering brings wisdom, but perhaps it just brings pain.

Michael hunched his shoulders diffidently and shoved his hands into his pockets. "How was your journey?"

They were shy with one another. They were like acquaintances, trying to find what common ground they shared.

"I went the scenic route…"

They regarded one another, puzzling over each small revelation: how they had changed, what they had become.

"You've lost weight."

Michael stared down at his chest and stomach, as if they were unfamiliar too. "Yes, I suppose…"

"I haven't! I've spent too long in Burgundy."

"I don't know Burgundy."

"It's very beautiful."

"We always went to Brittany for the holidays…"

"Delphine said." Colin hesitated, "She showed me her album. I saw pictures of…" When it came to it, he didn't have the courage to say her name, "Of her mum. She was looking very happy."

Michael glanced behind him and then glanced back. "Yes. Well…"

Neither of them spoke. They stood in loose proximity, like strangers disassociating themselves. "I need to post this," Michael produced a small package from under his arm. "It's a book," he said. "For my cellmate. To say thank you."

Colin watched him as he crossed the road, weaving his way between the cars, sliding the parcel into a post box, then weaving his way back, conscious of all the tremulous trajectories that children make, from their first, faltering steps to the long walk away from home.

Then they set off, heading for the park. "I'm sorry – for everything. That's what I've come to say. I thought that letting you go was in your best interests," the words came blurting out of him. "I loved you so. More than I loved your mother. I shouldn't say that, I know."

Michael was staring at the ground, listening to his Dad speaking, taking in the sound of his voice, the effect of it.

"I didn't want you to feel torn. I never wanted you to have to choose between us."

He remembered the phone call in the prison, his Dad's excuses: *parents sometimes have to make difficult decisions.* He half expected a kanga to tap him on the shoulder and tell him that their time was up. He shook his head. "It doesn't matter anymore."

"I tried to make it up to you, with Delphine…"

"It's forgiven and forgotten. Honestly. Let's put all of this behind us."

Colin made a sound; fighting the squall in his throat, the weather in his chest.

"Are you alright? Shall we sit down?" Ahead of them was a bench with a view out over the ornamental lake. It was a rustic fantasy: a cliff face, a waterfall, a small suspension bridge and a cluster of city trees that lacked the vigour of their country cousins. Nothing that day seemed quite real.

"How is she?" Colin asked when he had sat down and steadied himself and then because he couldn't stop himself, "How did it happen? Tell me. What did she do?"

Michael ran his hands over his scalp, fingering his stubble. "Charlotte was leaving," he said. "And I was very upset. That part of my statement was true."

Colin stared at the fringe of grass running down to the lake, wanting to hear and not wanting to know.

"We were standing on the landing. There's a little corridor that leads off it to Delphine's room. I kept asking Charlotte if she would stay. I thought if we could give it one more chance..." he tailed off. "You told me once that she would ruin my life."

"Did I say that?"

"Both of us were upset I couldn't let it drop and in the end she got angry. We were shouting and I was conscious that Delphine's door was ajar and I knew that she'd be listening, that she couldn't help but hear. I was shouting at Charlotte: *What about your daughter?*" I was playing dirty," he said sadly. "I feel so guilty about that. She said it wasn't about Delphine, that I should leave Delphine out of it; it was about the two of us. She turned to go and I gave one of those weird, animal cries – I called out her name – howled it."

Colin closed his eyes, seeking the retinal image of his boy standing vengefully at the top of stairs, but the picture had faded and gone.

"Delphine's door burst open and she came flying down the corridor at us. She was as wild as we were. She kept screaming, over and over again. She kept screaming *No*. She flung herself